DEAD ON DEADLINE

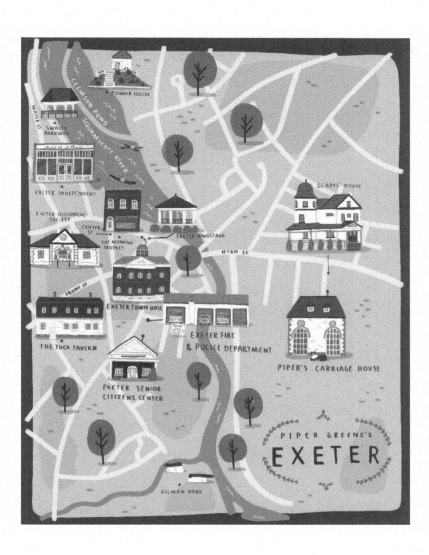

DEAD ON DEADLINE
A Piper Greene Exeter Mystery

Lara Bricker

Exeter Independent Press
75A Newfields Road, Exeter, NH 03833

Editor: Renee Nicholls www.mywritingcoach.net
Map: Alex Foster
Cover Design: Stewart Williams Design
Proofreading/Layout: Tom Holbrook/Piscataqua Press
Publisher Colophon: Lionel Hearon
Author Photo: Melissa Koren Wilson

Acknowledgments

There are so many people that have supported me on the journey to seeing this book in print. I'd been working on different versions of this book for years when we went into lockdown during the COVID-19 pandemic. My husband, Ken, who had watched me stop and start this manuscript countless times told me "Why don't you go finish that book?" in the summer of 2020. He put his full support behind me and gave me the courage to start writing again.

From there, my dear friend, Susan Nolan, became my first reader. I came to expect her daily phone calls asking when her next chapter was coming. While she suspects she knows her character in this book, she might be surprised to learn that she often falls into the role of my fictional Gladys in that she has always been one of my biggest cheerleaders since our days back in the old *Exeter News-Letter* newsroom.

My editor, Renee Nicholls, was instrumental in helping me finish this book. She is insightful, thorough, and knew just what needed to be done to take the manuscript to the next level. She also gave me the confidence to commit to going indie with this project. As an added perk, she shares my love of British mysteries.

Thanks to my beta readers, Kathleen Bailey and Renay Allen, both local authors, who gave great feedback on what did, and didn't work, in the story.

And lastly, thank you to this Exeter community that I've called home since 1998. I love living in a town that truly supports its local authors and makes independent projects like this possible.

Author's Note

Exeter, New Hampshire, my adopted hometown, is a real place. I've always said that our quaint downtown would be the perfect setting for a Hallmark movie—or a murder mystery. The murder mystery won.

The town of Exeter and its major landmarks are portrayed accurately in this book, as is the general history of the town. However, people and businesses are figments of my own overactive imagination. There was no Rev. Adams who led the first church, nor any Greene family who owned sawmills; I created them after researching early families in Exeter's history. The annual American Independence Festival is a real event, but aside from fake deaths during the mock battle, it's been a murder-free zone.

News stories in this book are fictional with the exceptions of past crimes detailed in chapter 34, including the death of a police officer, a convenience store shooting, and the disappearance of a young girl in Exeter, who the town still mourns for. Any other resemblance to actual events, locales, or persons, living or dead, is entirely coincidental.

CHAPTER 1

"Son of a monkey!" I yelled as I slammed on the brakes, almost hitting the elderly man who had strolled out in front of my car without looking. He seemed oblivious to the fact that he'd barely escaped two tons of heavy metal barreling toward him—or that he'd been seconds from meeting his maker. Instead, he continued to totter along at a pace that would frustrate even a snail as he peered ahead at the regiment of colonial reenactors.

You would think by now I would know better than to try to drive downtown during Exeter's annual American Independence Festival, the biggest event of the year, which included blocking off part of our main street. I glanced at my watch and quickly assessed my parking options. I had just minutes to get to my assignment for *The Exeter Independent.*

I was charged with writing a story about the festival, including the arrival of a George Washington role player on horseback and a reading of the Declaration of Independence by one of the town's elders. The reading of the Declaration, on the second weekend of July, was set to coincide with how long it took for a copy to reach town by horse and rider in 1776. Visitors and locals alike looked forward to the tradition, which would be front-page news in next week's paper.

I managed to ease Walter, the dependable Volvo my

widowed aunt had named after her long-deceased husband, through a narrow one-way street and into a parking space. I was just in time to see George Washington ride into town astride a lanky bay horse. I jogged across the street in front of him and took up position, notebook in hand, to jot down my observations. A few kids in black tricorn hats, who were armed with mock wooden rifles, trailed after George, looking like they could have traveled through time.

George's ride was essentially the same every year, but there was something thrilling about knowing your town played a part in the Revolutionary War. One of the town's elders climbed onto a wooden platform that was draped with a red-white-and-blue sash and unfurled a copy of the Declaration of Independence.

The crowd leaned forward to listen as he began. "When in the Course of human events, it becomes necessary for one people to dissolve the political bands which have connected them with another..."

My mind wandered as he droned on in a dull monotone, and I took in the crowd. There was a mix of tourists but also many of the long-time residents I'd known my whole life. One person I didn't miss seeing that morning was my boss, Charlotte Campbell, who took every opportunity she could to micromanage me, as if I didn't already know how to ask questions or write a news story.

At times, I couldn't believe I was back in Exeter, taking care of my octogenarian aunt, Gladys, and working at *The Exeter Independent*, where I'd interned in high school. But really, there was nothing I wouldn't do for Gladys.

I looked back at the man reading the Declaration. He was decked out in a colonial-era suit and black hat.

"And for the support of this Declaration, with a firm reliance on the protection of divine Providence, we mutually pledge to each other our Lives, our Fortunes, and our sacred Honor," he concluded.

The crowd cheered, and the fife and drum corps struck up a patriotic tune as they began marching in time toward the center of town. I followed along, as did most of the people who were ready to observe the next part of our freedom from English rule.

Suddenly, the group in front of me stopped.

"What's that?" a little old lady called out. She was pointing up toward the town hall.

I peered up at the top of the massive brick building and did a doubletake. It looked like a redcoat soldier was hanging off the edge of the roof. A rope was wrapped around the soldier's neck. I inched forward to get a better look. My gut lurched. That wasn't a role player. It was a body.

"Should we call the fire department?" someone asked.

But before anyone could answer, the rope let out a loud snap, and the body crashed to the sidewalk directly in front of me.

The crowd let out a collective scream of surprise and horror, but I couldn't breathe. I knew the body at my feet. It was Charlotte Campbell, my editor at *The Exeter Independent,* and she was clearly dead. She was probably the worst boss I had ever had but seeing her lifeless body and glazed eyes staring up at the sky was shocking to say the least. There was a rope around her neck, and she was wearing the cardinal-red colonial military jacket of a British soldier.

"Call for an ambulance!" someone yelled out. Around me people stood frozen in place, mouths agape as they gaped at the body.

Skip the ambulance—how about the medical examiner? I thought. Given the odd angle of her neck, it was obvious to me

3

that there would be no bringing her back. I knew I needed to move, but my feet were like blocks of concrete under me. After a minute, the ever-present busybody in me could not resist leaning over to get a better look, but my stomach did a queasy flipflop as I peered at Charlotte. I was going to have nightmares about her empty eyes staring up at me.

The people near me started to panic. A woman grabbed her child and shielded his face from the macabre scene in front of them.

"Stand back, I'm a doctor," an older gentleman announced. He leaned down next to Charlotte's body.

Someone else had the wherewithal to ask the crowd to back up and give the doctor some space. He held his fingers up against the side of her neck, then shook his head. My assessment had been right: nothing more could be done.

I surreptitiously snapped a few photos on my phone. The situation was awful, but I knew it could be a big scoop.

Within minutes, the blue-and-red lights of a police cruiser rounded the corner, quickly followed by one of the town's ambulances. Whereas the initial witnesses had panicked at the sight of the body, the police officer who walked toward us gave off an air of brisk efficiency.

"Everyone step back, please, and let the ambulance crew do their job," he said. He began unrolling yellow crime scene tape.

Two ambulance workers jogged over to Charlotte and exchanged a few words with the doctor, who was still crouched next to her. They looked at each other with a knowing glance. Like the doctor, they knew she was gone.

Some people in the crowd dispersed, but others, like the fife and drum corps, looked around anxiously, as if unsure whether to stop or continue their march around town. Duty won and they began their synchronized rendition of "Chester" by William Billings, the lyrics of which encouraged the patriots to be strong against the British tyrants.

Interesting choice of music, I thought. *Charlotte was certainly a tyrant. Did one of the locals take it upon themselves to end her reign?*

Charlotte had marched to her own drum as my boss and the editor of the local newspaper, but I could not imagine she'd killed herself. In fact, she was pretty much universally disliked, but enough for someone to kill her? And in such a public and elaborate way? It would have taken strength and determination. It was no easy feat getting up into that tiny cupola on top of the brick town hall. I'd gone up only once, to take photos of the downtown area, but climbing the well-worn wooden stairs had been such a harsh workout, my pounding heart had protested the entire way.

As the first members of the crowd wandered off, locals started to trickle in to get a look. Word traveled fast in a town of this size. I tried to blend in so I could take more photos as the police officers cleared the area for their crime scene people.

"Hey, Piper, maybe you'll write a book about this one day," the local bookseller remarked.

Oh yes, I thought, *because I have so much free time between taking care of Gladys and keeping up my job as staff reporter for the* Independent. But honestly, the return of Piper Greene to town wasn't all bad. Sure, some people flee the town they grew up in never to return, but Exeter was the type of place that settled into your blood. Between the quaint downtown, the old colonial architecture, and the close-knit community, many never wanted to leave. In the two months since I'd returned, I'd felt like I never left at all.

I glanced back at the colonial corpse of Charlotte. She was definitely one of the few people who never did seem to understand the love people had for the local community.

As I peered forward and quickly took photos, the police officers pushed the crowd back even more. One expanded the yellow crime scene tape, while another draped a white cloth over Charlotte's body. Before long, I'd been relocated to the edge of a crime scene that now took up half the downtown area. It was time for me to move on. Before I could write the story, there was someone I needed to see.

CHAPTER 2

It was a quick walk across the street to the cozy brick space that housed the Morning Musket. Not only did the Musket have the best coffee and pastries in town, but also it was owned by my best friend from high school, Jenny Dunbar.

While Jenny's specialty was breakfast pastries, her shop served as the hub of the town's news. If you wanted to learn anything about what was happening in Exeter, you made a stop at the Morning Musket.

Jenny took over the street level space in a building downtown from her parents, who had run a sandwich shop there for years. Fresh from a stint in France, where she had followed Armand, her college boyfriend, Jenny returned to town single and with a new love of breakfast pastries. Some of the locals had questioned her decision to change the shop's focus at first, but soon the townspeople were hooked.

Her croissants and scones had been selling out daily ever since she opened. I gladly volunteered as her assistant when she was experimenting with a new recipe. I was pretty convinced that her raspberry white-chocolate scones had magical healing properties.

I slipped in through the side door, which led right into the kitchen, as was my habit when I wanted to find out the news.

"Jenny," I called. "You are not going to believe what happened!"

Jenny was bent over, deep in concentration as she drizzled chocolate glaze over a tray of enormous croissants. Her curly red hair was pulled back in a headband with a few loose curls framing her face. We'd made quite the contrasting pair in high school: Jenny with her untamed head of red hair like a miniature Viking and me with my sleek black hair, always parted straight down the middle, like one of my Puritan ancestors.

I lowered my voice. "Charlotte Campbell's dead."

She raised her eyebrows in acknowledgement.

Of course she already knew.

But that didn't stop me from giving her a firsthand account of what had happened when Charlotte's corpse crashed to the sidewalk in front of me right next to the town hall.

"I mean, can you believe it? Right in the middle of the festival," I prompted.

She set the croissants aside and began flipping loaves of bread onto her large cooling racks. "That might explain the room full of historical reenactors out there wanting to eat."

She motioned to the front of the shop, where in fact it looked like the Revolutionary Army had set up camp.

I said, "I wonder if they've postponed this afternoon's battle?"

Jenny shrugged. Then she smiled knowingly and said, "Come to think of it, the festival had a bit of excitement last year too. During the reenactment of the colonists versus the redcoats, one of the Native American role players who showed up in a canoe came to shore and got knocked out by the handle of a soldier's rifle. Most people thought it was part of the act until the EMTs rushed into the middle of the battle. That would have been a good story for you."

I agreed. There was only so much you could say about a well-known battle where the "good guys" won year after year.

"To think we used to say this town was boring," I said. "Keep me posted if you hear anything else."

She raised her eyebrows and grinned. "Who me? I never kiss and tell."

But we both knew she was one of my best sources for what was really happening in town. People shared all sorts of news with her when they took a bite of her seemingly enchanted breakfast delicacies.

I walked around to the self-serve coffee table, filled a 20-ounce cup, and helped myself to a coffee cake muffin. It was going to be that kind of a day.

After I paid one of Jenny's assistants at the counter, I noticed that Winnifred Smart, our town historian, was nibbling a blueberry scone in the middle of the regiment of soldiers. The soldiers, as they often did when staying in character, had opted for the hefty pewter mugs they drank everything from.

"Hey, Winnie," I called to her, using her much-preferred nickname. Then I lowered my voice a bit. "Did you hear about Charlotte?"

She raised her eyebrows, much like Jenny had done. God, was there anyone who had not heard yet?

Winnie should have retired a decade or so ago, but it was hard to find a young person willing to spend their days in the bowels of the Historical Society building communing with dead people. And so, she stayed on, a human encyclopedia when it came to the town's early history, and an astute recorder of contemporary events and people.

Barely five feet tall, and weighing less than 100 pounds, Winnie reminded me of the woman who owned Tweety Bird in

Looney Tunes, but she was far from a demure little old granny. Her last name, Smart, was fitting. She was sharper than anyone else in town. Those in the know were aware that she was also a cutthroat poker player, part of a regular group that met at an undisclosed location once a month.

But she looked tired.

"You okay?" I asked, not wanting to mention the dark circles under her eyes. She motioned to the empty seat next to her, and I sat down.

"Just surviving another Rev Fest," she said with a wry laugh, using the former name of the festival. "It's the one week when everyone thinks they are an amateur historian or genealogist so they show up at the society trying to find out if Great Uncle Edward had a secret role in the fight for independence."

I knew that the only time she had ever been busier was when the famous Abraham Lincoln historian had come to town to research Lincoln's son's days at the private school in town. People had lined up in droves to get their books autographed by the historian, whom many recognized from the History Channel.

"You know, with Charlotte," Winnie said, also lowering her voice, "the problem isn't going to be finding someone who wanted her dead. It's going to be figuring out which one finally went through with it."

She had a point.

A new, shrill voice broke in. "You really shouldn't be gossiping about someone like that!" It was Myrna Smith, the woman I privately referred to as the "Cranky Yankee." As she walked past, she added, "You know what people say about *you*, don't you?"

Oh, did I ever. Piper Greene, always nosing into other people's business, digging up dirt. But honestly, aside from a handful of people like her, most folks recognized that it was my job, that I was fair, and that I had the best interest of the town at heart. Those who really knew me also acknowledged the benefits of my habit of intervening behind the scenes when I learned through the course of a story that someone needed help. It was the type of professional lapse that could get reporters fired at a big paper, but it was also one that locals grew to appreciate in a small town like Exeter.

I ignored the Cranky Yankee as she stomped out. Outside the coffee shop window, visitors to the festival continued to walk along Water Street. Across the way, an encampment with off-white tents and a smoldering campfire reminded me of the hardcore reenactors in colonial-era regalia who slept downtown in the tents throughout the three-day event. Young children carried wooden rifles and miniature felt hats. It appeared that not even death was going to stop the town's celebration of independence from carrying on.

After a few minutes Winnie excused herself and left, so I took my time chewing my muffin as I kept an ear on the regulars around me. There was a lot of speculation, particularly about some of the victims of Charlotte's nasty editorials.

Jimmy Malloy, our college intern, grabbed Winnie's chair, and plopped down at my tiny table. He said, "Chief Sinclair is out there now. He told me the state cops are coming in for backup."

Then he echoed my earlier thoughts: "I just can't imagine how they got her up there without anyone noticing."

Jimmy was my shadow these days. He was well over six feet tall and was gazelle-like when he walked, so much so that even I, with my long legs, had a hard time keeping up with him. His uncle, Hap, owned the newspaper and gave him a summer job, and although Jimmy was sweet, he was still a bit unsure about how to handle breaking news. He was prone to swiveling his head around like an owl to scan the room he was in, which reflected his anxiety more than his news sense.

"Did you see Charlotte at the opening reception for the festival last night?" I asked him. The event had been held in the upstairs area of the town hall, which doubled as an art gallery.

"Yeah," he said, his eyes widening in realization. "Do you think I was one of the last people to see her alive?"

I thought about that for a minute and opted not to answer, knowing how nervous he already seemed. "How did it go? Was there anything unusual?"

"I mean, it wasn't that interesting. There was some guy playing fiddle music," he responded. "And a big appearance by the George Washington role player. Charlotte was there alone, and then when she disappeared, I just figured she had left early. I didn't think anything of it at the time, you know."

"Was Andy shooting the event?"

He nodded. Andy Hathaway, our free-spirited, rugged photographer, tolerated the fluff pieces but was much more interested in nature photography. In his early 20s and unencumbered, he was known to pack up on the weekends to photograph moose and the occasional bear in the northern part of the state.

"We should look at those photos to see who else might have left early," I suggested. "Or find out who else was there so we can ask them if anything unusual happened last night."

Jimmy stood up and looked at me expectantly, simply awaiting his next orders, which was both helpful and annoying because I wanted to go off on my own and find out all I could without having him underfoot.

"Actually, we really need to go to the paper, see what Hap knows," I said of his uncle, "and find out what is happening next."

But Jimmy was already out the door before I finished my sentence, and given the length of his stride to mine, there was no way I could beat him to the office.

I waved to Jenny, who gave me a discreet wink as she rang out a customer. Then I trotted down the sidewalk after him.

CHAPTER 3

The newspaper offices at the edge of the downtown area were just a short distance from the Squamscott River, which first brought early settlers, including my mother's ancestors, to town back in the 1600s. They established the town in Native American territory, displacing the local tribe and relying on the tidal river to bring barges with goods and supplies.

Exeter had been the capital of the state during the American Revolution, and that independent streak ran strong in long timers around town. Sometimes it seemed this was nowhere more so than at the offices of the people who produced *The Exeter Independent*, a small, family-owned weekly newspaper that was beholden to no one, other than its role as watchdog for the community.

The paper was small but mighty, and when I went on to write for my college newspaper, I realized how educational my high school internship at the *Independent* had been. With that in mind, it wasn't where I had ever expected to find myself this far along in my career, especially after working at a paper 10 times this size just months before. Still, I was glad they had had an opening for a part-time reporter when I arrived back in town. I couldn't imagine sitting still and not writing. The publisher was understanding about those times I needed to skip out to check on my aunt, and my part-time schedule also allowed for that.

I'd been taking notes about the world around me as long as I could remember, though I had learned early on that sometimes my brutal honestly wasn't appreciated by everyone. That lesson was never more apparent to me than when my favorite notebook, which was filled with my keen observations of classmates, was discovered in junior high. I'd been ostracized for months after that, a movement led by the most popular girl in the class, whose ponytail I'd compared to a "bouncy old brown nag."

At the time, Jenny was the only one who had stuck by me, gently suggesting that maybe I didn't always have to be quite so honest.

When both of my parents were killed in a car accident the next year, my peers quickly forgot about Piper and her poison pen, and I thereafter became poor parentless Piper. As I went through high school, with Gladys's guiding hand, I learned to be more subtle when I wrote about people. But there were still times when my brain moved miles ahead of my mouth and I blurted out thoughts that were too blunt. Whenever I worked with Charlotte, it was a struggle to keep my lips zipped.

I caught up to Jimmy outside the front door of the newspaper, where Detective Richie Collins, a friend of mine from high school, stood guard.

"Sorry, no one goes inside right now," he said to Jimmy in his best big-scary-policeman voice, which he followed with a quick wink at me.

Jimmy backed away immediately.

"Really? Is that so, Detective Collins?" I responded. "If I just walk right in, are you going to arrest me?"

Jimmy was already turning to walk away, visibly uncomfortable with my comeback, not familiar with Richie or his sense of humor.

"Yeah, that's right. No pesky reporters are allowed in there right now," he said. "I've got my marching orders."

"Well, then you're in luck," I said, "because I am most certainly not a pesky reporter."

We grinned at each other.

"It's a good thing you're here," Richie went on. "The chief's in there, and he wants to talk to everyone who worked in the office."

I had suspected as much. Richie picked up his handheld radio from his belt and squeezed in the button on the side.

"Chief, I've got Piper and another one out here. Should I send them in?"

The radio squelched, beeped, and Chief Sinclair's voice came back.

"Yes, go ahead."

Richie held the door open, and we entered the tiny lobby of the paper, coming face to face with Clara, the paper's longtime receptionist and obituary editor.

"About time you two showed up," she began. "Hap and the rest of them are out back in the lunchroom, and I'm out here waiting for the next body to drop."

Typical Clara. Even the editor's death could not suppress her sarcastic sense of humor. After growing up in the northern part of the state with her French-Canadian family, she had moved to Exeter when her husband got a job at the now defunct shoe factory. Determined to keep busy, she had marched into the offices one day and told Hap Henderson's father, then the publisher of the paper, that she wanted a job. While she looked like everyone's sweet grandmother today, and in fact she was— her desk was covered in framed photographs of her many grandchildren—she had been around long enough to know what was, and what was not, an actual story. And she was not shy about sharing her opinions. She also had a direct line to news of the town's dead with the three funeral homes in Exeter.

"They've left me here like the bait or something," she went on. "That little uniformed guy out front isn't going to stop anyone who comes in here and wants to take me out."

This wasn't quite as overdramatized as you'd suspect. Last year a reader had marched in on the way home from deer hunting, bloody knife attached to the side of his camouflage pants, demanding to talk to Hap. Turned out he just wanted to discuss the nuclear power plant a few towns over, but the bloody knife, the outfit, and his ability to walk right in had left everyone a bit unnerved.

Despite that episode, there remained only a low counter to serve as a barrier between the newsroom and any person who came off the street. Even so, I will say that I had full faith that Clara could defend herself if a situation arose. Her hefty statue of St. Francis, for starters, was probably more lethal than a baseball bat.

The newsroom itself had not changed since the 1960s, aside from the addition of modern computers. Old wood-paneled desks sat atop beige tile, surrounded by worn brown carpet and sporadic stacks of newspapers. At the rear of the newsroom, the three private offices with doors were empty. The smallest on the end, which had been Charlotte's, had a strand of yellow police line tape across the door. The other two belonged to Hap and his brother, Dick, whose family had owned the paper for three generations. Their grandfather had established the paper back in the 1800s, determined to give the other paper in town some competition. It had worked; the *Independent* had been the only show in town for more than 100 years. Now, as papers across the country found themselves bought up and folded into larger news corporations, the Henderson brothers vowed to keep the independent in the local newspaper, turning down offers that came more often as the years went on. Dick was semi-retired and spent most of the summer at his lake house, leaving his office to collect dust in his absence.

"Let's head to the lunchroom," I said to Jimmy, whose tendency to pivot his head had hit a new speed record as he peered around the newsroom, almost as if he expected a murderer to jump out at any moment. There were times I worried his head might spin right off his body like a scene in a horror movie.

"Do you think she died in here?" he whispered.

"Only if someone then dragged her body over to the town hall," I responded.

We walked past the wide doors that led to the press room, the giant rolls of newsprint, and vats of ink, and into the cafeteria at the back of the paper.

Hap Henderson, clad in his trademark red plaid shirt and brown L.L.Bean loafers, stood as we entered. "Good, you're here," he said, putting a hand on Jimmy's shoulder.

Police Chief Frank Sinclair looked stressed, which was unusual for the veteran law enforcement officer. At about five foot ten, Chief Sinclair was barely taller than me. His kind eyes and grey hair made him look approachable, which he was. He was better known for his outreach at the schools and with the elderly than for his zest for writing speeding tickets. His approach epitomized community policing.

In Exeter, where it seemed residents valued history above all else, Sinclair was considered historical by many. He was the third generation in his family to serve as police chief in town, but while he was getting on in years, he had expressed no desire to leave his post just yet.

"Okay," the chief began. "Now that we've got everyone here. I want to make a few announcements so we're all on the same page."

Everyone must have referred to the newsroom, sans Clara. In addition to Jimmy and myself, the room contained the super-shy features writer, Sheila, and Nate, the sports editor and writer. It was unusual to see Nate, because he covered evening games and didn't come into the newsroom much during the day.

The only other person noticeably absent was Andy Hathaway, our photographer.

"Where's Andy?" I asked, before I could stop myself.

Hap shook his head and frowned. "Long story. I'll explain later."

Chief Sinclair cleared his throat and began. "So, obviously, you all know that Charlotte is dead. Now I know how you news people work, so I want to make sure there aren't any rumors. We are treating the death as suspicious, but it doesn't take a police officer to realize this wasn't a natural death. For now, we're going to need to get a statement from all of you."

He explained that the newspaper office was going to need to shut down while the state police crime scene technicians came in to process the scene and Charlotte's office.

He continued, "And I know this is going to be news, but for now, all information for story purposes is going to have to come from the state police contacts."

This was disappointing. I had a much better working relationship with the chief than with the state police, but it made sense given the situation. In the small state, murder cases were investigated by the state police and attorney general's office, with assistance from local police as needed.

Sinclair held his hands together and looked around the room. "So, this should go without saying, but please, for the integrity of this investigation, we need you all to stay apart and not compare notes before you give your statement."

Again, standard procedure, but come on, this was a room of small-town journalists. Of course we would not be able to resist talking about the case. The chief went on, pausing briefly to nod to Richie, who had just walked into the room.

"Now, Detective Collins here is going to take your preliminary statements, one at a time, and then we're going to ask you to work elsewhere while we process the scene."

For the second time that morning, Richie winked at me. "Miss Greene, why don't we start with you?"

CHAPTER 4

"Richie, come on, tell me what you know," I begged him once we were inside a small office.

"You know I'd love to, but I really can't," he said. I knew he was right, but there was nothing Richie liked more than spilling a good secret.

I may have been Piper with her poison pen in elementary school, but he was not an angel by a long stretch. An Irish Catholic, the youngest of eight brothers, Richie always seemed to be in the wrong place when something happened. But magically, he managed to talk his way out of most of those scraps with help from his big blue eyes and trademark dimples. While I'd turned my focus toward an English major at college, he'd joined the police force, eager in his own way to have a front row seat to all of the behind-the-scenes business in town.

"Well, you and I both know Charlotte wasn't exactly a beloved daughter of the town," I responded.

He nodded but didn't respond. Instead, he pulled out a narrow pad of paper and a handheld recorder, then gave me a look that felt like an apology.

"Sorry," he continued, "but with the state cops on this one, I've got to dot my *i*'s and cross my *t*'s. So, let's keep this as straight as we can."

He winked again, and I knew the real Richie was dying to dish about the case but had to keep up appearances. I was also starting to wonder why he was winking at me so often. Was he flirting? God, that would be something. Timing was everything. I'd had a short-lived crush on Richie in high school, but by the time I had confessed my feelings to him, he was dating someone else. When they eventually broke it off, I had left town for college. Jenny thought he was single but hadn't been able to confirm his status. I glanced at his left hand. There was no ring, but that didn't mean there wasn't a love interest in the picture.

Richie pushed the *on* button and the red light started blinking, indicating he was recording.

"So, let's go through: your role at the paper, how well you knew Charlotte, and where you were yesterday."

"Piper Greene. I'm a general assignment reporter at *The Exeter Independent*. I've worked with Charlotte for the past two months, so I didn't really know her that well. To be honest, she was not an easy person to work for."

I went on to detail Charlotte's unpredictable temper, her reputation for not understanding the town or its people, and her acerbic op-ed column, called "Charlotte's Turn," in which she publicly took aim at any number of groups and initiatives around town.

"I mean, she even took on the Senior Center when they wanted to fix the wheelchair ramp. She called it an extravagant expense. Can you imagine?"

Richie raised his eyebrows but didn't add any of his own commentary. I knew he had a soft spot for the elderly. He visited his 100-year-old grandmother faithfully every Sunday after Mass.

"So, yesterday, what was the schedule at the paper?"

"Well, we were busy, getting the paper out before deadline

and in time for some of our staff to get to the opening reception for the Rev Fest," I went on. "But I stayed behind, finished my story, and went home. Our intern, Jimmy, was assigned to cover the opening reception last night."

He scribbled in his notebook, then prompted me to go on. "So, other than Jimmy, who went to the reception from the paper, if you know?"

"Well, there would be the photographer, Andy; features writer, Sheila; and Charlotte, as far as I know. I left here just before dinner. It was just unfortunate luck that I was covering the festival this morning when. . ." I paused, thinking of how to say this gently. "Her body landed at my feet."

His eyebrows arched, and I knew that if he had not been recording our conversation, he would have inserted a sarcastic comment about that last statement. But he forged ahead.

"Anything unusual happen recently with Charlotte? Anyone who was more upset with her than normal?"

I shook my head. "Not that I can think of, but if I hear of anything, I'll let you know."

"Okay, I think that's going to do it for now," he said. He looked at his watch and pushed the stop button on the recorder. "I'm wrapping up this interview at 9:30 a.m."

Boy, that was quick, I thought, but I realized I did not really have any major information, and he had a lot of interviews to get through. I suspected the state police would circle back for longer interviews once they had gathered preliminary details from everyone.

Richie closed his notebook and stood up. "Seriously, if you hear anything, let me know. I can't guarantee that I can reciprocate, but I'd appreciate it."

I nodded, then turned toward the door. "Who should I send

in next?"

"How about Malloy," he said.

I sat out in the lunchroom while Jimmy went in. As I waited, I watched Sheila, who was typing on a laptop on the other side of the room. She was a good writer, but her shyness and timid interviewing style drove me bonkers. I wanted to yell "spit it out and ask the question" whenever I heard her on the phone working on a story. But apparently her subjects felt differently, and that nonthreatening style of questioning made them comfortable enough to share all sorts of intimate details. Don't get me wrong: she was a sweet person, and she seemed to be a good employee, but she wasn't my cup of tea, and I was relieved when she didn't cross the room to join me.

My phone pinged, and I opened a text from Hap, who was still in his office. He needed a brief story for the front page of the paper, and since I had witnessed the fall, he said I could have the assignment. I knew this would also be good experience for Jimmy, so I decided to wait until he was done.

Jimmy bounded back into the lunchroom a short time later. He indicated to Sheila that she should head in, and then he pulled up a chair beside me.

I said, "So, what did you tell him? Anything that might be significant?"

He shrugged. "I don't think so. Honestly, the same I told you earlier: the reception wasn't that interesting. Andy and I got what we needed for our story and photos and left."

"Same," I responded. "I wish I had some sense of what led up to this. I mean, that's not exactly a subtle way to kill someone, right? It was a message."

Jimmy did a quick scan of the room, checking to make sure we were alone before he answered. "Symbolic really," he said.

"She's a traitor, but to whom?"

"Exactly," I said. "That outfit plus the method makes me think she betrayed someone."

We sat in silence for a few moments, pondering that question. I could think of countless people around town who had no love lost for Charlotte, but none of them seemed capable of something like this.

Jimmy snapped out of the reverie first. "So, what's the deal on covering this?" he asked me. "I mean, I know she was the editor, but it's news, right?"

"Yeah," I said, standing up and grabbing my phone. "Hap just sent me a text. We need to get something up for the website as soon as we can. He asked me to write something quick, and given the situation, I think it would be good experience for you to tag along on this one."

Jimmy looked equal parts terrified and excited at the prospect of assisting with the coverage.

We headed toward the hallway closest to the rear parking lot just as Sheila was walking out of the interview area. Her eyes were red, and she dabbed a crumpled tissue to her nose. Richie was right behind her.

"Ms. Bradbury," Richie called, as he watched her leave. "Remember, discretion about our conversation, okay?"

That sounded significant. Did Sheila know something about Charlotte's death?

We followed her into the parking lot. I said, "Sheila, are you okay?"

She took a deep breath and opened the door to her old Volkswagen Beetle. "Sorry, Piper, I can't talk now, just the shock of it is too much . . . and Detective Collins said I shouldn't say anything just yet."

25

She slid behind the wheel and slowly drove away. I turned to Jimmy. "Something is definitely going on with her. We should go check on her, find out what's up."

"I don't know. I mean, are you sure? She seemed pretty upset," he said. "Like we should leave her alone for a while."

Oh Jimmy, he was still so green, not yet comfortable with following his gut and approaching people for difficult conversations, which came with being a reporter. To be fair, Sheila hadn't exactly warmed to Jimmy. From what I'd gleaned, she put herself through college and resented what she perceived as his free ride and supportive family, especially his uncle who gave him the job. I felt that this was exactly the time to talk to her, while she was still a bit on edge, and even though we were not really friends, I did want to make sure she was okay. Any day of the week, Sheila's long-flowing Bohemian outfits and undone wavy hair gave the impression she didn't spent much time on her appearance, but today, even for her, she looked a bit worse for the wear.

I nodded at Jimmy and held up my car keys. "I'll drive."

"Well, if you really think it's a good idea," he said.

"I do. Walter is just down the street."

As we walked around the corner, we came face to face with Grayson Adams, the chairman of the Select Board, our equivalent of a mayor. He was peering into a window at the rear of newspaper building.

"Glad I caught you two," Grayson began, as he beckoned us over. He was visibly distressed. "Is there any word about what happened?"

Grayson was an institution in town. His family dated back to the founder of Exeter, a Puritan minster who had arrived in town seeking religious freedom. Anyone who met Grayson for the first

Lara Bricker

time learned that fact within the first five minutes of talking to him. Frankly, it was a bit much, but as a reporter I knew there was a real benefit to staying on his good side. Through his position as a town father, he had a direct line to our police chief, and after a few drinks at the Tuck Tavern, he often spilled the beans.

"No word yet," I said.

"Awful, just awful," Grayson said. He kept shaking his head. "I can't believe this. Oh, Charlotte, Charlotte, Charlotte . . . "

Charlotte had not been kind to the select board in her editorials, but that was apparently water under the bridge now. For a stoic old Yankee, this emotion was a bit surprising. Grayson was typically a model of the old New England air of detachment. He was better known for his sharp eye toward trimming the town's budget than for any semblance of benevolence.

Inwardly I cringed, but I knew that in a town like this, we should probably include a comment from him in our reaction story in the paper. Jimmy did not seem like he'd made that assumption yet, so I forged ahead.

"A tragedy, just horrible," I said, reminding myself to slow down, even though I was eager to find out as much information as I could. "Would you be able to offer us a quote about what the loss of Charlotte means to the community? As tragic as this is, we will be writing about it."

Grayson blinked a few times and took a deep breath. "Yes, yes, you're probably right," he said, pausing again. "Well, I know the two of you can be trusted to take this on, so yes, I will send over a comment from the board this afternoon."

Boy, I thought, *all of this work before noon is a first for him.*

Good thing the Tuck Tavern was opening for lunch. We might really get an interesting quote if we hit him up after his first drink of the day. We might also find out if Chief Sinclair had told him anything off the record.

"Good to remember her in a positive light," he murmured, drifting away.

He wandered off down the sidewalk without saying goodbye. Jimmy looked expectantly at me, waiting for direction, but I was mulling over our interaction with Grayson. On the one hand, his positive comment about Charlotte would help assuage my guilt at not feeling more upset about her death. I mean, she was dead, and that was a tragedy, even for someone who had been as difficult to work for as she'd been. She wasn't coming back to try to micromanage me like I was a cub reporter with no experience, suggesting I should ask my questions a certain way, or picking apart my writing. But given some of her editorials aimed specifically at Grayson, it was impressive that he was able to feel the level of sympathy he had for her demise.

With Grayson gone, I was ready to move. As we approached Walter, I picked up the pace. We really needed to find out what Sheila had told the police.

CHAPTER 5

My cell phone rang before we made it much farther.

"Piper dear, I'm in a bit of a pickle," my aunt, Gladys, began as I answered.

When wasn't Gladys in a bit of a pickle? Just last week, she had toppled off her patio into the shrubbery during a particularly rousing rendition of "I Hope I Get It" from *A Chorus Line* after a few too many martinis. It had started as "Step, kick, kick, leap, kick, touch...again" but quickly dissolved into "HELP!"

Fortunately, I had been home to hear her shouting. My apartment was part of the converted carriage house at the back of her property, so I had been able to extricate her from the Mountain Laurel.

"You know I was shortlisted for the Rockettes, right Piper dear," she'd insisted, as I offered a hand and brushed off the leaves. "Oh, those were the days."

Did I mention she was wearing high heels while kicking? Just two months after breaking her arm? And that she's 80 years old? When she said she was in a jam, there really was no telling what that might mean.

"Is it an emergency, Gladys?" I began. "I might be hot on the trail of a killer."

"Oooh yes, that does sounds exciting, but I really do need

help," she said. She paused briefly before sighing heavily. "I'm in the tub and I can't get out."

I cringed and held my tongue. Taking a bath was exactly how she had broken her arm this spring, and her doctor had strongly suggested only showers, unless she had on-site help.

Of course, I could have just called the fire department to help her. But this was Gladys. She had a certain aura of civility that would simply not do with having the young firefighters see her in this state of duress—or more appropriately, undress.

I held the phone away from my ear and turned to Jimmy, who was still anxiously hovering next to me.

"Change of plan. I need to make a quick detour home. I'll text you when I'm ready to head to Sheila's place and we can meet there."

He nodded, then headed for his own car. "Okay. I'm going to get a coffee."

I picked the phone back up as I headed for Walter the Wagon, hoping Gladys was still there. She was; I could hear her splashing.

"Okay, stay put and I'll be there in a few," I told her.

She laughed. "Well, Piper dear, now where would I go? I'm stuck, remember? Thank goodness the water's still warm, but I'm starting to look like a prune."

It was still early, so at least I wouldn't be dealing with her daily cocktail hour. Gladys was like clockwork. As soon as 5:00 p.m. arrived, so did cocktail hour. One each night. Perhaps two or three on Saturdays when she entertained her regular gentleman caller, Stanley, and they got into singing showtunes together.

This time of year, she donned a scarf and her Jackie O–style sunglasses as she sat on her patio, martini in hand, and waved to her neighbors. Only those who knew her—or had been asked to mix up a martini for her—knew that she drank straight vodka from the glass.

"No need to ruin perfectly good Smirnoff," Gladys was fond of saying. She had been drinking Smirnoff since the 1970s when the brand was in vogue, and she would no doubt continue until she died.

I made a detour up High Street toward home, hoping I could help Gladys quickly and get over to Sheila's place before she put up some emotional walls. Something was niggling at me about Sheila's distress. I had a hunch that she knew something about Charlotte—otherwise, why all the secrecy?

High Street was peppered with old Victorians and colonial-era wooden homes, many with the historically accurate black shutters on white buildings, with a few converted into apartments. Gladys's home was both grand, with a turret on the side, and unique, with special features like an octagonal sunroom with custom stained glass on one window.

I found Gladys, still covered in bubbles, a vintage shower cap over her bright silver hair, with Sinatra playing over her wireless bathroom speaker. Her cell phone sat on the edge of the tub. She may have been getting on in years, but she was hip, even learning to use Siri on the phone when she had a question.

"Oh, Piper, thank God," she exclaimed. "I couldn't have handled it if you'd called the fire department."

That was an understatement.

"Okay, so first thing, let's drain the tub," I said, looking around for a towel or bathrobe. An industrial-size bottle of Chanel No. 5 perfume that harkened back to the 1970s sat next to her artfully arranged brushes and handheld mirror.

I handed her a silky pink bathrobe, which had been hanging from a hook on the back of the door. "Let's get you covered up,"

I said. I hoped the robe would be less slippery than the bubble bath as I pulled her out.

In a maneuver that was more suited to wrestling or pulling weeds, I managed to haul her tall, slim body up from the tub and over to the toilet, where she quickly sat down, shaking her head. I handed her an enormous pink towel, knowing that her fashionable bathrobe would barely dry off one arm.

"Well, good thing you're strong, my dear," she said.

I wanted to remind her about her questionable decision not to put up safety bars next to her tub after her fall this spring—the same fall that brought me back to town to keep an eye on her—but I bit my tongue. She was independent and putting up those bars would have been a sign of weakness. Too mundane.

"Well, I'm sorry to save you and run Gladys, but..."

"Oh yes, I heard about poor Charlotte," Gladys said, shaking her head again.

Gladys heard everything and had an institutional memory when it came to the inner world of the town. She added, "But then, she wasn't the most popular person now, was she?"

"No. But Grayson just told me and Jimmy all about what a loss her death is for the town," I confided.

Gladys pursed her lips together. I knew that just like the rest of us, she was tired of Grayson's constant need to be in the spotlight. "It's just not dignified," she often said.

For now, though, she seemed determined to keep those thoughts to herself. Instead, she raised her hand in a little wave to me. "Until we meet again, my dear. I expect a full report when you have time to stop by."

"You bet," I answered.

As I drove back into town, my mind kept wandering back to Gladys. She'd been there to pick up the pieces after my parents died, and there was nothing I wouldn't do for her. My brother had been too busy with law school to keep up our home, but Gladys had welcomed me with open arms into hers. Consequently, it had not been a hard decision to give up my job at the big metro newspaper when she broke her arm and needed assistance with the tasks of daily living. To be honest, I had been at the tail end of a bad breakup, so in many ways the move had come at a good time for me. I had also paused my potential book deal with a literary agent, although I had not given Gladys any of the details about either of those situations just yet.

Now I had my own rent-free space, but I spent most evenings with Gladys, just like the old days. She had grumbled about my decision to return home just as my career was taking off, but I knew she liked having the company. "Someone to check up on me, make sure I'm still ticking," she often joked.

The words "still ticking" brought me back to the present. Charlotte. I still needed to send a text to Jimmy. I slipped Walter into the next parking place and pulled out my phone.

"Meet me at Sheila's in five."

CHAPTER 6

Jimmy and I huddled outside Sheila's apartment door. She lived in a second-floor apartment in a converted colonial-era home on a side street by the tracks, where the train that went from Boston to Portland passed multiple times a day.

"Sheila," I called out, as I gave a gentle rap on the heavy wood. "Sheila? It's Piper and Jimmy. We just want to know if you're okay."

Oh, and was Detective Collins suggesting you know something about Charlotte's death? I added to myself. But I'd keep that question unspoken until we got a sense of how she was doing.

I gave another soft thump on the door, then waited impatiently. I really wanted to avoid another run-in with the downstairs tenant, a rather unpleasant older man who had told us to be quiet as we started up the stairs.

Beside me, Jimmy shifted from one foot to the other. *This is not going anywhere,* I thought. *Just how long should we stand here?*

Perhaps we could leave her a note. I looked down and realized I'd left my purse and notebook in the car in my haste to get to Sheila's apartment. Fortunately, I could see that Jimmy had his ever-present notebook in the front pocket of his button-down shirt.

I was about to ask for a piece of paper when I heard soft footsteps on the other side of the door and a chain jangling. The door opened a crack, just enough for me to see Sheila peering out.

"I'm really not feeling like talking," she said, so softly I had to lean forward to hear her.

I knew we would need to proceed cautiously with her.

"Sheila, you seemed pretty upset when you left your interview, are you okay?" I met her hazel eyes through the crack in the door. "Do you need anything? Or is there anything we can do to help?"

Sheila sighed, stepped back slightly, and opened the door. "Quickly! Clyde gets upset at new people." She ushered us into her kitchen.

Clyde, as it turned out, was her massive white parrot. And upset may have been an understatement. He sat on a wooden perch between the kitchen and living room, old copies of *The Exeter Independent* spread beneath him, covered in poop and a pile of stray feathers. Clyde began squawking at Jimmy and me, much like the way a watchdog would bark. Every few seconds, he ruffled up his wings as if he were about to take flight.

"Clyde, Clyde," Sheila cooed, then added, "he's just not the same since Bonnie died."

Was she for real? I had never had a poker face and tried not to smirk.

Jimmy didn't seem to get it. He asked, "Who's Bonnie?"

"She was his mate. They had been together for almost fifteen years. He's been so depressed, he keeps pulling his feathers out." She gestured to the feathers on the newspapers. "Someone online suggested putting poor Clyde on Prozac."

Seriously, a parrot on Prozac? I knew I had to appear sympathetic. I did not want to discourage Sheila from letting us stay for a few minutes.

"That's so sad," I said. Jimmy nodded.

Sheila shrugged. "Anyhow, the vet said that Prozac wouldn't actually help him. And so, I just deal with the feathers. What else can I do?"

As we continued to stand there awkwardly, Sheila floated around her tiny kitchen almost as if she were in a trance of some sort. Despite the summer temperatures, she wore a long-sleeve blouse, along with her trademark billowy skirt.

"Tea?" Sheila asked.

"No, thank you," I responded, though I really could have used another coffee.

Sheila twisted open a container and heaped a scoop of grey powder into her mug. "Moon balance supplement," she explained. "My astrologer says it helps my spirit when Mercury is in retrograde."

Oh yes, the astrologer in Portsmouth who led the alien abduction support group, which Sheila had written a story about after the annual UFO Festival in town. Sheila had made this woman her unofficial life coach. Now she often returned to the newsroom after visiting the woman's shop, eager to show off the latest herbal remedies she had picked up that week.

She took a sip and looked at me. "I know Charlotte was awful," she began. "You both know that too, but I think she felt like that was what an editor was supposed to be like." She gazed out the tiny kitchen window and added, "It was just such a shock to hear about her death."

I sensed an opportunity and leaned closer to her.

"Sheila, do you know something about what happened? It

sounded like Richie, I mean Detective Collins, thinks you know something important."

Now, if any other person in the newsroom had details about this, they would have been chomping to spill the intel. But Sheila wasn't a typical newsroom employee.

Instead of answering my question, Sheila added another sprinkle of moon powder to her tea. Her spirit was clearly going to be in tip-top shape. Perhaps it would help with her timid nature too.

I tried again. "Sheila, did you see her last night at all? I mean, aside from the opening reception at the town hall?"

Sheila turned toward me and looked surprised, as if she had momentarily forgotten I was there.

"I went to the office," she said. "I'd forgotten to bring home my laptop, and I needed it to write up my story about the new art exhibit today. I prefer to write articles here, where my flow isn't so hampered by the chaos of that place. So, I went back to the paper to pick it up last night."

She paused and took a shaky breath. "And she was there too."

So, wait, Charlotte was at the paper after the Rev Fest reception? But then, how did she get back to the town hall? How did she end up there, dangling off the roof, with the shadow of Lady Justice cast upon her? I pushed these questions away as the look in Charlotte's dead eyes flashed back through my mind.

Clyde started screeching again, more aggressively than before. Jimmy jumped, and then he backed away from the watch bird, edging closer to the exit.

"Are you sure Clyde's okay there?" I asked.

"Oh, he's fine, he's just expressing himself," Sheila said, cooing at him again. "Clyde, Clyde, be good."

I felt like we probably had a limited window of time before

Sheila got nervous again about telling us what she knew. She finally looked a bit calmer. Maybe there was something to that moon powder after all.

"So, you went to get the laptop and Charlotte was there?"

I let the statement hang in the room and waited. You can learn a lot in an interview if you sit and wait. The uncomfortable silence often results in people blurting out things they had not intended to say.

Sheila closed her eyes, clenched her jaw, and exhaled loudly. "You know, I'd really rather not say. I told the police what I know, and I want to leave it at that."

Jimmy looked uncomfortable, but I felt like a dog who kept catching the scent of a squirrel. Something was clearly up, but I was afraid to spook her. Still, I couldn't resist asking one more question. I just knew that Sheila wasn't telling us something important.

"So, did you see anything else or anyone else while you were leaving?"

Sheila shook her head. "You know, they are going to be really upset if they find out I talked to you."

"It's okay," I said. "We just wanted to make sure you were okay, and you know how it is, right? In a newsroom, we just can't hold back from asking questions. I didn't mean to upset you."

Sheila settled into a kitchen chair and took another sip of her tea.

After a long pause, I said, "Jimmy and I saw Grayson this morning. He's giving us a nice comment for a feature about Charlotte, her life, her contributions to the town, the paper. Do you have any suggestions of other people we should talk to? Know if she was seeing anyone?"

When she shrugged and looked back out the window, I took

it as affirmation and pressed on. "So, she was seeing someone then?"

"Well, I guess it might be okay to tell you now, given the circumstances," she said. After another long sip, she added, "I overheard her on the phone before the long weekend for the Fourth of July. It sounded like she was making plans to meet up with a man, like a date, not a work thing."

I waited, not wanting to spook her.

"And then, when I was leaving that night, she didn't leave in her car; someone picked her up."

Finally, we were getting somewhere. "Do you remember what the car looked like?"

She shook her head. "It was silver-blue and some kind of convertible, fancy looking."

This didn't sound familiar to me, but then, I didn't know what everyone in town drove.

Sheila continued, "When we came back to work after the holiday, I asked if that was her boyfriend. She just said it was someone she knew because of a story she was working on."

Wait, what? Charlotte was working on a story herself? Charlotte had always been far too busy micromanaging me to do any reporting. And really, it was not in her job description. She assigned news stories, gave a first edit, and handled the editorial page. This tidbit was a red flag, but of what I wasn't sure.

Clyde started flapping and squawking again, louder this time, more insistent. Why didn't she just put him in his cage? But then, just like that, Clyde was off. He dove toward my head, his beak opened wide, in full attack mode. I fell to the floor and covered my head with my hands. Jimmy scurried to the corner of the kitchen.

"Clyde, leave it!" Sheila yelled. I'd never heard her sound so assertive. She held out her arm, and seconds later, the disturbance was over. Clyde landed on her arm, calm as a sparrow, come back to roost.

"He's never done that before," she said, and I was relieved as she coaxed him into his cage. "I think it's your aura."

I held back from the sarcastic rebuttal I wanted to make. My aura? What was in that powder? Well, I wouldn't go there. Jimmy reached down to help me up.

"Thanks," I said, as I dusted off my pants.

Sheila was still fussing over Clyde, filling the water in his cage and murmuring to him. We'd lost our window of opportunity. It was time to go. Sheila might have more information, but today wasn't the day we were going to extract it from her.

"Sheila, we're going to head out now," I said, keeping what I hoped was a safe distance from Clyde who was eying the open door on his cage. "Thank you. Please let us know if you need anything. Anything at all."

Jimmy nodded his agreement. Sheila turned, the vacant, somewhat-dazed expression back on her face. "Okay then," she said quietly.

I hadn't done any real exercise since I returned to town, but I could still move when I needed to, and I practically skipped down the stairs to get away from the attack parrot before he could go for round two. In fact, I was moving so fast I almost tripped over the tattered rug at the bottom of the stairwell. Jimmy had to work to keep up.

Outside, however, he passed me. I said, "What the heck was that? Do you think Sheila was on something stronger than tea? Did you see her eyes?"

Jimmy didn't answer. He had already rounded the corner to the street.

"Piper," he called out, sounding concerned. "Why did you leave your car door open?"

My mouth dropped briefly before I muttered a few choice expletives under my breath. Walter had been laid bare. The driver side door was wide open. My purse lay upside down on the street next to the passenger door, its contents scattered on the pavement. What now?

CHAPTER 7

"Son of a monkey," I muttered, as I looked at Gladys's car. As angry as I was, I upheld my vow to cut down on actual swearing, which was, to put it mildly, a challenge. "I can't believe I forgot to lock it."

I had been so eager to get to Sheila that not only had I forgotten my purse and notebook, I hadn't locked the doors.

Jimmy paced around my car, his apprehension palpable as he digested the scene in front of him.

"Who would do this?" he asked. "I don't like this, Piper, I really don't like this."

I sighed. This was going to raise his anxiety to the same level as the morning he barreled into the newsroom convinced his uncle, Hap, and aunt knew he had snuck his girlfriend in for a sleepover. He hadn't been able to write a clear sentence all day and had been afraid to look Hap in the eyes for weeks afterwards.

Viewing the contents of my purse spewed all over the ground, I briefly wondered if I actually had bigger problems. Was someone trying to stop me from asking questions? I shivered ever so slightly, not from the weather but from wondering if our presence at Sheila's had triggered the incident. But given that it had only been hours since Charlotte's body had plunged to the ground, it seemed unlikely. Who was I kidding? It was probably some local teenager fishing for easy money in unlocked cars. The police ran warnings about them often on their crime stoppers page.

I bent down to pick up my purse and gather the contents. It was like a still art painting of a boring life. A pack of breath mints, Chapstick, a spare notebook, and a handful of pens. I had learned early on that it was always a good idea to have a spare pen or two on hand in the event one ran out of ink. A pencil was also necessary for those cold or rainy days when the ink could freeze up.

The little cash I had was gone, but thankfully my debit card was still there. The only other casualty was my lipstick, something I only wore a handful of times a year, which lay discarded in the road, its tip mashed flat. Well, there went my chances for gussying up before I hit the Tuck Tavern to pump the locals for gossip about Charlotte's mystery man. Guess I'd have to rely on my keen interviewing skills rather than my female prowess to find out what people knew. Or bring Jenny, who had become a magnet for almost everyone in town since launching her bakery.

Jimmy hovered like a mother hen. "We should call the cops, don't you think?" he asked.

I appreciated his concern, but that was the last thing I was going to do. Tell the police, so they could warn us off continuing to ask questions? Then they'd also know we had talked to Sheila. Detective Richie Collins was an old friend, but I knew he would not be thrilled to find me poking my nose into the investigation.

"No," I said, perhaps a bit too abruptly. "First of all, we were here, talking to Sheila, who wasn't supposed to talk to us. How is that going to look? Not good."

"But, Piper, we could be in actual danger," he said.

I tried to remind myself that he was still in college. He was probably scared. And it had been one of my first thoughts, too.

"Listen, we're not calling the cops, Jimmy. This is no big deal."

Jimmy crossed his arms over his chest, frowning. "Well, just remember, I wanted to call them." Then he shuffled his feet and muttered, "I don't think this is a good idea at all."

You are such a Nervous Nelly, I thought. I popped open the back of the boxy station wagon, where I kept all of my practical New Hampshire supplies: jumper cables, windshield washer fluid, a container of wet wipes. *You never know when you might need a wet wipe,* I thought, as I wiped off the lipstick on the side of the tube.

As we headed back toward town, Jimmy was still twitching and periodically looking over his shoulder. I dropped him off at his car and made my way back to the carriage house to wait for Grayson's quote before I wrote my story.

Top Editor Hung from Town Hall During Festival

By Piper Greene

EXETER__ Charlotte Campbell, the editor of The Exeter Independent, *was found dead on the sidewalk by Town Hall early Friday morning.*

Exeter Police Chief Frank Sinclair said onlookers at the town's annual Independence Festival got a horrific surprise when the body of the 55-year-old woman plummeted to the sidewalk next to Town Hall. She had been hung over the edge of the town hall. He declined to provide specifics, pending notification of next of kin, but multiple witnesses said she was wearing the trademark red jacket of a British soldier.

Sinclair said the death is considered suspicious and that more information will be released when appropriate.

"At this time, we have no reason to believe the public is at

risk," the chief said. "But we do ask residents to contact us if they have any information about this crime."

Campbell had been at the helm of the weekly newspaper for the past 4 years. "This is a tremendous loss for the Exeter community," said Grayson Adams III, Chairman of the Select Board. "Charlotte was a dedicated editor, a true professional, who will be missed by many. This tragedy is just absolutely unbelievable."

Officials from the County Medical Examiner's office were on scene to assist with the investigation. Sinclair said a press conference will be scheduled tomorrow.

Back in my apartment, I looked at the story on my laptop. It was brief, but I knew this was the kind of story that would grow legs once it got out.

I could only imagine the reaction to the story around town. A death—likely a murder—in Exeter, especially one of such a public persona, was big news.

But before I could get to the bottom of the question of Charlotte's death, I'd have to find out more details about her life. Frankly, I'd avoided getting to know her aside from the professional interaction I was required to have as a reporter working on stories she assigned.

I knew that she had become the editor at the paper while I lived in the city. In fact, she had taken over for the longtime editor who had trained me as a high school intern. Given the comments I heard when I was out on assignments, I knew there was no love lost for her in Exeter. Most people felt she just didn't understand, or care about, the town.

At the office, Charlotte was either over-the-top nice, which always felt phony, or she was a complete, raving witch. I learned that predicting which version of Charlotte would appear on any given day was impossible. She reserved her nastiest treatment of her reporters for when we were alone. I had gotten my first real taste of that side the day Charlotte had reprimanded me for interviewing a source on the school board she had told me to ignore—which of course had only made me more determined to talk to the person.

"Nobody, I mean *nobody,* goes behind my back like that. I don't care how long your family has been in town," she had warned me later on, after cornering me in the lady's room.

I had kept my cool and held my tongue, despite the temptation to point out my four-year journalism degree and my experience as a successful reporter at a well-respected metro paper. I knew I had an uncanny gut instinct when it came to knowing where to follow a story, and I had every intention of following it again in the future. She, on the other hand, had worked at a series of small local papers, at least as far as I could tell, and she relished the power of the pen more than the power of serving as a public watchdog. Unfortunately, she was also my boss.

Soon after my bathroom encounter, I learned I wasn't the first one to be on the receiving end of Charlotte's temper. One night over drinks after deadline at the Tuck Tavern, other newsroom staff had started sharing stories about Charlotte making threats toward them when no one was around. They told me that some of them had even talked about unionizing a few years earlier, which did not go far because everyone liked Hap so much, and frankly the staff was too small. The sports editor, Nate, had talked to Hap about their concerns, but there hadn't been any real change. Over time, they'd simply dropped it, calling Charlotte "Sybil" behind her back as an ode to the infamous psychiatric case of a woman who reportedly had sixteen personalities.

In fact, I knew that Charlotte had alienated most of the folks in Exeter. She had a proclivity for writing columns in her op-ed spot that did not sit well with the locals, who considered her a harsh, meddling outsider. Charlotte had even taken on one of the town boards last year, calling them out for illegal meetings after she spotted them eating breakfast together at the Morning Musket. They claimed they had only been speculating about the secret ingredient in Jenny's scones, but under state law, the meeting constituted a quorum.

Next, when Grayson was campaigning for a third term as chairman of the select board, she had strongly suggested that it was time for a change in leadership. This made his kind words about her even more unusual, but then it was in his public favor to appear benevolent. Charlotte had even taken on the very police who were now investigating her murder, writing an editorial lambasting the officers for getting a higher hourly rate of pay for traffic details. Personally, you could not pay me enough to stand in the blazing hot sun or a freezing cold blizzard all day directing traffic, but Charlotte said the town was squandering its money.

I also wondered about the new information from Sheila that Charlotte was possibly involved with a man, a mystery man, who drove a fancy silver-blue car. With everything that was going on, it seemed like he might show up soon—unless, of course, he had something to hide.

My phone pinged with a text message from Jimmy: "Cops are questioning Andy Hathaway."

My thoughts jerked back from Charlotte, almost universally disliked, to the mild-mannered photographer who was genuinely liked by everyone who met him. I responded immediately.

"Where?"

"The PD."

"Are you there?"

"No, he texted me."

I wasn't aware that Jimmy and Andy had become that close, but either way, I needed to find out more, something I knew Jimmy wasn't quite up for yet.

"Thx. Will head over now."

First Hap had refused to say why Andy wasn't at the newsroom, and now Andy was at the police station. Of course, he had been the photographer at the opening reception for the festival. Maybe they just wanted to review his photos. Then again, maybe he actually knew something. Hap had called Andy's absence a "long story."

Andy was a gentle spirit, and I knew he valued his job at *The Exeter Independent*, which seemed to be his first steady job after traveling around the country after high school. I had always enjoyed going on assignments with him, watching the kindness he showed as he photographed people. He was the last person I could imagine committing a murder. Still, I needed to see what I could find out.

I grabbed my purse, slipped my phone in my pocket, and strode out the back door, stopping when I heard something rustling behind me. I spun around and looked at the trees behind the carriage house. Oscar, the black-and-white feral cat that was constantly challenging my primary residence in the carriage house, peered down at me from a low branch. Nothing else seemed out of the ordinary, but still, something felt off.

I walked over to the edge of the yard, then scanned the area. My eyes came to rest on the ground, where a few leaves had fallen during the last big storm. A candy wrapper lay on the ground. It was a Zagnut, the vintage peanut brittle bar I remembered from my childhood, which only appeared in old-fashioned general stores these days. I had never seen one locally, but this was clearly new. The wrapper wasn't faded. In fact, it looked as though it had recently been discarded, with a few light-tan crumbs visible inside.

I knew the wrapper was probably nothing, but the situation with Walter the Wagon at Sheila's had me more on edge that I wanted to admit. As I climbed in the station wagon, I could not shake the eerie feeling that someone had been watching me.

CHAPTER 8

A colonial soldier was sitting on the bench in the lobby of the police station, holding an ice pack on his head. Seemed a bit early, given that the annual battle was not until the next day. But then, I'd already started the festival seeing a dead British soldier by the town hall, so nothing should have surprised me at that point.

"What happened to him?" I asked Cindy, the elderly receptionist.

"Oh, you know how they are," she said. "Sounds like a fight broke out in the encampment again—something about which side was going to win the battle, colonists or redcoats."

That would have been a comical story to write: the debate each year among the reenactors about how the battle would end. We all knew how the war ended, how the colonists eventually won their independence from the king, but they tried to mix it up each year, keep the crowd guessing. Honestly, I was kind of sympathetic to the debate. I mean, how many times could you do the same battle scene? And who wanted to play the losers?

"So, how are things with you?" I asked Cindy, a necessary approach in small-town newspaper life, where you got further with a request the friendlier you were with the receptionists.

"Oh, fine," she said with a sigh. "You know, my arthritis is really acting up, but I can't complain. Lots of others got it worse than me."

There was a limit to my ability to keep up small talk, and I knew I needed to get right to the point before she gave me an update on her husband's bunion, another frequent topic. Seemed insurance would not cover those repeat trips to the podiatrist, and she was just not having it. I never wanted to get old, when all you seemed to talk about was your health issues and what time your next meal was planned. Then again, Gladys chose to ignore talk of aging altogether, instead regaling me with stories of her dancing career.

I said, "So, I heard Andy Hathaway's here. Any chance I could talk to him?"

She glanced behind her desk toward the hallway, no doubt to make sure none of the officers were about to walk past.

"Sorry, he's still in with them, and from the sound of things, it's going to be a while." She paused briefly, then lowered her voice. "One of the highflyer defense attorneys is in there now too."

Now that was interesting on a few levels. It seemed unusual that a defense attorney would already be at the station if Andy were just being questioned as a witness. It also cost money for a retainer, and I could not believe that Andy, with his measly photographer's salary, could afford that.

"Wow..." I said, somewhat conspiratorially, hoping my tone would lead her to expound a bit more on how or why the attorney came to Andy's aid.

"I know," Cindy said, clearly understanding what I was thinking. "Showed up almost immediately. They seem to know each other well, too. He gave Andy a hug and everything when he went into the interview room—or so the chief's secretary told me."

I momentarily mulled this information over. A well-known defense attorney in the area knew Andy. Knew him well enough to show up at the police department immediately. And then hugged him, as if they were old friends. It did not make sense. But what did I really know about Andy's life other than our joint assignments at the paper? He'd never volunteered details of where he'd lived or worked before Exeter. I assumed he was just a bit shy. Still, this was a *very* interesting development.

"Hmm," I said. "Well, thanks, I'll check back in later."

I sat in the Volvo in front of the police department for a few minutes, contemplating my next move. I knew I wasn't going to be able to chase down leads on Charlotte's murder without Jimmy as a sidekick indefinitely. As the paper's most experienced reporter, I could keep it up for a while, but eventually Hap would gently suggest that I turn my attention back to Jimmy's on- the-job training. And in the middle of all of that, the Independence Festival was still ongoing. I really hoped Sheila, who was the actual features writer, might cover the festival if she recovered from the shock of Charlotte's death in time to return to work.

The inquisitive part of my personality could only think of one thing: finding out as much as I could about Charlotte, Andy, and the case before Hap reeled me in. I figured it would not hurt to poke around Andy's apartment to find out if his roommates knew what was going on.

I knew exactly where the well-maintained Victorian-style house that Andy lived at was located. The driveway was empty aside from a large black pickup truck with oversized wheels. I hadn't given it much thought before, but as I stared at the stately home, I wondered again about Andy's finances. He had a high-priced attorney and seemed to live in a *very* nice place.

I went up to the door and rang the buzzer. Nothing. I leaned forward, peering in the window, and was surprised to see gleaming hardwood floors. They were pristine, even by Gladys's standards. Nothing seemed out of place. What I could see of the house had a peaceful feel to it, like a yoga studio. Certainly not the type of place I would expect to find a single photographer. It also looked too big for just one person.

"I don't think they're home," a deep voice said, and I jumped.

A fit man walking two toy poodles had quietly moved up behind me. He was wearing a black hoodie sweatshirt, and I felt like I'd been busted by the neighborhood watch.

"Sorry," I said, reaching my hand out to him. "I work with Andy at the paper. I'm worried he may be in a bit of trouble."

The man smiled at me. "I'm Terrance, their neighbor," he said, gesturing toward a driveway behind us. "I live over that way."

The poodles were clearly not ready to stand around and chitchat. As they pulled him closer toward me, he said, "Fiona, Fancy, heel! Heel! It's not time!" Then he told me, "They're only puppies, still learning the ropes."

I looked around awkwardly, not sure if I should make a graceful exit or ask this neighbor another question. Then the dogs calmed down and he continued.

"This trouble with Andy," he began. "Does it have anything to do with him losing his job yesterday?"

Even if I had possessed a poker face, it would have failed me in that moment.

"What do you mean, *losing* that job? Did something happen at work?"

He hesitated, only briefly. "Well, I only saw him for a minute in the parking lot yesterday afternoon. But yeah, he said his female boss told him that his position was being eliminated. Downsizing or something like that. Honestly, I've never seen the guy so angry. He was using some words to describe that woman that I've never heard him say before."

My internal alarm bell started to ding. Andy lost his job, Andy was angry at Charlotte, and a few hours later, she was dead. But I couldn't bring myself to believe he could actually be responsible for killing her. It didn't fit with the Andy I'd gotten to know these past few months.

But goodness, considering that my job was to stay on top of information, how had this big news slipped by me? It explained why Hap had been so evasive. And were all of our jobs at risk?

The puppies' barks broke into my reverie. I said, "Before I go, do you have any idea when Andy's roommate is usually around?" I took a chance there, not actually knowing if he had a roommate, but assuming the place was too big for just one person.

He smirked. "Oh, that would be A-Train, but I'll let you experience him for yourself. You might try him later today when he's home from the recording studio. He's making an album right now."

I nodded and said, "What's his real name?"

The poodles started pulling Terrence toward the edge of the driveway, straining on their leashes and putting him off balance, which was a feat in itself given their tiny size relative to his.

"You know, I don't know. Never goes by anything other than A-Train. We call him A around here for short."

"Okay, well thanks. I'm Piper, by the way," I called to him, as he gave in and let the dogs trot over to the side of the driveway. "Good luck with the puppies."

Before he could respond, the puppies dragged him forward to continue their adventure.

I climbed back into the Volvo and contemplated my next move. Light was fading and I knew it was almost time to call it quits for the day. My phone vibrated with a text message. It was Jimmy.

"I heard something," he texted. "Sounds like Sheila wasn't the last one to see Charlotte alive. Andy was there too."

Oh, Andy. I really wanted to help him, even though it went against every bit of impartial journalism training I'd ever received. The thought of Andy being accused fired up all of my injustice-activist tendencies.

I wanted to head back to the police station, or even to find this A-Train roommate person, but as I drove back toward town, I knew I would have to set this aside for a few hours. It was, after all, the town's biggest weekend, and even with a suspicious death under investigation, some traditions would not be postponed. My brother was hosting his annual summer soirée on the river and shirking this family duty was never an option.

CHAPTER 9

Most years, I tolerated the annual party thrown by my brother, Chester, on the Gundalow Company's barge during the Independence Festival. He was a total stick in the mud, but it was the best vantage point to see the fireworks.

This year, I had no desire to go. I had barely spoken to him since he had refused to pitch in to help Gladys after her fall, claiming he was simply too busy at his law practice to get involved. He'd suggested that I had nothing going on, in a way that completely disregarded my burgeoning journalism career: "Surely, you could come home and help her out for a bit?"

Not to mention that Chester, a confirmed bachelor, had plenty of money to help hire someone local to check in on Gladys. However, in typical Yankee fashion, he would take that money with him to the grave, clenched tightly in his fists, before he spent it.

Now I planned to force myself to go to his party anyway, hoping I might pick up some tidbits about Charlotte while there. Chester did like to align himself with the who's who of the area business community, so it was more likely than not that I'd run into the people from the town with whom Charlotte had interacted the most.

Even more important, Gladys wanted to go, and she needed

a ride. She seemed to accept Chester for who he was, despite his selfish tendencies, something I had yet to master.

"He's a snob, but he'll come around," she had told me more than once.

I went home and changed into something more festive. Ten minutes later, Gladys was waiting for me in the driveway next to the car, which she lovingly put her hand on as she waited.

"Okay, Walter, let's go out for the evening," she said with a smile as she folded her long legs into the passenger seat. We found a parking spot not too far from the river, and then we walked to the site of the party, where Chester spotted us immediately.

"Well, well, if it isn't the fourth estate," he began, as he walked to the edge of the gundalow, a long, flat-bottomed wooden barge, to help us aboard.

"Chester," I said, before leaning in to give him an obligatory kiss on the cheek.

Chester Greene was an impressive man by most people's standards. Tall, with a full head of thick black hair, he looked much like our Puritan ancestors who were on display in the paintings in his library. He was dressed down, for him, sans necktie, but he still looked dapper in a white polo shirt and creased Nantucket Reds chinos. The only thing missing from this auspicious waterfront affair was a captain's hat.

"Aunt Gladys," he said, reaching out a strong arm to help her step onto the deck.

Gladys smiled politely and thanked him, but she didn't engage, instead teetering toward a makeshift bar set up in the middle of the barge, where beer and wine were on display.

I took a minute to find my footing on the boat, keeping an eye on Gladys, who was already clutching a glass of wine and making her way to one of the handful of chairs.

The wooden barge made a voyage to town each year from its home base in Portsmouth, a city on the ocean. Technically, it was there for an educational program during the festival, but during evening hours those with deep pockets, like my brother, were able to rent it out for private functions. The nonprofit that owned the barge used those funds to pay for routine maintenance and upkeep.

Chester was always in his glory during the festival weekend, which gave him a chance to share our long family history in town with anyone who would listen. I smiled at Gladys, took a breath, and looked around at the crowd. Chester had all the regulars. Currently, he was speaking with the dentist and his wife, who seemed to have no other purpose in life than her obsessive power walking. No matter what time of day I drove through Exeter, I spotted the woman. She walked three, sometimes four, times a day and still managed to survive on a diet of seltzer water and cucumber sandwiches.

Chester, who liked to keep the family name a steadfast presence in town, was in his glory. You would have thought our family line went right back to George Washington the way he talked and talked.

"You know, my ancestor came to town in 1647 and brought the town back to prosperity after that reverend left us high and dry," Chester said. "And then, of course, another descendant was our state's representative to the Constitutional Convention."

The dentist's wife nodded politely, but her eyes looked glazed.

"And you know," he went on, "Exeter supported every colonial protest against parliament's attempts to levy taxes on the colonies."

I bristled at his comments, especially since he made us all sound like a bunch of resentful revolutionaries and failed to mention any of the contemporary activities that made the town so special. Sure, we had a historical past, but a lot had happened in the nearly 400 years since then to modernize the town and its residents.

When the dentist and his wife managed to slip away from Chester, he stopped to talk with Emily, the petite woman who owned the Tuck Tavern. The tavern filled the same role in the evening as the bakery did in the morning: town gossip. I moved closer to join them.

"Piper is involved with that nasty business of the Campbell murder case," he told Emily. "Really, just unpleasant to be on the top of the homepage of our newspaper."

When he paused for effect, Emily perked up. "Any behind-the-scenes tidbits that didn't make the story online?" she asked.

Chester huffed and headed off toward the bar. I gave Emily my full attention and thought about what I might share. She seemed like a kindred spirit, and I decided to rely on my favorite technique to gather gossip: trading of information. I give out a crumb and the other person does the same. Maybe she'd share something that might help Andy.

"Well," I said, "I heard Charlotte was seeing a lot of someone in recent weeks."

Emily's eyebrows raised in acknowledgement, but she didn't say anything. I was going to have to work for it.

"Sounds like she confided in one of our coworkers," I continued, hoping to hook her.

Emily looked around. At the bar, Chester and another nearby guest had turned their backs ever so slightly to us, as they no doubt discussed some business dealing.

"Well," she said, "I did wonder about that when we started seeing her multiple nights a week, looking nice, if you know what I mean."

"Did you ever see her with anyone?" I asked.

"I didn't, but she had that look, you know, the glow you have early in a relationship," she confided. Inwardly, I cringed, realizing it had been a long time since I'd had that feeling. Outwardly, I leaned toward her with the type of eager face I hoped would encourage her to go on, which she did.

"You know, I'll ask Kevin. If anyone knows, it would be him."

Kevin Daniels, a down-on-his-luck tennis player, had returned to Exeter last year, and he worked a few nights a week at the Tuck Tavern. He was classically good looking, and business had picked up since he took over. It was like Exeter's version of Tom Cruise in *Cocktail,* though there would be no juggling of cocktail shakers here. Knowing the way this town operated, that would probably violate the Historic District ordinances.

Emily took a swig of her wine. Courage perhaps, or she was just stalling. Then she said, "I mean, he hasn't had an easy run of it since he came back, you know, after what happened."

That was an understatement. Kevin had returned to town after a brief run on the tennis circuit, where he'd made a name for himself not so much for his tennis ability, but for his tumultuous love affair with Maria Elsinger, his coach, which had ended rather dramatically during his final match when he broke his racket and stormed off the court because she had showed up in the stands with Kevin's rival.

Gladys chimed in from her chair near the bar, where she had clearly not missed anything. Her friend Stanley, a retired tailor, had arrived and was settled in a chair next to her. He was impeccably turned out as usual with his ever-present bowtie. He had one for every occasion, and this one had a pattern with tiny golden muskets.

"It's such a shame," Gladys clucked, shaking her head. "Last week, he was tipsy at the tennis courts. He hit the ball backward and just missed Pansy Bolton's head as she stood watching from the sidelines."

Too bad it missed, I thought. *It might have adjusted her attitude a bit.* Pansy, the head of the Rotary Club, wasn't my kind of person. When she wasn't tending her prize-winning rosebushes, she was looking down her nose at everyone else. I would have paid to see her get hit in the head with a tennis ball.

"You know, the only person we saw more than Charlotte lately was Grayson Adams," Emily added.

That didn't surprise me. The town's select board chairman was known to be there often, so I was curious why this had seemed worth noting to Emily.

"Really? Isn't that the norm for him?" I asked.

Emily shrugged. "Yes and no, but lately, even for Grayson, it was a lot."

Well, really, who could blame him for hiding out. Dealing with town business as chairman of the select board was a thankless job if there ever was one. The types of complaints and calls the board members fielded could get redundant, although some did make for quirky news stories, like the neighborhood feud that escalated until one neighbor painted her house with pink polka dots, in the historic district, just to annoy the other neighbor, a card-carrying member of the Daughters of the Exeter Revolution.

Emily emptied her wine glass and picked up her purse. "I've got to get back to the tavern," she said. "Keep up the good writing."

Chester, it seemed, had been eavesdropping. He called after Emily, "Well, it should be good writing. Top of her class in high school, accepted to any number of Ivy leaguers." He paused, sipped his drink, then went on. "Wasting herself at that newspaper, earning less than my receptionist does at the firm."

Gladys scowled at Chester, and when he went to greet new guests, she came over and patted my hand gently and then returned to her chair. Without saying anything, I knew what she was thinking. We had talked about my brother many times since I'd returned home: his attitude toward me, and Gladys's feeling that he needed to get knocked down a few notches. More than once, she had told me to just ignore him and walk away. "You've got so much to be proud of, Piper dear," she always said. "You're going places with your writing."

At my age, I should have moved past letting Chester get to me. I knew that he was the way he was; I wasn't going to change him. But knowing and feeling were two separate things. After our parents had died in the car accident, he hadn't even taken a break to make sure I was okay. He had stayed one day for their funeral and then went back to law school. I moved in with Gladys and didn't see him again until Christmas. We'd never been close given our age difference, but the little sister in me somehow still hoped that he might begin to fill a more nurturing big brother role, replacing the prickly and judgmental persona who was so prone to notice any mishap I made.

Thankfully, the annual fireworks display began, which broke my mood and helped me avoid listening to Chester ramble on about himself. I looked over at Gladys, thankful for all she had done for me and feeling good that I was able to reciprocate when she needed me most.

The fireworks continued in earnest, and I could just see the fire department set up on the other side of the river, next to the historic brick Powder House. The tiny square structure, whose claim to fame was providing storage for the gun powder that was eventually used in the Battle of Bunker Hill, served as ground zero for the firework setup.

Yes, Chester's party on the barge was a bit stuffy, but it was the best spot in town to watch the fireworks display.

As I looked around, I noticed that Stanley was now sound asleep. He must have turned off his hearing aids again, though I was surprised the thunderous shaking of the boat did not rouse him.

The fireworks were a success but were still over and done within 20 minutes. I quickly made the rounds with Gladys, giving people a farewell hug or handshake, using the excuse that I needed to get to bed.

That was partly true. I was exhausted, as much from being around Chester as from the excitement of having seen Charlotte's dead body. At the back of my mind, I also found myself wondering if this might be my ticket to a true crime novel, a general project I had briefly discussed with a literary agent before putting any book idea on pause when I moved back to Exeter.

"Nice display this year," Gladys said, as I took her arm to steady her. "The company, not such much. Stanley being the exception."

I nodded in agreement, and we walked in silence back to the car, passing the military encampment where the hardcore reenactors spent the night. They broke out in song as we passed by.

"There's a lusty liquor which Good fellows use to take-o; It is distilled with Nard most rich, And water of the lake-o."

I stopped to watch and listen for a minute, wondering if the injured soldier I'd seen in the police lobby was back and if the commonality of a good tavern song and a mug of beer had made him forget the events of earlier that day.

Our car was at the end of the park, and I found myself glad I had driven to the fireworks. After the day I'd had, the thought of walking home sounded impossible.

I flipped the switch to turn on Walter's headlights as I backed into the street. Right after I pulled onto the road, I had to slam the brakes so hard it felt like I almost put my foot through the floor of the car.

A disheveled woman with long white unkempt hair that went halfway down her back had stepped right out in front of us, more intent on eating a chocolate bar than on looking where she was going. I had just barely avoided hitting her.

"Oh, Piper dear, what a fright!" Gladys exclaimed, looking over at me.

My heart was pounding from the near miss, and I rolled down the window.

"Are you okay? You've got to watch where you're going."

The woman stared at me but didn't speak. Then she turned and ran the other way, a weathered backpack bouncing on her shoulders as she left. She certainly wasn't one of the historical role players.

"Well, what do you make of that?" Gladys asked. "She doesn't look like a local."

She was right. This was the type of town where between Gladys and me, we knew almost everyone, if not by name then by sight. And I knew I had never seen that woman before. So, who was she? And what was she doing wandering around in the town at night?

CHAPTER 10

As usual, I entered the Morning Musket through the door into the kitchen the next day, eager to find out what Jenny knew. I got right to the point, the encounter after the fireworks still on my mind.

"Have you seen a woman who looks really down on her luck around the river lately?"

Jenny looked up from a tray of cinnamon buns she was drizzling with a thin, white glaze. I knew the different types of glazes she used on different days, both from my addiction to the buns and from the story I'd written for the paper about her bakery. This simple mixture of powdered sugar, vanilla, and milk was not my favorite. I much preferred the thicker frosting with a cream cheese base and a hint of orange extract.

"Not that I can remember," she said, giving me a puzzled look. "More likely to run into that kind of person over near Portsmouth, where they've got the services to help, you know."

She was right. This reinforced my feeling that there was something significant about this woman, some reason that I should investigate her further.

She moved on to a tray of colossal croissants, artfully swirling chocolate sauce over the top before pausing to give me a conspiratorial grin.

"More importantly," she said, almost whispering, "any fireworks I need to know about between you and a certain blue-eyed detective? Was he there last night?"

My face flushed as she mentioned Richie Collins. She had been reminding me of that high school crush ever since I returned to town.

"No. I haven't seen him since he interviewed me at the newspaper after Charlotte's body was found," I said, trying not to take her bait.

She winked at me. "I confirmed with one of my regulars today that he's single, just saying. I mean, you two did always have a spark."

Normally I would tell her about my suspicion that he had been flirting with me during our interview at the paper. But I had sworn off romance after my last disastrous experience and wasn't ready to venture into the dating world quite yet.

"I don't have time for a love life right now," I reminded her. "I've got Gladys to look after, and not to mention, this murder investigation."

She rolled her eyes at me but shrugged and returned to the croissants. "Suit yourself," she said. "But I know what I see."

I put in my order—a bacon, egg, and cheddar sandwich on one of those giant croissants—and slipped out to the front of the house, stopping at the self-serve coffee station. The bakery was not as full as it had been during the festival, though a few role players in full garb remained. This year the organizers had extended the event to a full week of colonial-era events—a first—but it seemed that aside from the colonial soldiers in the coffee shop, most people had missed the memo about the expanded event. Exeter was working hard to build up its reputation as a historical destination, New Hampshire's version of Plimoth

Plantation or Colonial Williamsburg, but with only a small museum and Historical Society leading the charge, we weren't there yet.

I took a seat in the corner, my favorite type of place to sit, and placed my chair back against the wall so I could see all of the comings and goings without drawing attention to myself.

First things first, I thought, taking a long sip of coffee. And another. And another. I always struggled to function until I'd gotten at least half a cup into my system. It was odd that Jenny had brought up Richie, because he had texted me that morning with what he called a friendly tip: inquire about the autopsy from the medical examiner's office. "You didn't hear it from me," he had added, with a smiley face, winking emoji. The medical examiner's office would be my first stop.

Then I needed to find out what was going on at *The Exeter Independent.* I knew the murder was my top story, but at a paper of this size we all had to multitask, and I had a feeling Hap would have some other stories for me to write this week. But first, I really wanted to find out more about Andy. Had he been released from police custody? Between his layoff and Charlotte's death, the timing did look suspicious. And who was the mystery man with the fancy car?

My sandwich arrived and I looked around as I nibbled my first bite. Winnie Smart from the Historical Society was in her usual spot. As town historian, Winnie wrote a monthly piece for the paper about the town's history, interesting people who lived here back in the colonial days, or even more modern residents. So I had a sense that she probably had a file about Charlotte over at the Historical Society, since Charlotte had held a public position in the town. Winnie often remarked that the reporters working on *The Exeter Independent* were writing the first draft of history, and I knew she kept clippings of past issues of the paper.

"Morning, Winnie," I called out.

She looked up, gave me a tired smile, and placed her teacup down. "Well, we survived another year of this festival," she said. Then she paused, clearly remembering about Charlotte, and added, "Well, most of us anyway."

I slid over to the table next to her, rearranged my breakfast, and leaned in a little closer. "So, how well did you know Charlotte? I wasn't living here when she moved to town, and honestly, I kind of kept her at arm's length at work if you know what I mean."

Winnie chewed a piece of her bran muffin, ruminating like a cow chewing a tough piece of hay as she worked through her own morning roughage.

"Well," she said, "she worked in Portsmouth before coming here, you know. Covered their city hall before being promoted to assistant editor. Can't really say why she'd go from a larger paper to a smaller one like ours, but maybe she just wanted the prestige of being the big fish in a little pond."

She chewed some more then added, "I really didn't have much to do with her. Sent my column directly to Hap. But you hear things, if you know what I mean."

I leaned closer. "Such as?" I said, hoping she would go on.

"Oh, you know, that there was some concealed reason why she wasn't ever going to be able to move up to a big paper, something that kept her at the local level," Winnie said, her eyes brightening as she shared these details. "I always got the impression that there was something in her past that she would prefer to remain in the past."

Could it be something worth getting killed over? I wondered.

It was hard to stay calm at moments like this. Part of my personality always wanted to know everything—immediately. When I got that feeling in my stomach that I was on to something, I went full speed ahead.

"How did you hear that?" I asked. If I could identify the source, I might be able to track down first-hand information.

"Well, here and there. You know, people who came into the Historical Society from other towns, other places where she worked before here." She paused. "But I can't really remember who said what; I just filed it away in the old vault." She pointed to her head.

This was slightly disappointing, but since Portsmouth was just a few towns over, it was a great place to start. I also felt a pinch of satisfaction knowing that something in Charlotte's past had kept her working at a small-town newspaper. After all, she'd been hanged in a traitor's jacket. Surely, I could eventually discover why. In a small-town, after a while, no one really had an iron-clad secret.

CHAPTER 11

I wasn't able to head to Portsmouth until late that afternoon. Unfortunately, I had forgotten about the rush of vacationers heading to Maine, and I was stuck in traffic on the interstate for so long that the office of *The Portsmouth Clipper* was closed when I finally got there. First thing Monday morning, I hopped in Walter and headed that way again.

As I pulled into the parking lot, I was impressed with their setup. It was a far cry above the tiny brick building off Water Street that housed *The Exeter Independent.* Not only did they have a spacious newsroom, complete with a kitchen stocked with free snacks, but they had a state-of-the-art digital photography area, and multiple photographers.

It seemed the only thing the newsroom didn't have was any information about Charlotte. The current editor was out of the office, and the only people left in the newsroom hadn't worked there when Charlotte was the editor. The receptionist had let me into the newsroom only because I knew some of the locals from the informal monthly meetups for journalists at one of the bars in the city.

"You need to find Todd Tisden," the petite brunette who covered the City Hall beat told me. The only problem with that was that no one knew where Todd was. According to my bar friends, he was kind of a free spirit, prone to traveling the country with his truck camper or hitching a ride on a large yacht out of New Castle when it went south for the winter and they needed an extra crew member.

Todd, it seemed, had worked with Charlotte and openly disliked her. At the time, people chalked it up to Charlotte cracking down on his "loosey-goosey" approach to reporting: coming in at noon, leaving for hours, and not communicating with Charlotte about what he was working on.

"He's a real character," the city hall reporter said with a smirk. "We all kind of wondered how he kept his job, you know, with the way he vanished when he was supposed to be on deadline."

"It seemed," she continued, "that Todd had some sort of dirt on Charlotte, something that he was holding over her, something that gave him—as he described it—job security. He never told anyone what it was, but we had all speculated that it must have been big for Todd to get the get-out-of-jail-free card with Charlotte that he seemed to have acquired."

This seemed to echo the speculation that Winnie had told me about.

"You have *no* idea where he is?" I asked.

"Last we heard, he was working on a banana plantation somewhere warm," she replied.

Now, I can't lie, the idea of tracking a man who lived on a yacht and worked on a banana plantation did sound like an intriguing prospect. But, given my current salary at the paper, the fact that I was knee deep in my own investigation into the murder, and my heartfelt commitment to taking care of Gladys, it wouldn't be happening anytime soon.

When I got back to my carriage house, I did a quick online search for Todd Tisden, browsing through social media, but I

71

came up empty. It didn't surprise me, given what the helpful reporter had described as his tendency to go off the grid, but aside from links to articles he'd written, I came up blank, which only made me want to keep looking. There had to be some clue about where he was living, but it seemed like the guy had vanished like someone in the witness protection program. I left him a message at the last phone number his coworkers in Portsmouth had found on file and hoped I might get lucky.

Just as I was on the precipice of going down another level of rabbit hole with my online searching, which I knew could end with hours of my life that I'd never get back, my phone buzzed with a text from Jimmy. He wrote that he was with Andy, who wanted to talk to me.

I met up with Jimmy and Andy at the parkway along the Squamscott River, where just days earlier the Gundalow had docked during the Independence Festival. We met up at the end of the park, on a small hill that gave us a view back toward the downtown section of what I liked to call our little Puritan village: old wooden houses built in the 1700s, interspersed with solid, brick buildings. From there, I could see the top of the historic brick town hall, where Charlotte had met her end, and the steeple of the town's oldest church, which was visible above the rest.

My family had been members of that Congregationalist church since their early days in Exeter, when my mother's ancestors arrived on the river, built a sawmill, and brought prosperity to the town. Chester was fond of recounting how—most annoyingly—after establishing the church, the minister had returned to England. It had taken years for the town to find a replacement. You would have thought Chester had been in charge of human resources, the way he complained. Still, despite

Chester's gripes against the original minister, my family were longtime members of the church, and I'd spent many a Sunday as a child in its Sunday school.

But I didn't have time to think about Chester's grumbles right now. I brushed some crumbs off the bench and sat down with Andy and Jimmy.

For the most part, Andy Hathaway looked like he always did. He had on his regular uniform of neat Levi's, a blue cotton polo shirt, and his brown leather docksider shoes. Only occasionally did we see Andy in something other than long jeans or khaki pants. But he was always neat and tidy. Jimmy and I had been known to joke that his legs must be the color of a vampire given that they never saw the light of day. Still, there were pronounced lines around his eyes today, a hint that the ordeal was taking a toll on the normally laid-back photographer.

"Oh, Andy, I am just so sorry about your job," I began.

"Yeah, thanks," he said. "I mean, it's not surprising, but on top of everything else, it's been a rough couple of days."

I wanted to be sympathetic, but I also was chomping to get to the news. *What happened at the police station? And why was a high-flying defense attorney at the police station with him like it was old home day?* I was pretty certain that Jimmy, who looked even more uncomfortable than usual, hadn't asked.

"So, Andy," I continued, "do you need anything from us? I mean, have you heard anything else from the paper? Now that Hap's doing double duty as owner and editor . . ." I paused, not wanting to say what I imagined we were all thinking: *without Charlotte's salary to pay.* "Maybe they won't let you go."

Andy shrugged. "Your guess is as good as mine," he said. "But the timing couldn't have been worse, and the cops are really fixated on that."

According to Andy, right before the opening reception for the festival, Charlotte had decided to eliminate the staff photographer position and have reporters take their own photos. The festival was supposed to be his last gig. She told him to shoot the event, process the photos for the Sunday paper, and clean out his desk.

"So, I just wanted to get out of there," he told us. "You know, get the photos uploaded, get my gear, and leave."

When he had gone back to the newsroom to pick up his stuff, Charlotte had returned. He said she had clearly enjoyed more than a few Pinot Grigios, and she had started accusing him of stealing camera equipment from the newspaper.

"It was mine, my own gear, my own lenses, things I wanted to be sure I didn't lose," he said. "You know, the way she made it sound, I wasn't going to be able to get back into the newsroom after that last assignment."

He paused, clearly annoyed with himself. "I shouldn't have let her get to me, I know, but I just couldn't help it," he said. "I yelled, and she yelled, and then, well, you probably heard that Sheila showed up."

I kept my face neutral. Sheila hadn't mentioned that she'd seen Andy and Charlotte arguing when she talked to us about going back to get her laptop. Though to be fair, she had been quite upset the day we went to her apartment. It could have slipped her mind.

The police told Andy that he was on the surveillance footage outside the offices. There were no cameras inside the building, but two had gone up outside recently. Hap had them installed after a particularly disgruntled reader showed up outside, in a van festooned with handmade signs complaining about the paper's coverage of local government, and spray painted some choice expletives on the sidewalk. The cameras went up too late to catch that man in the act, but Hap felt it was better to be prepared for future incidents.

"People don't respect journalists like they used to when I was your age," he told me when I asked about the cameras, before adding, "it's a darn shame it's come to this in a town like Exeter."

Andy went on to explain that he took his gear, left the newsroom, and thought nothing of it until he heard about Charlotte's death.

It sounded plausible, especially given my gut feeling about Andy's innocence, but something was niggling at me. "Andy, I went down to the police station when I heard you were there," I began. "And I heard you had an attorney, that high-priced one from Portsmouth. How do you know him?"

Andy looked out at the river, where a great blue heron had just swooped down and landed on the shallow side. It poked its beak forward and speared a fish, which it swallowed in one gulp.

"We go way back," he said, in a way that made it clear he was not going to elaborate. "And his presence really saved my hide, for now."

I glanced at Jimmy, who looked even more nervous than before if that was possible. His right leg was jiggling a mile a minute. I knew I had a reputation for plowing ahead like a bulldozer, even when the interviewee was clearly uncomfortable and reluctant to share anything else. Andy hadn't seemed upset, but I knew I should dial it back.

"Well, I'm glad the lawyer was with you," I said, a bit softer.

"Yeah, me too," Andy said. "But he wouldn't be happy if he knew I talked to you two."

I returned my gaze to the heron and tried to process what Andy had shared. He had been at the paper, he had engaged in a fight with Charlotte the night she was murdered, and he did have a motive, albeit a weak one, in that she had fired him. But, honestly, if that was the best Chief Sinclair and his crew could do, then we were never going to find out the truth. Surely, there were other suspects in the case, those with a much more convincing motive. And if I was going to find them, I needed to find out if Andy had any leads that I could chase down to help his case.

"So, anything else, Andy? I'd really like to help you if I can."

Jimmy finally chimed in. "Me too," he said, nodding enthusiastically. I suddenly realized his kindness might actually be his superpower. If he leaned into the part of his personality that plainly helped little old ladies across the street and brought stranded cats down from trees, he could learn to get great inside information as a reporter. Sources would love that nice polite Jimmy Malloy.

"Thanks," Andy said. "It's such a mess. I'm also worried about my roommate. A-Train is still on probation. He doesn't need to be roped into any of this now."

Oh yes, Andy's roommate whom the neighbor walking his dog had told me about, the one who was at the recording studio when I stopped by Andy's house.

"Why's that?" I asked, knowing he would eventually tell us but not wanting to wait for his piecemeal style of information sharing.

"Well, A-Train was with me when I went back to the paper that night," Andy explained. "He needed a ride home from the studio, and I'd offered him a ride."

Jimmy broke back into the conversation then, and I tried to look sympathetic as I listened to him awkwardly reassure Andy that of course we'd help him, that of course we knew he wasn't a murderer. I couldn't believe when he actually asked Andy where we might find A-Train, and once the address was revealed, I could hardly wait until I could head over. I knew I had to discover what A-Train had to say about that night. But I can't lie, I was also going to find out where he got that nickname.

CHAPTER 12

That afternoon, my search for Andy's roommate, A-Train, took me into a quiet residential neighborhood on a road heading out of town. It was a more modern neighborhood by Exeter standards, in that it was not made up of several-hundred-year-old wooden homes. The street I was driving along had mostly single-story, ranch-style houses, including some that had not been changed since they were built in the 1960s.

I spotted the house number Andy had given us and tapped Walter's brakes so I could take in the house where A-Train had his "studio." It was like a trip back in time, complete with a combination of dark-brown and brick trim with a hint of brick facade—the kind of place that screamed "makeover" on any number of shows on HGTV.

I grabbed my notebook, smoothed my hair down more out of habit than due to stray hairs, and walked up to ring the doorbell. The slight older woman who answered the door had on a matching pink pantsuit and perfectly curled silver hair.

"Hi, I'm looking for A-Train," I began, feeling more than a bit ridiculous that I did not know his real name.

"Oh, you mean George Jr.! He's in in the garage," the woman said. She stepped onto the front steps and pointed to a door on the side of the home that led to a single-car garage. I had to wonder if I'd find a Studio 54 disco theme inside given the overall vibe of the place. She led the way, shuffling slowly over the patio pavers that formed a path to the garage.

"Georgie, your little friend is here!" she called out as she opened the door.

"Nana, how many times have I told you, it's A-Train now," a voice grumbled from inside.

She looked at me, unperturbed by his grievance. "He's a big music guy now, wants a new name," she said. She shrugged and added, "Who knows. I wiped his bottom when he was a baby, so he's always going to be Georgie to me."

I thanked Nana and headed in.

"A-Train?" I asked.

"Yeah."

A-Train looked like a teenager. He could not have weighed more than 100 pounds, though the fake gold chain around his neck might have added a pound or so. The white tank top he had on hung down, exposing his collarbone and skinny arms, even though he had a black button-down shirt draped over himself. I found myself wondering how someone like this had come to live with Andy. If I went by appearances, they didn't seem to have anything in common.

"I'm Piper. I work at the paper with Andy."

"Oh yeah. He said you'd be by," A-Train said, dramatically holding both of his arms out to the side as if he were summoning something from above. Without warning, he started rapping what was probably the worst excuse for music I'd ever heard. But then, he was living in New Hampshire, which was not exactly a rap music hub.

"He didn't do it, no he didn't do it, he didn't do it, no he didn't do it.

"Can't you see that this is just so foolish?

"We're in America, America, the land of the free and brave.

"Oh, you know, it's wrong, oh so wrong, that it's Andy you've got to save!"

This was a first for me, a rapping interview subject. "So, you like rap then, huh?"

He looked at me as if I were clearly from the same century as his nana and continued.

"A-Train is my name, and you know, you know, I don't play no games."

Really, was that the best he could come up with? God, a third grade could make up better rhymes. But I smiled at him and offered a question. "So, you record music here then?"

A-Train shrugged. "Yeah. It's my Nana's place, but even though I live with Andy, she lets me record here, you know so I can check up on her and stuff."

Lucky Nana, I thought, as I looked at the mishmash of recording equipment that left no place for the Ford Escort station wagon in the driveway to fit inside. "So, A-Train, I work with Andy, but I'm trying to help him out a bit, you know, so I'm wondering if you can tell me about the night of the Independence Festival reception? Andy picked you up here when he left work that night, is that right?"

"Yo, yo, yo, he did, he did, Andy is my best kid."

I hated to interrupt his little rap game, but seriously, it was even more annoying after the first time. No wonder he was still recording in Nana's garage. Poor Nana! I hoped she could turn off her hearing aids to protect herself.

"Sorry, A-Train, but I'm having a hard time understanding you when you rap your answers. Can you just talk normally? Please? And do you mind telling me your given name?"

He let out a big sigh. His shoulders slumped, and he had a look of defeat as he glanced over at me. "You're the boss," he said. "It's George. George Connifey."

I wrote down his name in my notebook, then pushed ahead. "So just walk me through that night. When Andy picked you up and where you went."

"Well, I was here," he said, lifting his arms to the side in his studio. "And so, well, I don't have my license, so Andy usually gives me a ride home when he's done with work."

Poor A-Train. His life didn't sound like it was getting any better than his awful rap lyrics. I looked over at him expectantly, indicating he should go on.

"So, he picked me up here and told me about how he'd lost his job." A-Train, aka George, paused, looking momentarily thoughtful. "He loved that job, you know."

I did know that about Andy, though it surprised me that A-Train, who seemed a bit immature and living in his own musical world, understood that as well. "So, then he says he had some of his equipment there. He figures he'll just go back, pick it up when no one's around, you know to bug him or ask questions. So, we stopped at the newspaper."

I looked up, trying to maintain eye contact while at the same time writing my notes.

"So, what time did you do that, if you remember?"

"Well, it must have been about eight, maybe eight-thirty."

"So, did you go in with him?'

"Nah, I stayed in the car. I had a phone call to return."

"So how long was Andy inside?"

A-Train paused, clearly concentrating, before he answered. "Maybe five, ten minutes tops."

"Okay. And how did he seem when he came back to the car?

Anything different?"

"He wanted to get out of there, you know, I think it was just too much for him to be there after she fired him. He just couldn't deal, you know?"

I made a star in my notes next to this. Andy wanted to leave ASAP. This could be a normal reaction, or it might be something the police would latch onto as a suspicious fact because he seemed so eager to leave.

"Did you see anyone else when you were there, A-Train? Any other people? Any other cars in the parking lot?"

He came to life a bit. "You know, there was one car there. A silver-blue-type convertible. Old one. Really old, but nice. Had some sort of vanity plate, something about Love-15."

I got a jolt—that kind I got when I knew I was about to receive juicy information.

"Did you see anyone around the car? Any other cars?"

"Nope, that was the thing. The parking lot was empty, except for the silver-blue convertible—I think it's what you call a roadster—and the newspaper delivery trucks out back."

"So, you didn't see anyone around the silver-blue convertible then?"

"Nope. Everything was really quiet, but then Andy said it was usually a quiet night there because the paper was already done for deadline except that because of the festival, he had to upload some photos after the deadline—you know, because it was considered big news that week and all."

Oh, I did know. Until Charlotte's murder, breaking news for *The Exeter Independent* was usually a wayward turkey causing a traffic jam, or the occasional ice rescue in the winter when one of the overzealous fishermen stayed out in his ice-fishing shack a day too long in warm weather and found himself floating down the river. The festival was a big deal in town.

I turned back to A-Train, hoping I'd get a nugget of information that would help Andy.

"I know this may seem obvious, but I have to ask: did you see anything else, anything that seemed off that night?"

George, aka A-Train, shook his head emphatically. "No way! I can't believe they're saying that, man. I mean, Andy is the last person to do something like that. The dude meditates and stuff, you know?"

Yeah, because definitely, no one who meditates could commit a murder, I thought. Still, I remained pretty certain that Andy was innocent. I folded my notebook closed and slid a business card out of my pocket, handing it to him.

"So, give me a call if you think of anything else," I said. "I appreciate it, really."

He slid the card into one of his baggy pockets. "Sure. I mean, Andy's a good guy. And honestly," he said, as he looked around, "if he goes to jail, I might have to move in with Nana again."

Given how my own move back home with an older relative was going better than expected, I was tempted to tell him it wouldn't be that bad. But I didn't want to give him any reason to bail on Andy, who would need extra rent money now more than ever—assuming A-Train had some source of income. I gave him a little wave as I turned to go. As if he'd been doing everything in his power to hold himself back, he held his arms out to the side once more.

"Yo, yo, yo. He didn't do it, no, no, no, he didn't do it."

"Well, thanks again," I said, turning to leave. The detail about the silver-blue convertible was niggling at me. I knew that Love-15 was a tennis term, and I knew one person who was all about tennis, or had been all about tennis: Kevin Daniels, the bartender at the Tuck Tavern. But was that his car? For all I knew, it might have belonged to Pansy Bolton, of the Rotary Club, who was also obsessed with tennis. A standout vintage car would be just the type of accessory she would buy for herself.

As I reached the garage door I turned back, realizing there was one last thing I needed.

"Sorry, A-Train," I began. "But I meant to ask you another thing. What time did you get back to your place with Andy that night? I'm assuming you went straight back after he left the paper."

A-Train gave me a sheepish shrug. "Yeah, well, so Andy dropped me off about nine, maybe a few minutes after, but then he left."

Wait, what? That didn't make any sense. "Did he say why? Or where he was headed?"

A-Train looked like he really didn't want to answer. I waited. He looked down and mumbled, "He got a phone call and said he had something he had to take care of. He didn't say where."

Oh, this wasn't a good fact for Andy. *Something he wanted to take care of* sounded suspicious, like something the police would interpret to mean permanently taking care of an editor who had fired him. I hated to ask the next question, but I knew the police would eventually ask A-Train themselves, so I wanted to be prepared for what they might find.

"So, what time did he get back from this thing he had to take care of?"

A-Train closed his eyes, took a deep breath, and groaned. "You know, I'd rather not say."

Oh no.

"A-Train, I want to help him, remember? Better I find out than the police."

He sighed loudly. "It was the morning, okay? He didn't get back until the morning. And honestly, he didn't look good, if you know what I mean. Like he hadn't slept at all."

Oh, Andy. This was not the type of information I had been hoping to learn. And why, oh why, would Andy send me here to talk to A-Train if he knew this was what I was going to find out?

I raced out to my car and was driving back toward downtown Exeter before I realized I had forgotten to ask the origins of A-Train's nickname.

CHAPTER 13

After the craziness of the past week, I was looking forward to hiding out in my cozy carriage house and having a bit of quiet time. But no sooner had I taken off my shoes when I heard a persistent *rap, rap, rap* on the side door.

Gladys stood on the other side, decked out in her weekend entertaining attire, complete with a vibrant silk scarf around her neck, a sure sign that her regular gentleman caller must be visiting.

"Oh, Piper dear, do come up and have a martini with me and Stanley," she began, confirming my suspicion. "We're dying to hear the latest on the big murder."

They must have reached critical mass for showtunes for the evening, and what better way to pass the time after a few cocktails than speculating about murder? Especially one where, so far, no one seemed terribly upset about the victim.

I was exhausted, but the prospect of Gladys's trademark hors d'oeuvres from the fancy gourmet shop downtown did entice me. That way, I could get off without having to prepare something at home. Cooking for one had its ups and downs, and tonight, when I felt like putting my feet up, the idea of making food seemed a bit much.

"Let me freshen up and I'll be over in a few," I told her.

"We will wait with bated breath," Gladys said. Then she teetered back across the walkway that led from her house to mine.

My carriage house home was painted a dark purple that was actually a deep violet called Amethyst Reflection, according to Gladys. Her large Victorian-style home out front was also a shade of purple. "The color of royalty," she told me more than once, and a way to make a statement amongst the white houses with black trim that dominated much of the town.

The old front doors of my living space, which once opened to allow large horse-drawn carriages in and out, now boasted two enormous windows that gave me a grand view of Glady's back garden from my living room. (Of course, in Exeter's frigid New England winters, they also let in a lot of cold.) One wall of the room had a long kitchen and butcher block island, the other opened into a small office nook, while a set of narrow stairs led to my loft-like bedroom upstairs.

When I'd moved in with Gladys after my parents died, I lived in her big Victorian out front. She'd converted the carriage house when I was at college, using proceeds from some antiques she had found inside that had more value than she had realized. She had rented it out for a few years, but after the last tenant moved out, she had left it empty. I think that at some level she was always hoping I'd come back home.

I changed into capris and a button-down shirt of light cotton before heading out. I knew I would be underdressed compared to Gladys and Stanley, but it was the best I could do. They were seated on the white, wrought-iron patio chairs behind the house, martinis in hand, Sinatra playing in the background. Stanley had on a bowtie with tiny dancing penguins this evening. Though he was a man of few words, his dedication to decorum endeared him to Gladys. She often marveled at his continued independence. He still drove his immaculately maintained antique Cadillac and stopped for cocktails at the Tuck Tavern. Though he had clearly lost weight and muscle mass with age, he used his skills as a tailor to take in his suits, which still fit perfectly.

"What can I get you, Piper dear?" Gladys said, standing and walking toward her outdoor bar cart. "I've got a pitcher of martinis and some white wine."

Given that I was bordering on exhaustion and wanted to stay awake to eat, I decided to skip the high-test martini and opted for the wine.

Gladys patted the seat of a chair next to them. "Now come sit and tell us what's going on," she said. "You know Stanley and I could use some excitement, something to spice up our lives."

I took a long sip of the wine and eyed the tray of food next to them, picking up a napkin and a jumbo shrimp cocktail. Just how I liked them. Perfectly chilled and seasoned with a hint of Old Bay spice.

Glady nodded encouragingly toward me. "So, what do you know?"

"Well," I began. "Not a lot so far, which is maddening to be honest."

I told her about Charlotte firing Andy, how the police had questioned Andy, the rumors of Charlotte meeting with a mystery man, and what I'd learned from A-Train. "And there was this car, A-Train mentioned, some sort of antique silver-blue convertible with a vanity plate," I said. "I didn't recognize the description, but it could mean that another person saw Charlotte the night she was killed."

Gladys clapped her hands together. "Oh, Piper dear, I'm surprised you don't know that car!" She paused for effect. "That was Cameron Daniels's pride and joy. I suspect Kevin got the car after Cam died."

Kevin's grandfather, a contemporary of Gladys, had died a few years ago.

"But why would Kevin have been at the newspaper that night?" I asked, more to myself than to Gladys and Stanley. I dipped another shrimp cocktail into the extra-spicy cocktail sauce and popped it into my mouth. I chewed slowly, savoring the crustacean.

"Well, that's obvious, Piper dear," Gladys said, sitting up a bit straighter. "Kevin is the killer."

Oh, Gladys, I thought. *This is not a game of Clue with Kevin in the newsroom with the candlestick.*

I said, "But that doesn't make any sense, Gladys. I mean, why would Kevin want to kill Charlotte? It wasn't like they had anything to do with each other, as far as we know."

Gladys gave Stanley, who had dozed off, a gentle nudge with her elbow. "Stanley darling," she called, and he startled upright. "You go to the Tuck Tavern a lot. Ever see Charlotte Campbell there talking to Kevin?"

Now that Gladys didn't venture out as often as she used to, she often treated Stanley as her personal scout. Stanley had his own stool at the Tuck Tavern, emblazoned with a brass nameplate, which recognized his years of patronage.

"I'm afraid I can't really say," Stanley apologized. "My eyes aren't what they used to be. But, you know, I had seen that Charlotte there a lot lately. And always dressed to the nines if you know what I mean."

Gladys nodded approvingly. There was nothing she hated more than the trend of women to go out in public in yoga pants or jeggings.

"Back in the day," she told me more than once, "people dressed, really dressed, if you know what I mean, Piper dear."

"Now, you know who would know," Gladys said now, "that Pansy Bolton. Granted, I can hardly stand to be around her more than five minutes with all her talk about her tennis matches and those dratted rosebushes, but nothing gets past her. I know she's a regular at the Tuck Tavern, isn't she, Stanley darling?"

Stanley nodded, then leaned forward to get a handful of nuts.

Jeepers, Gladys, I thought, *could you put anything more hazardous out for him?* I was afraid he might choke on the nuts or break his dentures. I kept an eye on him as he worked the nuts very slowly before swallowing.

"Have you seen Pansy lately?" I asked Gladys. She shook her head no.

Guess I could just drop by the Tavern and talk to Kevin. Maybe I'd take Jenny as my wing woman. I shared my idea with Gladys, who looked positively giddy at this prospect.

"Stanley dear, let Piper use your stool when she goes, so she has a prime vantage point."

But Stanley had dozed off again. Looked like the rest of the shrimp were mine.

CHAPTER 14

Jenny was on board with my idea, so the next night we made plans to meet up. I decided to walk over to the Tuck Tavern, which would give me a chance to stretch my legs, and if I got lucky along the way, I might even hear some tidbits about Charlotte from other locals out enjoying a summer evening stroll.

I stopped when I reached the center of town next to the impressive bandstand across from the historic town hall. I couldn't help gazing over at the roof of the town hall. Why would someone use such a public spot to kill Charlotte? And how on earth did they not only get her stuffed into that jacket but also out the window and onto the roof without attracting attention?

I pondered what the police knew, and if Richie Collins would give me any more tips. I also wondered if Jenny was right about him being single, but I was not sure I was ready to find out. After my last relationship fiasco in the city, I'd decided to focus on myself for a while. But at the same time, I couldn't help feeling a little spark when I thought of his deep blue eyes and dimples.

I plunked myself down for a minute on the steps of the bandstand. Newcomers to town often mistakenly called it a gazebo; locals knew it best as the home of the oldest brass band in the whole country. On Mondays in July, Exeter took on the appearance of a Norman Rockwell scene as residents brought chairs downtown and sat in front of the town hall to hear the band play songs of a time gone by.

It was hard to believe that the very spot where folks like Gladys enjoyed the old standards was just a few yards away from the spot where Charlotte's body had landed on the day she was murdered. It was equally impossible to believe that one of Exeter's citizens might have carried out the murder.

After a few minutes, I passed the large library at the private school and cut down a narrow side street toward the Tuck Tavern. The popular bar and restaurant were housed in one of those old white colonials with black shutters that Gladys found so dull, complete with candles in the windows, which seemed more appropriate for the holiday season but stayed up all year round. In the summer, the early birds got one of the big rocking chairs on the front porch, a prime spot to catch up on the news of the town as people entered. It was named for Amos Tuck, a significant antislavery politician and a founder of the Republican Party, who was a prominent citizen of town in the 1800s. The tavern had the feeling of a colonial-era establishment with old ecru walls and bronze light fixtures. It was the kind of place you'd expect to find a beef pasty or shepherd's pie on the menu but instead catered to the traditional New England seafood and beef lineup that the older clientele demanded.

The intimate dining room was like a throwback to the 1800s. It reminded me of the themed restaurants I'd visited with my parents at Colonial Williamsburg when I was in elementary school. The only thing missing were the role players dressed like tavern barmaids.

Jenny waved me over from a seat at the side of the bar, where she had already amassed a fan club of eligible—and not eligible—men of the town. Some things never changed. Back in high school, she had been a magnet for the cute boys, while except for my never-consummated flirtation with Richie, I'd been a draw for the boys in the chess club.

Jenny waved off her admirers and patted the stool next to her.

"So, tell me," she said, leaning in with a mischievous look. "What's my cover story?"

She was always up for an adventure, which probably accounted for why she had followed her nomadic boyfriend, Armand, over to France after college. I'd always been a bit more reserved but had come to appreciate being best friends with someone who pushed me out of my cautious comfort zone.

"No cover," I said, trying to hold back a smirk. "Just two single ladies out on the town catching up. So, what's new?"

She paused to take a sip of red wine, another carryover from her time in France. "Same old, same old," she said. "I've been interviewing for some more help in the kitchen to keep up with the catering orders. It's really taking on a life of its own."

As usual, she was understating the extent of her success. Her catering orders were coming in so fast that she was now working after hours most days to finish them. Our outing was a rare evening away from her bakery. She'd been so busy with her business that she hadn't even been to the horse barn, which had been her second home as long as I'd known her.

"That's fantastic, Jenny," I said. "I'll be able to say I knew you when."

She grinned at me. "Get that true-crime book written and published and I will say the same about you."

"Maybe someday," I replied. I thought, *I'll need to find out who the killer is first.*

I glanced over behind the bar, where the other reason for my visit, Kevin Daniels, was shaking a silver cocktail shaker. He looked a little worse for the wear around his eyes but was still attractive by most people's standards, with straight white teeth, short brown hair, and a fit physique. Even so, there was something about him that rubbed me the wrong way. He always had a chip on his shoulder. But for now, I pushed that aside and slipped into fishing mode. I caught his eye and raised my hand, indicating I wanted to order.

"What can I get you?" he asked.

"How about a Sauvignon Blanc?"

"House okay?"

Guess he didn't know what it was like to be on salary at *The Exeter Independent*. Of course I wanted the house wine.

"Yes," I responded.

Across the bar, Grayson Adams sat alone. He smiled in acknowledgment and got up to walk to our side.

"So, what's the news?" he asked, holding what looked like a gin and tonic, with two wedges of lime.

He slid into an empty seat next to me, and Jenny winked at me. She knew me and my penchant for picking up choice kernels of news at bars. People didn't realize I was always storing away these little nuggets, compiling a mental dossier on everyone I met, like an elephant who remembered everything. Grayson was usually prime for the picking when it came to town gossip.

"Well, not much more than we knew the other day," I began. I didn't want to let him know what I was working on just yet. As the chairman of the select board, he had a direct line to the police anyway. "Chief Sinclair said more information should be released next week, and they are waiting to hear from Charlotte's family about funeral arrangements. But other than that, not much."

Grayson sipped his drink and looked around before leaning

a bit closer to me. "I heard they took her computer, something about what she might have been working on, something important. Any idea what that was?"

That was news to me. Charlotte had not worked on a story in years, but those op-eds of hers were usually enough to make her the most unpopular person in town. But wait, Sheila had told me the same thing: Charlotte was working on a secretive story.

"I haven't heard that," I said. "But then, the cops are being pretty tight-lipped with me."

He looked disappointed, and I could tell I'd served my purpose.

"Well," he said. "I should be getting on. I've got an early day tomorrow. They're unveiling a new marker to commemorate my family's role in founding the town, something they were supposed to do during the festival, but, well, it was delayed given the situation. And between you and me, there may be an Adams Day celebration this fall."

Typical Grayson. He was all about his family's role in the town's history, just like my brother, Chester.

"Well, good luck with that," I said, as he returned to his original seat. I could only imagine what Adams Day would entail and how bloated his ego would become if it came to fruition. Chester would be gunning for Greene Day next.

On the other side of the bar, I spotted Stanley, who was eyeing a thick slice of prime rib but suddenly noticed my presence. He looked at Kevin, then back at me, and smiled knowingly. Perhaps he was not as daft as I thought. I mean, he did hang out with Gladys, who was one of the sharpest people I knew.

"So, have you heard from you-know-who again?" Jenny asked, and I knew she was referencing Richie. "I'm telling you, I have a feeling about you two."

I generally shared everything with her, but I was still too focused on the murder investigation to think about having a love life.

"We'll see," I said, popping a few of the rosemary-seasoned nuts from the dish between us into my mouth.

Kevin glanced around the bar, eyeing the drink levels of his customers, and came back to me. "You doing okay? Need a refill?"

With Jenny on one side and the other stool empty, it seemed like a good time to bait the hook. "Well, actually," I said, lowering my voice, "I wanted to talk to you, give you a heads up on something we heard at the paper."

This was the fun part. Watching his expression go from nonchalance to confusion to concern. I continued, "So, it sounds like someone told the police they saw your car at the newspaper offices the night Charlotte was killed. And . . . " I paused for effect, "the police are going to want to talk to you."

A woman on the other side of the bar was trying to get his attention, holding an empty glass up. Kevin looked at her, then me, and grumbled "I'm going to take a break in a few, while the hostess covers for me. I'll meet you out back. "

Ooh, just like the movies, I thought. Meeting in a darkened alley. I finished my wine and got up, ostensibly to go to the lady's room. Jenny gave me a covert thumbs up as I walked away. I waited five minutes and then slipped out the side door to the parking lot, where I came face to face with the antique silver-blue convertible that Kevin had inherited from his late grandfather.

"So, what's this about?" Kevin said in an edgy tone as he walked out from behind the corner. "I really don't want to get involved in any of this."

I explained that a witness had seen his car— I gestured to the vehicle next us—at the paper the night Charlotte was killed. I added that as far as we could tell, he may have been the last person to see her alive.

"Some folks are speculating that you knew her more than you let on," I said, using my least threatening voice to imply that I was on his side. "I mean, I know it's all circumstantial, and probably nothing. But I just wanted to let you know, you know, before the police came calling."

Kevin grimaced and shook his head, again. He looked angry. "I knew I shouldn't have gotten involved."

"With what?" I prompted.

"Nothing," he said.

"Doesn't sound like nothing," I continued.

"It's not important now," he said. "Because nothing's going to come of it. I should have known better."

What had he been involved with? It was hard to tell from what he had said if it was a personal thing or a professional thing. Either way, it didn't take a detective to know it wasn't just "nothing" as he'd said.

"Is there anything I can do to help?" I asked.

He looked confused. "Like what?"

I resisted the urge to meet his annoyance with my own and reminded myself that I'd get more information if I didn't burn this bridge by snapping at him.

"You know, tell the real story, in a way that gives you a chance to tell your side of whatever this situation was you got involved with. Maybe under the umbrella of a story about your work teaching tennis at the rec park now and your tennis career?"

He paced around, and I found myself looking at the back entrance to the funeral home next door. There was a hearse in the driveway, maybe the very one that had picked up Charlotte.

My mind wandered as I waited for Kevin to stop pacing. What had happened to that soldier outfit? Where had it come from in the first place?

Kevin sighed loudly and then glanced at his watch, still clearly agitated. "I don't need your help," he finally muttered. "I've got to get back to work, I can't think about this right now." He turned to leave.

"Well, let me know if you change your mind," I called out. Seconds later, Grayson Adams walked out the side door.

Grayson glanced at me, looked at Kevin, and frowned. I wondered if he was regretting his decision to stay out late when he needed his beauty sleep before the big event to unveil his family plaque. Or, perhaps Kevin, as the town's best bartender, knew too many of his secrets.

CHAPTER 15

As soon as I got word that the crime scene people had finally cleared out of the newspaper office, I made a beeline for the newsroom and my desk. Working from my carriage house was fine, but there was something to be said for being in a newsroom with other people who felt the same buzz of excitement from being part of the news.

In the reception area, Clara was milking the gallows humor of our situation. She suggested we should get shirts that said "I survived the Rev Fest," which I cautioned her not to share when Hap was around. He had a great sense of humor but was the type of decent person who would never make fun of someone's death. He'd no doubt seen enough of the townspeople injured or otherwise during his work as a volunteer firefighter in town.

While I was eager to be back in the hub of the news with an eye on the downtown area's happenings, Sheila and Jimmy both looked lukewarm at best about being in the building. Jimmy occasionally glanced at Charlotte's former office with a look that would give any sad puppy a run for its money. Sheila was as reserved as I'd ever seen her, and I wondered if being back in the newsroom, where she had been one of the last to see Charlotte alive, was getting to her.

Sensing that the others were not up for chit-chat, I slid behind my desk, booted up my computer, and contemplated what I needed to work on throughout the rest of the day. I wanted to find a follow-up story on the murder, but knew I first had to take a photo at the Council on Aging.

The unique ring that indicated someone had dialed my direct line brought me back, and I answered right away because only a few people had that secret number.

"Oh, Piper, do I have a scoop for you," Detective Richie Collins said, his voice almost giddy. "And it's one you're not going to believe."

He only paused a split second before he blurted out, "Charlotte Campbell isn't actually Charlotte Campbell."

"Wait, what?"

Richie, it seemed, could not wait to share the details. I guess he had moved on from the whole plan to keep things super tight-lipped while the state police were involved.

"I know!" he uttered, without stopping to take a breath before he went on. "It was like it was a pen name. Apparently, her real name was Carlotta Cabanovich, but at some point, she changed her last name to Campbell. She thought it sounded more like a journalist and she wanted people to remember her, and she Americanized her first name. Or at least that's what her parents told the chief."

Well, it wasn't unheard of. There was a popular anchorman on TV who had changed his name to Brian Smith from a long European last name that was hard to pronounce, although later he changed it back after he decided to embrace his heritage. So, I could see a potential reason why Charlotte had changed her name.

Richie went on. Apparently, the detail had come to light when they were trying to find her relatives to notify them of her death.

They had pulled her driver's license information in the police motor vehicle database but couldn't find anyone named Charlotte Campbell. At that point, they went through her personal belongings, and boom, there was her driver's license with the name Carlotta Cabanovich.

A double identity, I thought. *This was going to be good.*

I said, "Well, I have to admit that Charlotte Campbell does have a much better ring to it."

Richie replied, "I guess, but it seems kind of strange that no one at the newspaper knew about it, don't you think?"

Well, perhaps Hap knew, but he respected her desire to keep it private, I thought. *Or perhaps she changed her name because of the early trouble that the elusive Todd Tisden at* The Portsmouth Clipper *ferreted out.* For a brief second, I wondered if he was really on a banana plantation.

Focusing back on the present, I said, "So, what's the deal? Will her family be organizing a memorial of some kind? Something in town?"

"Doesn't sound like it," he answered, sounding slightly disappointed, and I could almost feel his Catholic faith cringing at the loss of this type of ritual. "They live down in Connecticut, near Mystic, and they are going to do something local from the sounds of it."

Mystic was a nice spot, touristy but with a rich seaport history. While I had not exactly gone out of my way to get to know Charlotte when we worked together, it was not the place I expected her family to live.

"So, any news on the autopsy, or . . . " I hesitated, "when they'll release her body to her family?"

He paused too. Then he said, "Well, you didn't hear this from me because it needs to come from the state cops, but it sounds like she was dead before she was hanging off the side of the roof. Strangulation."

That was interesting. So, she had been killed first and the scene had been staged.

"But here's an interesting detail," he went on. "And I'm trusting you not to burn me on this one. Medical examiner says it was a ligature strangulation, almost cut through her whole windpipe."

Oh my, that was an ironic detail. The woman who spoke her mind, who cast judgement in her editorials and op-ed column, had her hot air snuffed out. *And, yikes,* I thought to myself, *the amount of muscle and persistence needed to carry that out would have been significant.* Would that make it a man? Not necessarily, but I couldn't imagine a woman carrying out such a personal, and brutal type of killing. At a minimum, it would have taken a heck of a lot of strength or adrenaline.

"Well, thanks," I said. "I owe you big time, Richie. I appreciate it."

There was a brief silence on the other end as he cleared his throat. "How about you come by my place this weekend?" he said. I thought I detected a nervous undertone to his voice. "Have dinner and tell me what you got up to in the big city."

"Wouldn't that look bad if the state cops found out?" I blurted out before thinking. "You know, consorting with the enemy and all?"

"Who says they would have to know?"

Now that was the Richie I knew, the one who was always ready to take a chance and somehow never got caught. Still, he was technically a source, and getting involved was not allowed. Though to be fair, it was hard not to be involved with the people you knew in a community of this size.

"Sure," I said, catching myself before too much enthusiasm came through. "That would be great. Let's touch base on Friday."

"Whatever you say, kiddo," he said. Then he hung up.

Kiddo? Any thoughts I'd had of romance quickly flew out the window. God, he probably thought of me like his little sister or something. I'd have to run this by Jenny and get her opinion.

Next to me, Jimmy groaned. "I can't believe I have to go cover this story about the Adams family's legacy."

Oh, yes, I thought. *Grayson's plaque.*

He added, "It's a total grip and grin."

I smiled, noticing that some of my expressions were rubbing off on him. The infamous grip and grin was one of those community photo ops, often with a large fake check passing between hands, or a line of people clutching plastic gold shovels at a groundbreaking ceremony, holding hands and smiling for the photo, aka the grip and grin. In the newsroom, they were a dreaded assignment. No doubt the photo would find itself framed on Grayson's wall of family history by week's end.

"Well, it could be worse," I said. "You could be me, headed out to take a picture of the Council on Aging's new board of directors. All due to the fact that we no longer have a staff photographer."

Jimmy laughed. "Well, maybe you'll see their leader, Olive. I've heard that she's always good for a story idea."

Oh yes, Olive was one of my community page frequent fliers. As head of the Council on Aging, she took her duties seriously, including their work to bestow on the town's oldest resident a replica of the *Boston Post* Cane, a uniquely New England tradition started in 431 towns in 1909 by the *Boston Post* newspaper. People in other parts of the country probably thought we were nuts, but this was Exeter, and we loved our history.

Behind closed doors, however, I called the cane the death stick. I mean, really, everyone who got the cane died. It was like the grim reaper coming for you when that stick landed in your hands. Frankly, I'd say no if they showed up and tried to give it to me. But alas, every new recipient seemed thrilled and posed for a photo with a replica of Exeter's original cane, which was kept at the Historical Society. Every time Exeter's current oldest resident passed away, I got a call from Olive letting me know that she was looking for the next lucky recipient.

"That's right," I told Jimmy. "I think the current *Post* Cane holder is 104, so we may have a story soon."

Before I headed out to meet with the Council on Aging, I devoted a bit more time to my new mission to confirm why Charlotte had changed her name. I pulled up an online search and punched in *Carlotta Cabanovich,* the name that Richie had shared. A link to a 20-year-old story in *The Rockport Report,* the newspaper from a tiny coastal town in Massachusetts's Northshore area, came up. I clicked and got the dreaded *404 not found* message that showed up when a website was no longer active. I clicked on a few more hits and got the same response, noticing that the byline and name were what was called a cached web search result, the kind that showed a snapshot of a website before it was taken down.

Drat.

It was still early, so I decided to make a quick stop over at the Historical Society on the way to the Council on Aging event. I knew Winnie had access to regional newspaper archives through a subscription service the society had for her own research. Hap always insisted that *The Exeter Independent* didn't have the budget for "luxuries" like that. Fortunately, Winnie was a great resource for these kinds of projects, and she always seemed excited to see me enter the front doors of her building. Not only was I a good four decades younger than most of the people who frequented the place, but I was actually still breathing, unlike all the personalities from Exeter's past whom she communed with in the basement paper archives as she did her research. I mean, everyone needs to be among the living from time to time, right?

The yellow-bricked Exeter Historical Society building was initially designed for use as Exeter's Public Library and Civil War Memorial until the library outgrew the space and moved across the river. It sported two chimneys, one on either side of the large arched entranceway. It was open to the public only a few afternoons a week, but I knew that if the door was unlocked, I could go in anytime and find Winnie.

The door was unlocked, but the place appeared deserted.

"Winnie," I called out. "Hello?"

I walked through the front room, past the Abraham Lincoln sesquicentennial poster commemorating his trip to Exeter to visit his son Robert Todd Lincoln when he was a student at the private school in town. Still no Winnie. I peered at the door to the basement archival area, which, I had to admit, did not look like an inviting place to go. In fact, it looked more like the type of place you went in a horror movie right before the killer with an extra-large shiny knife slashed you.

But if Winnie could venture down those stairs at 75 years old, I could surely do it at half that, right? I made my way down the narrow wooden stairs, spotting a light in the distance, then stopped dead in my tracks.

I was face to face with a twin to the Lady Justice on top of the town hall, and she had seen better days. The wooden statue had originally been painted white but was mostly now rotted and falling apart. Half of her right arm was gone, along with her chest, the end of her nose, and her mouth. A black blindfold was covering her eyes, and her left hand, which should have been holding up the scales of justice, only had a chain.

"Oh, Piper, what are you doing here?" Winnie said, nearly startling me out of my skin as she suddenly tottered toward me from a spot near the back.

"I had a question, some research," I began. Then I stopped and pointed at Lady Justice. "But, what is that? Is that actually Lady Justice?"

Winnie nodded.

"What happened to her?"

"She was hit by lightning a few times," she explained. "That does a number on you."

You don't say, I thought. "So, the one there now, it's not the original?"

She shook her head. "Oh, good heavens no. They replaced the original one several generations ago. Then they replaced the replacement with this wooden one, which also came down a good 20 years ago."

Interesting. Not sure it had anything to do with Charlotte's death, but, yikes, I was going to have nightmares about the one in the basement. I followed Winnie up the stairs and briefly paused to look back. I'd heard this was where Winnie's secret poker games took place, but nothing looked out of sorts. Back in the light of the first floor, Winnie turned to me.

"So, what can I help you with?" she asked.

I knew I was taking advantage of her generosity a bit, but I did always help her get her history press releases into the paper, so I justified to myself my request.

"Any chance I could use your regional newspaper search

tool?"

I told Winnie about Charlotte's pen name and her given name, Carlotta Cabanovich, and then I explained that I wanted to look at old editions of the *Rockport Report* to see what I could learn about her career as a reporter before she changed her name.

"Oh, no problem at all," she said. "I could stand the company. This reminds me, I just got a copy of her obituary, which I'm including in the file I've started on her death."

I must have looked surprised. She said, "Oh yes, I keep a file on everything for our records, even murder." She held up a manilla folder that was labeled "The Murder File" in big black letters. There was something about a tiny septuagenarian maintaining a murder file that I found almost comical, but I kept my thoughts to myself.

"Can I see the obituary?" I asked.

"Oh sure," she said. "Your obituary is your final biography, you know. You should really write your own."

Well, that was morbid.

"Wait, have you written your own obituary, Winnie?"

"Well, I'm not going to let my son do it," she said, looking pointedly at me, "You do know him after all."

Oh, did I ever. Winnie's son was an IT computer guy. He was a few years older than me, and the idea of him writing anything creative was a stretch to say the least.

I scanned Charlotte's obituary.

Charlotte Campbell born Carlotta Cabanovich, 55, of Exeter, died unexpectedly last week. A career journalist, Charlotte had been the editor of The Exeter Independent *for the past five years. She began her journalism career as an intern at the* Mystic Story. *After graduating from Northeastern University, Charlotte took a job as a staff writer at the* Rockport Report. *She is survived by her parents, Yvonne and Henrick Cabanovich, of Mystic, Connecticut. There will be no funeral at this time. Burial will be private at a later date.*

Well, that didn't tell me much.

"See what I mean," Winnie said. "Trust me, start your own now. You never know when your number is up. Best to be prepared."

I didn't want to jinx myself, but maybe she had a point. Who knew what Gladys might choose to write about me? And Chester? I shuddered at the thought.

"So, about that newspaper search," I asked.

Winnie set me up with the old desktop computer in her office, which was in a room that doubled as the kitchen. She logged me in and wished me luck.

Okay Charlotte, I thought to myself, *let's see what you were up to back then.*

CHAPTER 16

It didn't take much searching with Winnie's program to find out why I hadn't found any archives for the *Rockport Report*. As it turned out, the reason I had gotten the *404 not found* error message was that the newspaper was defunct.

It had been sold about a decade prior, at which time their website was taken down. Like many small-town newspapers, news for the community was now farmed out through short articles in larger regional papers, with a story or two about the town's news but nothing like it had once been.

Luckily for me, Winnie's subscription search tool seemed to have a lot of the old editions of the paper, including stories by Charlotte, in their online database.

Using her real last name, Cabanovich, it seemed that Charlotte had written most of the weekly newspaper. The images of the front page typically had four of the five stories written by her for the better part of three years.

"Rockport Selectmen Shoot Down Liquor Exemption Request"

"Police Crack Down on Bootlegging"

"Selectmen Take Up Water and Sewer Project"

"Misuse of Funds Found in Sewer Department"

Like Exeter, Rockport was an old New England town, but

unlike our little village, it had a prime location on the Atlantic Ocean, making it a picturesque seaside tourist destination. The red-painted fishing shack on the side of its harbor, known as Motif # 1, was perhaps the most photographed and painted building along the Massachusetts coastline. On his study wall, Chester had a large watercolor of the shack, which he had purchased in a silent auction last year to benefit Exeter's new library project.

Rockport was artsy but also conservative. It had been a dry town for almost 200 years. *It wasn't like you had to go far to get liquor,* I thought wryly. Rockport was located right next to Gloucester, a hardscrabble fishing town known for having any number of establishments that catered to the hard-drinking, hard-living, blue-collar folks who spent weeks at sea and returned to port ready to let loose a bit. Most people in Rockport simply bought their alcohol across the town line and brought it back over.

I had a soft spot for Rockport because my parents used to take me and Chester there every summer for a week. It was probably the last time I remember my brother and I really getting along as we spent our days in the ocean and our evenings walking around Bearskin Neck. I liked to think a bit of nostalgia accounted for why he'd bid so high on that painting last year and not simply his desire to outbid Grayson.

I knew from living in Exeter, my own little Puritan village, there were secrets everywhere. And it seemed that Charlotte had found that out in Rockport as well. Just when I thought I'd seen all I could see of small-town politics and mundane meeting coverage, my heart jumped. Her next series of stories homed in on a scandal on the town's select board, including its chairman, a man named Hank Tarr.

Lara Bricker

"Tarred and Feathered: Selectmen Chairman Suspected in Skimming Scheme"
I leaned forward, reading as fast as I could. It seemed that Hank Tarr, a local frame shop owner who had been a longtime member of the board, was suspected of funneling money from the town's budget for his personal use. "This suspected malfeasance was brought to our attention by reporter Carlotta Cabanovich of the *Rockport Report,*" the police chief was quoted as saying. "Whose diligent review of the line items in the town's budget identified certain irregularities."

Wow. I paused for a minute, thinking that the early Charlotte was already operating like the person I'd known: always out to accuse local boards of doing something illegal. I kept reading. Tarr denied any wrongdoing, but Charlotte clearly believed his cry of innocence was just the last-ditch effort of a guilty man to save face, and she plowed ahead with her rather inflammatory exposé. The story went on to explain that given Tarr's relationship with the town and the police department, which was technically under the selectmen's control, the case had been handed over to the regional district attorney's office for investigation.

I clicked again, looking for the next article, but only found several with slim details, which indicated that at the time, the investigation was still ongoing. No charges had been filed and no new information was being released.

Next up, I found a piece that focused on Tarr's business: a framing shop near the harbor that locals had been boycotting, including some who stood out front with signs that called him a crook, a swindler, and a cheat. Tarr was quoted in the article, again asserting his innocence. He also said he was worried his shop might go out of business.

111

Drat, I realized, as I looked at my watch. I was going to be late for the Council on Aging. I knew that their leader, Olive, ran a tight ship and stuck to her schedule. This meant they met promptly at noon once a month in the Senior Center for a light lunch—finger rolls with egg, tuna, or ham salad—followed by a speaker at half past the hour. They were lining up to leave at 12:55 on the dot.

"Winnie," I called out. "I've got to go, but any chance I can swing by again?"

Winnie unfurled herself from her chair in the corner, where she'd been sipping herbal tea and reading a periodical. She peered over my shoulder, looking at the sensational headline about the selectman Tarr in Rockport.

"Guess it shows this happens everywhere," she said. "I have a similar file on some funny business in town here back in the 1980s, back when that convenience store owner was taking bribes."

I vaguely remembered the story, which happened when I was in elementary school. The convenience store owner, who also sat on the town's planning board, had all sorts of illegal meetings in the stocking area behind the store. It came out that he took bribes from developers to help their projects get approval. I only remembered because my family's law firm, then led by my father, had represented him at trial, which had meant a lot of evenings when my father was late coming home for dinner. As a young child, I'd gotten used to my father's role as a defense lawyer, even though some of his clients were definitely not going to win a Citizen of the Year prize.

But that was neither here nor there. Small towns were not immune to corruption. Spend one week in *The Exeter Independent* and you'd learn that.

"You know what, Piper," Winnie went on, "I'll do a little work on this later today for you. My file's still a bit thin." She held up the manila folder and gave me a wink. "And it is my job, after all, keeping track of both the living and the dead in town. All parts of history."

I got up and thanked her, knowing there was no one in the town, aside from maybe me, who was such a diligent a researcher. There was nothing that irked Winnie more than sloppy or incomplete work. I knew she would find sources to confirm everything she dug up, and then maybe a few more for good measure.

As I hurried down the sidewalk toward the Senior Center, my mind kept going back to the stories about Tarr. What had become of the selectman and his case? Had he been arrested and charged? Charlotte's career trajectory after this type of exposé also didn't add up. A story like that, an investigative piece from a small, notoriously close-mouthed town, would surely be a launching pad for a correspondent job for one of the big Boston metro papers. And yet she had changed her last name and landed at *The Portsmouth Clipper*. I wanted to unravel the thread more, but it was going to have to wait. It was 11:50 and I was expected, along with the others, promptly at high noon.

As I silently cursed the Council on Aging assignment, I wondered if Hap might reconsider his decision to get rid of Andy. Being a stand-in photographer was really putting a crimp in my plan to track down a killer.

CHAPTER 17

I settled back into my desk in the newsroom the next morning and started to write up a short article about the Council on Aging and their new board's priorities. Directly after their meeting, I had needed to cut the workday short to drive Gladys to an appointment with her Reiki master. She swore the treatments were what kept her nimble. I just hoped this wouldn't encourage too much dancing on showtunes night and lead to another injury.

I typed a sentence about the council's efforts to attract new members with a discount coupon to a sandwich shop in town. I knew the story wasn't exciting, but I also knew the members would rush out to buy the paper anyway. To some extent, it pleased me to know my articles were eagerly anticipated by readers, even if the work wasn't what I'd envisioned during journalism school.

I looked up when I heard a loud groan from the reception area. Clara was like the warning scout who forged ahead of the platoon on a military operation.

"Oh God help us, here comes old Arnold," she called out.

The name instilled amusement in some of us and fear in others. Jimmy immediately jumped under his desk. "Don't let him know I'm here!"

It was saying something that Jimmy, well over six feet tall and agile, was hiding from a ninety-year-old man who barely topped five feet. But such was the life of a small-town reporter and their regular town personalities.

Recently, Arnold, a vocal member of the local taxpayer group, had been sidetracked from his obsession with fiscal responsibility by a breakthrough in the automotive world: accident-preventing smart headlights. He'd been after Jimmy to write a story, despite Jimmy's repeated insistence that this was really not a local Exeter story.

"Is that Jimmy around?" asked Arnold, as he marched up to Clara's desk. Not only was he short, but he was also wiry. "I have a good story for him."

Clara shook her head, almost apologetically, as if she hadn't just helped Jimmy go underground. "Sorry, Arnold, but he's out on assignment. Can I take a message?"

This wasn't Clara's first rodeo. There was a reason she had lasted three decades at the front window of the paper. She was at times as protective of the young reporters as she was of her own grandchildren, shielding them like a mother hen.

Arnold peered into the newsroom, as if seeking another target, but after glancing at me and Sheila Bradbury, he shook his head.

"No, I'll try him again," he said. "I really think he needs to get ahead of this story I have for him. It's going to be big, really big, changing the course of automobile travel for generations to come."

Better Jimmy than me.

Arnold always had a cause. At last year's Town Meeting, he was always the first to get up and protest any spending he saw as extravagant, like the street sweeper repair or the new ambulance.

"That ambulance is only fifteen years old, practically brand new," he'd argued loudly.

Winnie's husband, who was also Exeter's fire chief and on the brink of retirement, had quickly told Arnold that at his age, the ambulance service was the last thing he should be nickel and diming. "Let's see how you feel when it breaks down on the way to the hospital," he'd told Arnold. The motion for repairs had passed.

"Is he gone?" Jimmy whispered.

I watched out the front windows of the paper, where Arnold marched along, looking aggrieved that his plan to expose the headlight story had been thwarted yet again. Then he stopped at his white Buick LeSabre, the type of boat-like car the retirees just loved, and climbed in.

"Almost," I said, watching as he slowly, ever so slowly, edged out of the parking space, narrowly missing the car parked next to him. His seat was about an inch away from the steering wheel, and from where I sat, it looked like he had a booster seat in there to see over the dashboard.

"What's the matter, Jimmy?" Clara called over, smirking as Jimmy crawled out from under the desk. "Do you really need me to protect you?"

Jimmy gave her a sheepish smile. "I can never get away; it's an hour before he stops talking," he said. "And I just don't have it in me today."

I had to admit he had a point. It was an hour of your life you would never get back when you got stuck with one of those talkers, especially when there was no legitimate story.

I was thankful that Jimmy and I sat behind Clara, which gave us a buffer when every member of the public with a story idea marched into the foyer. Sheila's desk was behind ours. Nate's desk was usually empty.

I glanced back at the offices in the rear of the newsroom. Charlotte's office was still locked up, a strip of yellow crime scene across the front.

Behind me, Sheila was on the phone, though it was often hard to tell with her who was leading the interview. Her long blonde hair was pulled into a messy bun, and she had on a frilly white tunic shirt with long, loose sleeves, like a character out of King Richard's Faire. Personally, I felt that long sleeves should be banned in the summer, but I didn't have a look to curate like Sheila did.

As I eavesdropped, she murmured, "Well, only if you're comfortable talking about it." It was a miracle she ever got any details at all for her stories.

I leaned toward Jimmy, now back at his desk but still nervously glancing at the door.

"So, did you find any story ideas in the police logs this morning?" I asked.

One of his intern duties was to check the logs each day. It saved me the time, but it also taught him to flag reports that might be worth following up on. He picked up a stack of papers on his desk.

"Well, there's been a string of car break-ins, mostly over by the train tracks, during the past week."

Now that got my attention, and I rolled my desk chair toward him. "Wonder if that's what happened to my car at Sheila's?"

He shrugged, and I decided to prompt him. "Why don't you follow up on that? Might be a good short story, along with a helpful PSA for people in that area to lock their cars."

I sent my story and photo on the Council on Aging to Hap for his review and then briefly returned my focus to the Rockport angle on Charlotte. Even though I was taking the lead, I decided to share what I'd learned with Jimmy. Half the fun in finding out a good tidbit was watching someone else's face when you revealed what you had unearthed.

"So, Jimmy, in other news, I might have a lead on Charlotte's time in Rockport," I began. I updated him about what I'd learned at the Historical Society with Winnie's database program, and I explained that she would keep looking for more details of Charlotte's work at the paper there.

"I'd love to go back over there today, see what else I could turn up," I told him, "but, alas, it's the annual rubber duck race."

Depending on which way the tide was moving in the brackish river, the Friday afternoon rubber duck race could be over in minutes—or hours. Participants bought a duck and got a number, which was on the bottom of the duck, and then waited to see whose duck was first to cross the finish line, which was set up in the water in front of Swasey Parkway. Money raised went to a different charity in town each year.

Jimmy perked up as I confided my plan. "After the duck race, I'm going to work on a story about this Rockport thing, as a follow-up to Charlotte using a pen name. Maybe I'll talk about her early career or something," I said.

Just then, my phone rang on the direct line, which went straight past Clara and to my desk. I only gave the direct line number to people I wanted to hear from.

"*Exeter Independent*, this is Piper."

"Piper, are you really going to let Grayson get away with this? I mean, this plaque is too much! And don't even get me started on his plan for the Adams Day celebration—"

So, not really *just* people I wanted to hear from. Also, Chester.

For the next five minutes, he ranted nonstop about the big

front-page spread about the unveiling of the new plaque recognizing the role of Grayson's ancestors in our town's history. Chester didn't understand that it was news—that despite his personal feelings, a plaque commemorating the family who founded the town was always news in the tiny paper that covered the town.

"Not my area," I told him, when I eventually managed to get a word in edgewise.

"Well, he's just insufferable! Really, this has taken it to a new level!" Chester grumbled.

"Take it up with Hap," I told him, knowing full well he had likely cornered the publisher already at last week's Sunday brunch at the Terrace, a much grander spot than the Tuck Tavern.

"You know," Chester went on, "being a Greene, you should really understand where I'm coming from."

I wanted to say, "Get over it! Stop with the three-hundred-fifty-year-old feud and move on!" but I knew from a life of living with Chester that he could hold onto a grudge for years. He'd go to the grave cursing Grayson's family.

"Sorry, I've got another call coming in," I lied. "Talk soon."

Seconds later, my private line rang again.

"Hey, Scoop," Richie began. "If I were you, I'd take a little walk out by the boat launch."

My pulse quickened. A tip!

"Thanks," I said. "Anything you can tell me about why?"

He paused. "Not about this, sorry. The state cops are heading things up. But there was some news on the search inside the town hall you might find interesting."

"Yes?" I prompted.

"So, they think some wire that was found up in the attic

section could be the murder weapon." He lowered his voice. "But you didn't hear that from me, right?"

"Absolutely not." I was well versed in how to protect my sources. "I owe you, big time."

I slid my notebook and camera into my purse and glanced at Jimmy. He was on the phone, and honestly, I was glad. I wanted to tackle this on my own. But before I could head out, my phone rang again.

"Exeter Independent, this is Piper."

"Piper dear," Gladys began. "Stanley just called. He was on his way to the eye doctor, you know, down by the ice cream place, when he saw a few police cars out in the parking lot out back. He said they were next to a red Toyota pickup truck with a kayak in the back. His report was that it looked juicy. Actually, he said, 'Tell Piper.'"

My stomach flipflopped the way it did whenever a big story was unfolding before me. First Richie, and now even Stanley, telling me to head down to the parking lot by the river.

She continued. "Oh, Piper dear, do you think it's part of the murder? How exciting for Stanley."

Exciting for Stanley, but not for the truck's owner—Andy Hathaway.

CHAPTER 18

As I walked toward the parking lot behind the boat house, I felt a growing sense of dread. I was certain that the red truck belonged to Andy. I had gone on more than one assignment with him in that very vehicle. He always kept the kayak in the back for those times he headed out on the river to pursue his nature photography.

I stayed discretely along the edge of the lot as I watched the scene unfold. It wasn't the Exeter police, that much was sure. Two unmarked black Dodge Chargers that screamed *undercover state police vehicle* were parked behind the truck, along with three plainclothes detectives clad in khaki pants and polo shirts. The only indications of their profession, aside from the short trademark cop haircuts, were the gold badges clipped to their belts.

Andy stood on the edge of the parking lot next to the river. He was holding his phone to his ear and looking more than a little worried.

Oh, Andy, I thought, *the odds are not in your favor.*

I scanned the area. The parking lot was full, I suspected, because of all of the people headed to the rubber duck race along Swasey Parkway, on the other side of the boathouse. I watched as an Exeter police cruiser drove into the parking lot and stopped behind the unmarked cruisers. It was Richie, who gave me a wink when he stepped out of his cruiser but didn't make a move to come talk to me. I got it—he had to be discreet when the state cops were around—but there was something thrilling about getting a tip and playing it cool when we saw each other. Perhaps we *could* keep a romance under wraps if things ever went in that direction.

I glanced at my watch. This was the second time this week that my duties for the Community News page were taking me away from something I would much rather be doing. If I played my own shadow investigation into Charlotte's death right, it might even land me the type of book deal I'd been working toward before returning home to help Gladys.

But I knew I couldn't miss taking the photo of the ducks in the river. Nor could I miss the subsequent plucking of the winning duck from the water by members of the fundraising committee, who gleefully held it up, the same way every year, and called out the winning number over a bullhorn from their tiny motorboat.

On my way out of the parking lot, I spotted Darby Jones, Andy's attorney, walking briskly toward the scene. Once again, I was curious as to how Andy had secured a lawyer of such renown, but I put those thoughts aside for the moment when I reached the crowd of people grouped near the fence in the park.

The duck race began the same way it did every year, and I halfheartedly snapped a few photos, wishing once again that we still had a staff photographer. Then, as the ducks floated toward the finish line in front of the covered pavilion on the park, they picked up speed, as if they were making a break for it.

Out in the motorboat, a 15-foot Boston Whaler, Pansy Bolton, the current president of the Rotary, looked panicked as she grabbed the fishing net to scoop up the first duck across the finish line. In her haste, she toppled over the edge of the boat and into the water. This time I gleefully snapped photos, thinking there was some karma in seeing someone like Pansy soaking wet and brought down from her high horse.

The problem escalated when the other person in the boat didn't throw the life vest quickly enough, and Pansy got swept down the river with the army of yellow rubber ducks. She could clearly swim, but the tide was going out and she didn't have the strength to get back to the boat.

At this rate, Pansy might be the first across the finish line set for the ducks.

Eventually, the fire department showed up in their rescue boat and plucked a sopping wet Pansy from the water, and I got some great photos. Community news was getting more exciting by the day.

Unfortunately, the winning duck was never recovered. In the excitement of plucking Pansy out, everyone had forgotten the ducks, which continued floating down the river toward the next town, Newfields. It looked like this year, they'd just have to pull a winning number from a hat.

I raced back to *The Exeter Independent*, where I sat down immediately and wrote my story.

Duck Disaster
By Piper Greene

EXETER__ The town's annual rubber duck race for charity turned into a race to rescue one of the organizers who plunged into the river at the finish line.

Pansy Bolton, president of the Rotary, appeared to lose her balance while leaning over to scoop up the winning duck, and she was swept away with the current.

"I tried to grab her, but she was just too fast," said Tom Stone, of the Chamber of Commerce, who was also on the boat. *"Before I knew it, she was flailing and flapping like an actual duckling."*

Spectators along the riverbank tried to call out directions to Bolton, who was surrounded by the large raft of yellow ducks as she floated out with the tide.

"It was hard to see her at times, what with her hair being the same color as the ducklings," said Tina Sherman, who witnessed the misadventure. *"It looked like she just couldn't get ahead of the tide, and the guy in the boat was on his own, so he didn't seem to be able to get to her and drive."*

The fire department dispatched their rescue boat to the scene and made quick work of fishing Bolton out of the water. *"She was a little wet, but no worse for the wear,"* the fire chief said. *"This is just another example of how having the right equipment can help us save lives."*

Bolton declined to comment other than to say she hoped her mishap didn't take the focus off the charitable nature of the duck race. This year's event raised a record amount for *The Exeter Neighborhood Table*, a local food pantry that relies on community fundraising and support.

I shared the dramatic story with Clara, along with my suggestion for a photo caption, "Bop Goes the Bolton," knowing that Hap would never let that go to print.

With the story done, I finally had time to ponder the event in the parking lot before the duck race. What had the police been looking for in Andy's truck? I didn't want to take advantage of Richie, but I was eager to chat him up, off the record of course, to find out what he knew. I really wanted to ask Andy directly, but I was doubtful of how much, if anything, he'd tell me. And I also needed to get home. Gladys had left me a message, requesting—no, rather insisting—that I stop by for dinner so she and Stanley could hear the latest on the "big murder," as she called it now.

"Oh, and dress nicely Piper," she'd instructed, before hanging up. "Stanley and I have a little surprise for you."

The surprise turned out to be Stanley's nephew, Carson, who was visiting his uncle and staying at the bed and breakfast downtown. I arrived at the back patio to find the three of them sitting there, and Gladys had the look of the Cheshire cat as she introduced me to Carson, a bespectacled intellectual type with blonde hair. Stanley was impeccably dressed as usual, donning a crimson red bowtie with blue elephants.

"Carson's an art history professor in California," Gladys explained. "And what a dear to come all this way to visit his uncle, don't you think?"

I smiled, knowing full well what Gladys and Stanley were up to with this little dinner. Gladys often remarked about my single status and her disbelief that a good catch like me was not taken yet. "Let them wine and dine you, Piper," she usually told me when I demurred. "No one's saying you have to marry anyone."

Carson was definitely not my type, and I had my vague flirtation with Richie to figure out, but I still had to give the two of them credit for trying.

"Maybe you could show him around town, Piper dear," she said, looking at me and then back to Carson. "Piper's in the middle of a big murder story, you know."

She took a delicate sip of her martini and raised her eyebrows as she gave Carson a pointed look, clearly waiting for what she hoped would be his impressed reaction.

"Oh yes, I saw that here in the paper," he said, gesturing to a stack of *Exeter Independents* on a side table. He wrinkled his nose, the way someone might if they smelled dog poop. "What a nasty bit of business."

I looked back at Gladys, who, to give her credit, seemed to be realizing that Carson was a bit of a stuffed shirt. I mean, didn't this man realize what a big deal this was in our town?

"Oh, I don't know," Gladys continued. "She wasn't the most popular person in town, and it gives your Uncle Stanley and I something to mix up our routine, isn't that right, Stanley?"

But Stanley, as per his norm, was dozing off again. Clearly, his big trip to the eye doctor and his from-the-scene report about the police search of Andy's truck had drained him.

"Stanley might even be a witness now, isn't that exciting," she went on, giving him a gentle nudge. "Right there, minding his own business, when he found himself face to face with the authorities this morning. Now, I haven't been that close to a murder since my days as a model."

Gladys looked thrilled to share this tidbit, clearly loving that she and Stanley had a line on the case. She often embraced the chance to reference her days in the city, back when she'd been discovered as a model in her 40s after her dancing career came to a close.

Carson looked like the last thing he thought his uncle should be doing was being face-to-face with anything other than a rousing game of cribbage.

"So, what did you learn, Piper?" Gladys said. "Did that truck belong to the killer? Did Stanley help your investigation?"

I explained that the truck belonged to Andy, it looked like they were doing some sort of search warrant, but I hadn't been able to stay because of the duck race.

"So," I finished, "I do think it was something, but we'll have to wait to find out what the police are able to release publicly."

Gladys paused, asked if anyone needed a drink refill, then excused herself to get the salads. Carson started telling Stanley about his latest research, authenticating a French painting, and to be honest, I started to tune him out. I briefly considered suggesting he visit Jenny to talk about all things France, but I decided she'd never forgive me for foisting him off on her. Not wanting to have to engage any more than absolutely necessary, I picked up the stack of *Exeter Independents* from the table. With all of the excitement of Charlotte's murder, I'd never looked at the issue of the paper that came out before her death.

There looking back at me was Grayson Adams, his photo along with a story previewing the Independence Festival, written by Sheila. He was extolling the merits of the festival and the value of keeping Exeter's Revolutionary history alive for future generations. But, as per normal, it seemed he could not resist mentioning yet again his family's role in founding the town when his ancestor eight generations back sought religious freedom in the area. Exeter, he went on, was the only town in New Hampshire that was founded on the principle of religious freedom, when that relative was banished from the Massachusetts Bay Colony after being convicted of preaching on the wrong day.

"So, really, with our role in the early days of America's history, and the Revolutionary War, Exeter could become the next Colonial Williamsburg or Plimoth Plantation," Grayson was quoted as saying. "Rather than a pit stop on the way to Old Sturbridge Village."

Ooof, that wasn't going to land well with the locals. The story continued inside the paper, but before I could finish, Gladys reappeared with a tray and four carefully arranged Caesar salads.

I hoped she left out the anchovies in her dressing but knowing what a stickler she was for the tableside preparation of the Caesar dressing at the fancy Italian restaurant in Portsmouth, I suspected I'd have to stomach the fishy addition to my evening.

She placed her tray next to the table and eyed the newspaper. "Oh, he's such a braggart," she said. "Really, Piper, I don't know why the paper gives him the platform they do."

I took a bite of my salad. Yep, as I suspected, extra anchovies. I concentrated on keeping my face neutral and swallowing the dreaded oily fish that in my world should have no place on the table. I took a generous gulp of water to wash it down.

"Well," I responded, "he *is* chairman of the select board, and he's on the board at the museum that organizes the festival."

Gladys grimaced. "Well, that may be, but he is just pretentious to a fault, and honestly, I've grown tired of him. I mean really, Piper dear, when someone's whole identity is tied to an ancestor who died over three hundred fifty years ago, really, that's a bit tragic."

She was starting to sound like my brother, Chester, though to be fair, he was also stuck in the past, back when the Greenes on our mother's side arrived in Exeter and brought prosperity to the area through their sawmill.

Gladys polished off her martini and ate the olive from the bottom of her glass. Clearly, this was going to be a showtunes night whether Stanley, or Carson, wanted to take part or not.

"I mean, look at you, Piper dear. You're a Greene. Half of this town has historic buildings with plaques honoring your ancestors, but you never carry on like Grayson," she said, standing. "That's the proper way to be, not like that puffed up pompous popinjay."

Oh, she was on a roll. I loved it when Gladys rolled out her repertoire of old expressions.

Carson looked surprised by her display of words, clearly not used to seeing a woman of her age so free with her opinions, or martinis.

Stanley nodded in agreement and added, "And he really needs a good tailor. None of Grayson's shirts fit properly across the chest."

Stanley, like Gladys, was a stickler for decorum and the understated New England way of life, not the persistent preening that dominated Grayson Adam's days.

"Mark my words, Piper," Gladys said. "Without that last name, he wouldn't have amounted to anything."

CHAPTER 19

I started off the next day at the Morning Musket, where I made quick work of bringing Jenny up to speed on the case and Andy, but most important, on my dinner the night before with Gladys.

"He was such a dud, honestly, it would have been like dating someone's grandfather," I moaned as I told her about Carson.

Jenny tucked a wayward curl behind her ear, then looked up from the tray of macaron cookies she was frosting. She was meticulous as she spread amaretto-scented frosting on one cookie, then lined a second cookie up on top, like a sandwich. My stomach growled just looking at them.

"I think it's sweet," she said. "I mean, can you imagine the conversation between Gladys and Stanley as they tried to become matchmakers? I would have paid to hear that."

She had a point. I could only envision how Gladys had told Stanley her big plan, then choreographed our dinner. With that in mind, if she had been expecting Carson and me to get cozy after dinner, then the stinky anchovies in her homemade Caesar dressing might not have been the best choice.

"And then there's Richie, who makes no sense," I said, as I filled her in on his platonic use of "kiddo" in our last phone call. "He mentioned getting together once but hasn't said anything since. Honestly, I think he changed his mind and doesn't know how to tell me."

Jenny set her bag of frosting on the counter and looked right at me. It was the same look she used to give me in high school when I got completely stressed out about a big assignment.

"Piper, take a big deep breath, seriously," she said, as she put both hands on my shoulders and gave me a squeeze. "You're obsessed with this murder investigation; don't you think he's in the same boat? Be patient."

I knew she was probably right, and honestly, until recently I'd been content to avoid any thought of romance. But those long-ago feelings for Richie were coming back fast and furious and, along with them, all of my old insecurities about being the tall, plain-old Piper I'd been in high school.

Jenny handed me a plate with a gigantic chocolate-drizzled croissant. "Here, go out, sit, relax, and enjoy," she said. "Winnie bought your breakfast this morning. Sounds like she's feeling flush after her last poker game."

I took the pastry out front, where I spied Winnie in her regular seat, a blueberry lemon scone before her. I sat at the table next to her and her eyes lit up. I sensed she had news to share, and I soon learned that it wasn't about her winning hand at poker.

"I heard there might be a break in the case," Winnie said, between bites.

I leaned closer.

"Oh, do tell."

She paused, swallowed, sipped her tea, really taking her time. "Well, I saw, the police chief's secretary at walking club this morning."

The Women's Walking Club was a pack of ladies over 65 who knew everything that happened in town, mostly because they walked around and kept tabs on everything—from the new sewer plant to the person who was building a simply scandalous non-historical house to the home where a man was killed in a murder-suicide a few years back. "The murder house," they called it, according to Winnie.

Winnie set the teacup down and continued. "Well, so all I know is that the chief's secretary said they got some sort of evidence, something yesterday, that matches something else," she said. "Like a connect-the-dots type of thing."

Hmm. I was definitely going to ask Richie about that as soon as I could. It sounded promising.

A shrill voice broke in, which startled me. "What business of that is yours," Myrna Smith huffed as she passed our table, reminding me how she earned her "Cranky Yankee" nickname. "Really, that's the police's job, and all this gossiping will come back to bite you."

Before we could respond, she harrumphed and stalked out of the bakery, closing the door so tightly that the bell echoed through the whole space.

"Has she always been that miserable?" I asked Winnie, knowing they had graduated the now defunct, all-girl's seminary school in town together. The building had burned decades ago, but those who had attended the school still had a yearly reunion, and a collegial bond.

"Since the first grade," she responded. "Always the first to tell the teacher when one of us did something wrong."

What a way to live, I thought, thankful I would never be like that.

I placed my focus back on Winnie. "So, did you find anything else about Rockport, about what happened with the Tarr case? Or any mention of Charlotte?"

Winnie looked frustrated, and I hoped I wasn't asking too much of her. She said, "Not yet. I got sidetracked by Grayson, who showed up and wanted to confirm something about when his minister relative returned from England the second time. You know," she paused, "when he went to lead that other church."

The other church had been across the border into Massachusetts, and some townies, my brother included, never got over him leaving the town he had founded for the state he had once fled.

Winnie sighed in exasperation before she went on. "You'd think he'd already know all about that, what with his obsession with genealogy, but no, he wanted me to pull some old files, way in the basement vault, and by the time I got done with that, it was time to go home."

I agreed with her assessment; his behavior seemed odd. I had also thought there was nothing about the history of the town that Grayson didn't know. So, what was he up to?

She changed the subject and said, "I'm going to do some looking later today on that Rockport angle." Her grin left no doubt she loved to dig up information. "Which reminds me, I think I met the curator from their Historical Society a few years back at the *Moby Dick* marathon in New Bedford."

Most people couldn't wait to be done with *Moby Dick* when they read it in school. Not Winnie. After becoming fascinated by whale oil lamps, particularly the period when they might have been used in town, she convinced her husband to take her to New Bedford one summer to do more research. The next thing he knew, she'd entered the lottery to read an excerpt aloud from the book during the once-a-year event at the New Bedford Whaling Museum. She had been positively giddy when she returned from the reading, which went on for 25 straight hours until the entire book was read.

The bell dinged again, and I looked up to see Carson wandering in. I made eye contact with Jenny and gave her an ever-so-slight sign toward him. She raised her eyebrows in response, and I could tell she was trying not to laugh.

I turned back to Winnie and decided it was time to head out before I got roped into showing Carson around town as Gladys had asked.

"Well, keep me posted," I said, knowing I didn't need to ask, because given her interest in her thickening murder file, I suspected she'd be deep into her research before the end of the day.

I took the back way from the Morning Musket to the paper, through the parking lot and around to the entrance of *The Exeter Independent*, stopping to look at the front page of the paper in the display racks in the lobby. My photo of Pansy Bolton popping up in the middle of the rubber ducks, her bottle-blonde hair drenched, was front and center with the headline I'd officially suggested: "Duck Disaster." Glancing at it quickly, I realized that she really did look like the mother duck, a lighter shade of yellow amidst the tiny waterfowl armada. I wondered if Hap would catch heck for that when he saw her at the next Rotary meeting.

"Where's Hap?" I asked Clara. I knew I had to fill him in on what I'd learned about the case and our coverage going forward.

Clara gestured to the rear of the newsroom, where Jimmy was in Hap's office with the door closed.

"How long have they been in there?" I asked Sheila. She was bent over her desk and closer to Hap's office than I was.

She looked up. "Oh, I don't really know," she said. "They were in there when I got here."

A minute later, Jimmy barreled back into the newsroom, slid into his chair, and began flipping through his notebook like something was on fire.

"What's up?" I whispered.

He didn't look up, still flicking his notebook at a pace fast enough to power one of those cartoon flip books I used to have in elementary school. He said, "I made a mistake on someone's name and title, and I could have sworn I wrote it down here."

I sympathized with him. There was nothing more horrifying than realizing you'd made a mistake that went to print. It's why I always repeated names and spellings back to people when I finished an interview. I'd learned the hard way too.

I headed for Hap's office before he had a chance to leave. He was settled behind his large desk and dressed as usual in an outfit that could have been ripped from the pages of an L.L.Bean catalog. I caught the slightest whiff of tobacco smoke from the pipe he was known to smoke on deadline nights.

"What's up?" he asked, and I sat down in a chair opposite him.

I filled him in on the wire found in the town hall, the search of Andy's truck, and my suspicion that it was connected. "But I only know about the wire off the record," I confided.

Hap gave me an apologetic look. "You know we can't run that without official confirmation."

He was right, but it was so frustrating, especially when I knew I had a juicy tidbit and could potentially scoop the other media, in this case the Boston papers that were covering the story. I went on.

"And I know Andy couldn't have had anything to do with this, but his lawyer, Darby, hasn't called me back." I knew from my experience covering court cases at the metro paper that official quotes on a case usually came from the defense lawyer. Andy would have instructions not to say anything on the record.

Hap sat thinking for a minute. "You know, I think Sheila wrote about Darby a while back. His collection of boats in bottles. Maybe she has another number for him, a cell phone perhaps?"

Inwardly I groaned, but outwardly, I thanked him and headed back into the newsroom to talk to her. She perked up at the mention of Darby and his boats.

"Oh, he was lovely," she said. "It helped that I knew about the process. My uncle had a collection of them growing up."

Sheila went on, a wistful expression momentarily crossing her face, at the mention of her uncle. "Darby said it was almost like therapy for him, a break from the intensity of his work, you know."

I refrained from giving my opinion on just how boring the hobby sounded. Instead, I pushed ahead with my original intention in talking with her. "Do you think you could give him a call, see if he'd be willing to talk to us?"

"Sure."

She typed in a number and hunched over the phone, then soon mouthed over that it had gone to voicemail. She left a message for him.

"I saw your piece on Grayson," I told her. "Boy, he's something, isn't he, with all of his colonial credentials and talk."

Sheila shrugged. "He's just passionate, you know, just his dedication is so strong to keep the town's history alive."

That was one way to put it, and she was probably the only one in town not annoyed by his constant mentioning of Colonial Exeter and its Revolutionary War history. But that was so typical of her. She never said a bad word about anyone or talked shop in the newsroom about frustrating personalities like I did.

"So, what are you working on now?" I asked, more out of politeness than actual interest.

She looked intently at me, the way she got when she had a new cause to embrace. "Well, Piper, listen. Listen to this. It's going to take some work, but it's important work."

She went on, "I've had some tips about a homeless camp in town, out next to the town forest. I think people would be shocked to know we're not taking care of our citizens, here in a town like this."

This reminded me of something. "You know, that's really interesting. Last week, I saw a woman who looked really down on her luck. Almost hit her with my car after the fireworks. And it was odd, you know, because that's not the type of situation we see in town."

Sheila was on a roll. "That's what I'm getting at, Piper," she said. "I think I saw that same woman, but she walked away before I could get close enough to talk to her. Left in such a hurry that she dropped a candy bar wrapper, a Zagnut if you can believe it."

I bolted upright in my chair. "Wait, did you say a Zagnut wrapper, like the ones with a red wrapper and big yellow lettering?"

She nodded. "Yes, why?"

I wasn't ready to share that with her. "Just something I haven't thought of since I was a kid," I said. "You don't see those in stores much anymore."

She nodded. But my mind was racing, ten steps ahead, as I digested what she'd told me. It was true: I hadn't seen a Zagnut bar in years—until I found one behind my carriage house the night where I'd felt like someone was watching me. And now, Sheila had seen this woman drop one. It didn't take a rocket scientist to reach the conclusion that this mystery woman had been lurking behind my carriage house. But what was she doing there? And more important, did I need to be afraid?

CHAPTER 20

I could not stop thinking about what the mystery woman had been doing in my backyard. She had looked harmless, but it was unsettling to think she might have been watching me. I decided to run the situation by Richie when I talked to him and ask if he thought I should be concerned. I also needed to check in with him to find out if there was anything new in the investigation that the police might be willing to say on the record after the search of Andy's truck. I grabbed my phone and dialed his number.

"What's the scoop?" I began when he answered. "I'd love to write about something other than next week's select board meeting."

He laughed. "Not much I can say officially," he said. "But things are moving along quickly now."

The police, it seemed, were most interested in Charlotte's treatment of her employees at *The Exeter Independent*. I knew they had interviewed all of us, but it sounded like back at the barracks, they talked a lot about who she might have wronged at the newspaper. The state police especially were really starting to finger Andy as their prime suspect. The search of his truck had yielded a piece of wire that matched the wire found in the town hall. Wire, Richie said, that the forensic people thought could have been used to strangle her.

But the clincher, he told me, was Andy's past.

"He had a record, Piper," he said, in a voice so low I could barely hear him. "Did you have any idea?"

Obviously, I had no sense of that type of history in Andy's life, but I wasn't ready to jump on the guilty train with the state police just yet.

"Did you find out for what?" I asked.

Richie groaned as if he was struggling with how much he could share. "Sorry, but I can't say anything else. It was mostly a juvenile record, and it could be my job if I say anything about that."

I knew from being born to a family of lawyers just how serious for police and attorneys the consequences of talking about juvenile records could be. But my curiosity was in high gear again, and my mind was already thinking of next steps I could take. In fact, I was so distracted by the news that I thanked Richie and hung up before I asked him for his opinion on the strange woman in my backyard. I realized he also had not mentioned his invitation to get together again. It was disappointing, but probably for the best. I wasn't ready to get my hopes up, especially with everything else that was going on in my life.

I turned to Jimmy and filled him in, only to watch his face recoil in horror when I shared that Andy had some sort of record. Jimmy had probably never even had a late library book.

"Just because someone has a record doesn't make them a killer, Jimmy," I cautioned him.

"Well, that doesn't sound good, Piper," Jimmy said.

I wondered how horrified Jimmy would be by my record, my underage alcohol possession at the all-girls college I attended. Given his sunny suburban upbringing, I suspected the closest he came to crime was watching reruns of *The Wire*.

But Jimmy aside, I was chomping to get moving. I knew I had to be careful with how I asked questions about Andy's past and his record, especially since it was information that came to me *way* off the record. But I could not stifle the feeling that I should go talk to him, maybe hint that the police were focusing on him, and see if there was something I could do to help.

I had an interview to do later in the day about a new pop-up taco stand, so I had a bit of time to follow up on the murder. As our intern, Jimmy was relegated a litany of tasks that were mundane but necessary to earn his stripes. Even though his uncle was the publisher, he had to go through the same training as any trainee. That day, he was charged with compiling the community calendar: the listing of clubs, organizations, and upcoming yard sales in the area. I made sure he had everything he needed, grabbed my purse and notebook, and slipped out the back door of the newspaper offices.

The more the police focused on Andy, the more I wanted to clear his name. In my gut, I just knew he could not be a murderer. I fancied myself a good judge of people, and nothing had ever made me feel like he was the type of person who could have a violent streak.

I walked the back way to Frank's Foto, a tiny camera repair shop where Andy had been working part-time for a few months. I don't know how he had fit it into his schedule when he was still at the newspaper, but he seemed to have a soft spot for the owner, Frank. Frank had run the shop for 50 years, and he even used to take freelance photos for the newspaper back before Hap hired a staff photographer. He'd suffered a stroke last year and his adult kids, who all lived in town, had pitched in to help him at the shop, a situation that had left many downtown watchers wondering just how long he'd be able to stay open. Andy liked

Frank, and the older man let him display some of his nature photography at the shop.

The chime on the door dinged as I walked in. Andy was behind the counter, wearing a white polo shirt and reading a magazine. He didn't look surprised to see me, more exasperated, likely because I kept showing up.

"Hey, can we talk?" I asked, noting that I was the only one in the shop other than him.

He pursed his lips together. "Darby is really on me about not talking about the case," he said. "And I know you want to help, but Darby knows what he's doing."

He was right. In the world of criminal defense in New Hampshire, Darby Jones was one of the best. And because of that I knew he had given Andy good advice; I'd been expecting that.

"I know. So, how's this, you don't have to talk, just listen to some information that I want to share with you."

He glanced around, as if checking to make sure no one was listening. No surprise, it was still just us in the shop. Sadly, with the uptick in online shopping and digital cameras, Frank's Foto was a dinosaur in the retail field, and the slow trickle of people in the shop was probably barely enough to make rent on the space. I quietly told Andy that I'd heard the state police were calling him their top suspect.

"So, you know, I'm on your side, Andy," I began. "I don't think you had anything to do with this, but give me something I can work with, something I can find to convince the state police they're on the wrong path."

I knew one of the other really incriminating details was what A-Train had told me: Andy had not come home that night. "So, I know you didn't sleep at your place that night, Andy, you've got to know that's not good, right?"

His shoulders slumped. "I know, but I can tell you, Piper, I wasn't even in the area that night. I definitely was not around at the time they think she was killed. I was over at Hampton Beach."

I asked for details, but he did not want to share where he was, or with whom.

"It's personal," he insisted. "Not something I want to get into."

I thought, *Whatever it is, is it worth going to jail for by not sharing it with the police?* It didn't make sense. I mean, was he moonlighting at the beach? Or maybe—I knew this was a stretch—he had a love interest he did not want us to know about.

"Or was there nothing going on there," I imagined the police saying in an accusatory tone, *"because Andy was actually back here in Exeter, wrapping a wire around Charlotte's neck to guarantee her cruel voice was silenced forever."*

Just then, Frank appeared, walking with the deliberate pace of someone with one arm paralyzed by his stroke, which put him off kilter but did not stop his determination to keep moving. He smiled when he saw me.

"Oh, Piper, I just loved that photo of the duck race, a keeper that one!" he said, with a laugh.

His body might have been slowing down, but Frank still knew a good photo when he saw one. I hated to respond in front of Andy, knowing that the only reason I got that photo of Pansy Bolton was because he lost his job. But Andy had abruptly walked out from behind the counter to the far side of the store, where he was bent forward with his phone pressed to his ear.

"Again?" Andy was saying in a tone of frustration I'd never heard him use before. "This is the second time this month. I can't always be there when this happens."

He let out an exasperated groan. "Fine, sit tight and I'll see what I can do."

That definitely did not sound like a casual phone call, and I was dying to know what it was about. Sure, it could be something as benign as his rapping roommate, A-Train, needing a ride. But something told me it was more than that.

"Everything okay?" I asked him, as he rejoined me and Frank.

"Yeah, everything's fine. Just a change in plans for today, that's all."

He did not elaborate, and I got the sense he was not going to do so.

"Well, good luck," I said. "And remember, let me know if you change your mind about what we talked about."

His smile seemed genuine. "I will, and I do appreciate it, Piper, I do, but you understand the position I'm in."

I did—at least to a degree—but that didn't stop me from making a plan. That little girl inside me, the one who used to write down what the neighbors did every day in the spiral notebook, was clamoring to come out. I returned to the newspaper parking lot, got into Walter, and waited. All the time, I kept an eye on the narrow driveway exit from the parking lot by Frank's Foto, only pausing to munch on some of Jenny's homemade granola, which I kept in the car as an emergency snack. I needed sustenance for this mission.

When Andy's truck finally pulled out of the parking lot and turned right to head east later that afternoon, I gently eased the station wagon into traffic a few cars behind him, making sure to keep the kayak on his truck in sight. Then I followed him straight out of town.

CHAPTER 21

I followed Andy through several little towns, on winding back roads with few houses or streetlights. It was a good thing I had a full tank of gas. I was starting to wonder if we would end up in the ocean by the time he stopped. Eventually, he took a left onto a two-lane road that went all the way from the Massachusetts border to the Maine border. Then he sped up.

It seemed like he was taking a very roundabout back way to Hampton Beach, a seaside community that harkened back to a simpler time with colorful arcades and a boardwalk. In the winter months, there was often an uptick in area drug busts due to the plethora of inexpensive off-season rentals, but on Friday nights in the summer, the traffic slowed to a crawl along the beach's strip, which often included everything from Canadian tourists to gangsters from Massachusetts.

"Hey, even gangsters go on vacation," one of the old-time police officers at the beach told me once.

As I followed behind Andy, I tried to piece together who he might be going to visit and why he had been so secretive when he took that phone call at the photo shop. He had more than doubled the time the drive to Hampton Beach normally took from Exeter, and I couldn't imagine it was because he knew I was tailing him. Maybe he needed time to clear his head before he got to wherever he was headed.

Eventually, he slowed and pulled into what looked like a drive-in motel. A large white sign with illuminated green lettering advertised it as the El Dorado Motel: "Rooms for a night or a lifetime."

Well, that's certainly equal opportunity, I thought.

I drove past the entrance, turned into a drive-through coffee shop on the other side of the road, and quickly parked Walter in a spot where I could watch what Andy was doing. The El Dorado looked like a washed-up skeleton of its heyday many decades ago when places like this housed legitimate tourists headed toward New Hampshire's Atlantic coastline to stop for a night, not a lifetime.

The motel was shaped like a U, with a narrow central courtyard area and an illuminated red arrow that pointed to what must have been the office. Andy drove to the far end of the hotel, as if he knew exactly where he was going, and went into one of the rooms.

Andy had told me he was in Hampton on the night of Charlotte's murder. It seemed likely that this was the place. But what was he doing here then—or now? It did not fit with what I knew about Andy. I didn't want to stereotype, but the El Dorado definitely looked like the kind of place where it wouldn't be too hard to find drugs or alcohol any time of the year. *The challenge,* I thought, *at a place like this, would be avoiding them.*

I continued to peer across the street, wondering what Andy was doing inside. If only I had binoculars. My imagination was out of control as I waited. Drug deal? Secret romantic rendezvous? Big story? Patience was not my strong suit.

Finally, almost an hour later, Andy exited, stopped, looked around the courtyard, and drove away. By that time, the only thing ready to burst more than my curiosity was my bladder. I waited until he was out of sight before I made a quick pit stop at the bathroom of the coffee shop and then drove across the street.

I steadied my hands as I opened Walter's heavy driver side door and looked around. It was not like I had never been around the odd sketchy hotel when I'd been a reporter in the city, but I still felt hesitant to proceed. If Andy found out I was snooping into his private life without his permission, it would ruin any trust he had in me, no matter the outcome.

The parking lot area suggested not only that people could stay for a lifetime but also that cars could too. Some of the clunkers lookers like they had been there since the place opened. A small crowd sat around one of the chipped picnic tables in the courtyard. Like the table, most of the people had seen better days. An empty 32-ounce bottle of Keystone Light sat in the middle. A small, scruffy-looking dog was asleep under the table.

I knew that the longer I stood there without moving, the more suspicious I looked. This was one of those times where I had to just act like I was supposed to be there and knew exactly where I was going.

I'd seen Andy go in the second-to-last door, toward the end of the building, so I walked that way. I paused outside, leaned in a bit, and listened. The wood-paneled door had a long crack, and the sound of the TV inside was crystal clear. It sounded like Maury Povich. Did people even watch that anymore? I banged on the door.

Nothing.

Banged again.

Nothing.

I felt more and more uneasy the longer I stood there. I glanced back at the table of people in the courtyard, and I remembered the lyrics from that kid's song, "One of these things doesn't look like the other." I was sure I stood out like a sore thumb, and a few people stared back.

I turned toward my car, which was a few feet away, quickly planning out how I could make a quick getaway if I needed to do so. Just then, the door to the hotel room clicked open.

I found myself staring into the face of an unshaven and haggard version of Andy Hathaway.

The guy said, "You from probation? Joey moved. He's down the street, that Gentle Breezes place now."

"No. My name is Piper, and I work with Andy."

He looked confused. "And he told you to come here?"

"Not exactly," I said. "Can I talk to you about something?"

He looked both ways, beckoned me inside, then bolted the door the moment I crossed the threshold. There was a bed, one wooden chair with a threadbare cushion, and a tiny dresser.

"You can't be too careful around this place. They're always listening to you around here," he said.

He shuffled toward the bed and pointed toward the chair, but I remained standing. I had a rule about not sitting on soft furniture in places like this, which always made me worry about bedbugs.

"So," I began, "as I said, I work with Andy." I paused, trying to find a diplomatic way to ask the next question. "And I have to ask, are you related? You look just like him."

Well, aside from the uncut hair, the beard, and the downcast aura he did.

He said, "I should be. I mean, we are twins after all."

I couldn't have been more shocked if he had told me aliens had deposited him there. Andy had a twin brother. A twin brother who lived in a place like this and looked like he was

148

about as different from the quiet and conscientious photographer as could be.

He must have sensed my surprise. "Yeah, hard to believe, I know," he said. "I don't always look like this. I'm going through some things right now."

I quickly learned that his name was Charlie and he lived here, in the efficiency hotel, looking like the mirror double of Andy and yet worlds away. He pulled out a cigarette.

"You mind?"

I hated the smell of cigarette smoke on my clothes, but in times like this, I knew it was pointless to say anything.

"That's fine," I said.

Charlie inhaled deeply, then looked to me as if he were waiting for an explanation of my presence there.

"So, there are some things going on with Andy," I said. "And I want to help him. Things with the police that don't seem fair."

Charlie plunked down on the bed, which sagged heavily in the middle under his weight.

"I had a feeling something was bothering him," he said. He ran his hands through his hair and looked down at the frayed carpet. I decided to forge ahead with my reason for being there with hopes he would open up.

I told him about the murder, about Andy losing his job, and about how the police now had some evidence that they felt linked Andy to the murder.

"The problem is, he won't tell anyone where he was that night," I went on, "and I think he might have been here with you that night."

A look of realization passed over this face, and I pounced without taking a breath. "So, he was here then?"

Charlie nodded. Then he went on to tell me that he had

149

blacked out that night, so he didn't actually remember anything after checking into the hotel and calling Andy. He'd arrived at the El Dorado after his wife had dumped him for her dog trainer, Gustav. She had immediately changed the locks and wouldn't let him back into their home. The only place he had been able to find to stay with the cash he had on hand was the El Dorado.

"So, I'm not proud of it, but I got reunited with Captain Morgan that night," he said. "I'd been sober for almost ten years until that night."

He shook his head sadly at that admission. "So, I know Andy came to help, he told me afterward, but the last thing I remember was dialing his number and pouring another drink."

Charlie clenched his hands together, sighed deeply, and went on. "Our dad had a taste for liquor. Didn't start out that way, but after our mom left, he lost his business and, well, let's just say, it wasn't good. I swore I wouldn't be like that, and then," he shook his head again, "it seemed history repeated itself."

My desire to help Andy was momentarily overrun by my curiosity about Andy and Charlie's upbringing. "Is your dad still around?" I asked.

Charlie shook his head. "Nah, he died a while back. Honestly, it was a relief as awful as that sounds."

"Oh, I'm so sorry," I said, and I was. I knew from experience what it was like to lose a parent. In my case, both parents.

"Thanks," he said, taking a long drag from his cigarette. "So, it's been just me and Andy since then, aside from the occasional Christmas card from our mom."

Charlie explained that Andy was helping him out with the rent at the El Dorado while he figured out his next steps. He didn't want to get Andy in trouble by sleeping at his place. Apparently, the landlord was a real stickler for the number of people who lived there. Andy got a great deal on the rent in exchange for helping with maintenance and didn't want to risk losing his housing. Charlie usually worked as a carpenter, but he was between jobs, and his estranged wife had left him high and dry.

"Yeah, she drained the accounts buying some prized dachshund for Gustav if you can believe it," he said. He gestured to the room and frowned. "So, I'm here until I get on my feet again."

I understood why Andy couldn't use Charlie as his alibi on the night of Charlotte's death. I mean, who was going to believe a man who couldn't remember anything other than the type of drink he poured that night? But maybe there was another way to verify that Andy was there.

"Anyone else around that night?" I asked him.

"Heck, if I know," he said. "I was out in another orbit that night."

Ugh. Well, that wasn't going to help. But, knowing that this was where Andy was the night of the murder was a start. I wondered if there was a surveillance camera outside the office. Not that the management would tell me, but perhaps Andy's hotshot attorney, Darby, could get ahold of it.

I edged toward the door, not wanting to overstay my welcome.

"Well, thanks so much, Charlie. You've been a big help, really. I do appreciate your time."

"So, is this going to help him then, show the truth?"

I didn't have the heart to tell him no. "I think so," I said. "But for now, can we keep this between us? I don't want to tell Andy until I know for sure."

Charlie stamped his cigarette out and unbolted the door, reminding me again that he had to watch what he said around the motel. It seemed that his troubles had also triggered a case of paranoia. I slipped out the door, then gave him a little wave.

"Well thanks again. I'll be in touch if I need anything else."

He slammed the door hard. The lock clicked back into place. I breathed a sigh of relief that I was in one piece and glanced at my watch. I would hazard a guess that I had gotten in and out of the El Dorado in less time than most.

CHAPTER 22

As I got ready for work the next morning, I couldn't stop thinking about Andy and his brother, Charlie. I was so distracted by the brothers, I decided to walk to the newspaper. It would give me time to clear my head a bit and try to make sense of things before I settled into the day's news.

I made my way across the patio walkway from my carriage house and paused for a minute just as a black-and-white flash caught my eye. It was Oscar, the feral cat that Gladys had been feeding behind the carriage house. The large tuxedo cat clearly had a hidden route to get inside the building, and a few times since I'd returned to New Hampshire, I'd woken up in the middle of the night to find him staring at me as if letting me know this was his domain, not mine. We were working out an accord. I gave him cat treats, and in exchange I told him not to kill me in my sleep.

"Hey kitty, kitty," I called softly. He stopped and narrowed his eyes at me for only an instant before disappearing into the greenery in the garden.

I cut through the yard to the sidewalk and headed for downtown, putting in my earbuds to signal to passersby that I was not available for conversation. I wanted to ponder the case.

Given what I'd learned, I sensed that Andy was protective of his brother, especially considering that his twin had just fallen off the wagon. The fact that he was also helping Charlie pay for the hotel room was also weighing on me. Losing his job at The Exeter Independent wasn't going to impact just Andy, but also the sorrowful man I had met at the El Dorado. If I was Andy, I'd have no love lost for Charlotte, who had laid him off at the very time he was helping his brother out.

But even I knew that there was no way Charlie could be a reliable alibi for his brother. He couldn't even remember what happened that night. For all I knew, Andy never actually showed up at the hotel. No one else saw him that night. I surmised that the police, or possibly Andy's attorney, could ask for surveillance footage to confirm the account, but I also knew the hotel wasn't going to let just anybody, aka a curious reporter, view the tapes.

It seemed like the chips were stacking up against Andy, and I found myself hoping the police would investigate all the existing angles. But if there were any others, I hadn't figured them out yet. I didn't even have any other suspects. Sure, Charlotte had written an editorial calling for new leadership on the select board after Grayson's third term, but it hadn't stopped him being reelected, and just recently he'd had nothing but appropriate things to say about Charlotte's death.

The most obvious place to look for suspects and motives still seemed to be Charlotte's past in Rockport. The way she had changed her pen name after working there just seemed dubious, like she didn't want to be found in Exeter. But unless someone was a supersleuth, it was unlikely anyone even knew she was in town.

And then there was the mystery man Sheila had mentioned— the one that Charlotte went off with over the Fourth of July holiday in a car that looked a lot like Kevin's. It didn't sound inconsequential, especially when I added the intel from the owner at the Tuck Tavern, who had mentioned that Charlotte had been out on the town more often than normal and seemed to have a certain glow. She was dressed to the nines on those outings, per Stanley, which lent some weight to the theory. So why hadn't this mystery man materialized? Especially after her death. Wouldn't he be mourning in some way?

I was so caught up pondering who in town Charlotte might have been having an affair with that I almost missed seeing the homeless woman with the backpack. She was sitting on a bench downtown. I recalled that Sheila really wanted to find someone to interview for her story about homelessness but that she hadn't been fast enough to talk to this woman. I was still wondering if she had been in my backyard, but I also figured it wouldn't hurt to try to talk to her and get a sense of what she was up to.

I slowed down and smiled. "Hi, I don't think we've met. I'm Piper. I work at the paper over there." I gestured toward the long brick building.

"Not interested," she said, abandoning the bench and walking briskly down the sidewalk that followed the river out of town.

Well, that went well.

Clara was particularly jovial when I walked in the front doors of the newspaper that morning. "We've got a good one today," she began, before I even got to my desk. "A letter to the editor from a man who is upset about the fantasy booths being unsanitary."

Dear God. The fantasy booths were a legal version of a peep show, a few towns over, in an area known for selling fireworks, tattoos, and a peek at the ladies in the booths. I pushed aside thoughts of what I had heard happened in the fantasy booths and got to the more obvious question: how could anyone who went into a place like that think they were sanitary?

"I mean, can you imagine?" Clara continued. "That's like complaining about cigarettes giving you cancer. You know when you go in there what you're in for."

She had a point.

Jimmy slid into his seat next to me and wrinkled his nose at the last comment. The poor guy was going to need therapy after hearing everything we discussed in the newsroom.

"So, I found out something about Andy," I told him.

I filled him in on Andy's brother, the reason Andy hadn't gone home that night, and my worry that our former colleague was looking more and more like a suspect. He shared my concern and leaned toward me. "So, what are you going to do?"

"I guess keep up with my police sources, see what they can tell me off the record, figure out whether there are any other angles," I responded.

By police sources, I meant the blue-eyed detective, Richie, and I punched in his cell phone number.

"Hey," I began. "Just checking in."

He laughed. "Sure, you are. You never call, you never write, and then there's a murder and you remember your old friend," he said. "What do I get out of this deal?"

I knew he was teasing. I was tempted to mention his invitation to get together for dinner but decided to wait for him to bring it up. I lowered my voice. "Anything new you can tell me for background, off the record?"

"Well, the state police forensics people have her laptop," he said. "Now, I can't tell you what, but there was something on the laptop, something they told the chief had strong evidentiary value."

Crumbs of information drove me crazy. "Can you give me a

hint? A tiny hint?"

He paused, and I thought he was considering it. "Sorry, Scoop, you know I'd love to help you out, but the state cops are really keeping a lid on things," he said. "I guess I can say it had something to do with a story she was working on, a story that would have huge implications in the town."

Sheila had also mentioned that Charlotte was working on a story. It really didn't make any sense. She only wrote her op-ed column and served as the eyes for *our* stories, editing and making suggestions on content. She had not written an actual news story in years. If she had been working on something in secret, something that was so big that she had not told anyone in the newsroom, it must have been a deep-sourced story. I wondered if Hap knew about it.

"Huh," I said. "And you can't tell me what."

"Sorry. I probably told you too much as it is," he said. "They've been dropping strong hints lately that they find it suspicious that the local paper is getting such good details. I told them that it's a small town and people know everything, but I'm not sure they bought it."

Ugh. I hoped that wasn't a sign that my off-the-record intel was going to dry up.

"Listen," he said. "I've got to run."

We said our goodbyes, and I contemplated what he'd told me. What kind of story had Charlotte been working on? With her computer gone, there was no way to know. So, short of waiting for the police to release more information, I could only hope that whoever she was writing about might come forward because they thought the story needed to be told.

I spent the rest of the afternoon doing some phone interviews for an article for the community section on a new adopt-a-spot program in town. It was what I called a quick-hit story, and I wrote it up before I went home.

Floral Follies

By Piper Greene

EXETER__ There is more to the town's new adopt-a-spot garden program than growing it green.

Volunteer gardeners also want to grow it yellow, pink, red, and all the colors of the rainbow. And they take their unpaid gig seriously.

"Now, I know some people might think to use petunias and marigolds, but really, does that fit in with the character of a town like this?" Agatha Stanley asked. "I mean, really, Exeter deserves more than that."

Stanley detailed the flowers she chose for her spot in a park by the river. "Now, I went with hollyhocks and irises, the same flowers used by our colonial ancestors when they brightened up their gardens," she said.

Mitch Owens, a retired carpenter, got into the program when he fixed up a rotted flagpole by the historic Powder House on the river. When he noticed there were no flowers by the flagpole, he set to work adding some marigolds.

"They're good for the butterflies," he explained.

Maude Sanderson, another volunteer gardener, said she sought to bring a contemporary feel to her garden. "We are a historical town, but that doesn't mean we can't bring some new touches in here and there," she said.

Sanderson created a tiered flower garden by the library that, she said, was influenced by a painting she saw in Paris.

"It's meant to be a piece of art," she said. "Something the townspeople can be proud to show off when visitors walk through our town."

Pansy Bolton, known regionally for her championship rose garden, declined to plant roses in her spot, saying they were too difficult to transplant. "You really have to know what you're doing, which I do," she said. Bolton planted petunias in a red-white-and-blue color scheme.

The town's public works department was thrilled with the extra help, which Director Jason Purdy said will help keep their landscaping budget in check. "We love to see the creations these volunteer gardeners have made," he said. "If you have a green thumb, and some time, give us a call and take on a spot."

I managed to leave out the snide remarks about garden spots a few of the ladies thought weren't up to snuff, and finished up the article. Again, it was not an exciting story, but it was one that showed the good things in town. It was almost dinnertime by the time I finished up and sent my article over to Hap for his review.

I had a plan for dinner but needed to make a quick stop at home to freshen up and check on Gladys before I headed out. She was comfortably ensconced in her library reading that John McCain biography, and I said a quick hello en route to the carriage house. I changed into a nicer blouse and added a touch of lip gloss before I headed over to the Tuck Tavern to schmooze Kevin. If anyone knew who Charlotte was seeing, I knew he would, and there was still the matter of his car being at the paper the night of her death.

The tavern was practically deserted when I walked in. It seemed I had missed the early rush, and the later dinner crowd had yet to arrive. There were a few diners in the main dining room, quietly eating their baked scrod or crab imperial, signature dishes of the chef, and just two people in the bar area, a couple I did not recognize, sitting close to each other and deep in discussion.

Kevin had his back to me when I sat down, watching the news on a tiny television behind the bar. He looked slightly apprehensive when he turned and saw me.

"What now?" he asked. "Please tell me you're just here to eat this time."

Okay, so I was going to have to be strategic with him. He was clearly still spooked from my last visit. "Yeah, I'm starving," I responded. "It's been quite a day at the paper."

I would need to ease in and let him come to me this time. He slid a menu toward me and took my drink order. I glanced at my watch and realized I had just made it into their daily happy hour food specials, so I ordered a roasted vegetable flatbread. I was trying to eat more vegetables and it seemed like a good compromise.

"Yeah," I went on when he handed me a water with lemon. "This case with Charlotte's murder is really heating up."

I watched him. He was starting to nibble the bait but was clearly not ready to give in.

"I guess," I lowered my voice, even though we were the only two people at the bar, "they found some information on her laptop, a story she was working on, that is pretty explosive."

Well, that got his attention. "And," I went on, sensing he was curious, "it sounds like she was seeing someone on a pretty regular basis, but no one knows who it was."

He raised his eyebrows. "The cops tell you that?"

"I never reveal my sources," I told him. "But I know you must see a lot here, know a lot of the behind-the-scenes drama the rest of us don't know about after people get a few drinks in them."

"I never reveal my sources," he shot back at me.

Touché.

He was a tough one to crack. My flatbread arrived, and though usually I never ate mushrooms, they weren't half bad when combined with caramelized onions and asparagus. I ate slowly, hoping that perhaps Kevin would change his mind and reveal his sources, or his secrets. But when he brought me my bill, wordlessly, and turned back to watch the tiny TV, I knew it wasn't going to be that night.

"Well let me know if you think of anything you think I should know," I said as I stood up.

But I knew that was about as likely to happen as me winning the lottery.

CHAPTER 23

I had just hit the snooze button on my alarm the next morning when my cell phone rang. I debated letting it go to voicemail, but the number was vaguely familiar, so I answered.

"Piper, Jack Harper here."

Well, that was a blast from the past I never expected to hear from again: my former literary agent. He'd been frustrated to say the least after what he termed "all the work" he'd put into me when I told him I was taking some time off to help Gladys. Jack, a graduate of the elite prep school in town, had immediately gravitated to me when he learned I was from Exeter. The nostalgia for those who went to the school in our little Puritan town seemed to grow stronger with age.

"Jack," I said, working to keep my voice neutral. "It's been a while."

He got right to the point.

"Listen, I just saw a story on the AP wire about that murder in your town. I know you were taking some time off, but that has true crime book all over it."

No kidding, I thought. And how ironic that he was contacting me, not knowing I had already been considering that as I conducted my own investigation into the murder.

"So, here's the thing," he went on. "I've got an editor who is hot to acquire some true crime. People eat it up, and journalists are often the ones to write them."

But not, I imagined, *journalists whose credits included the garden club and the rubber duck race.* But I did not mention that just yet.

The case had it all, he told me, because it happened in a small town, a town with some prestige, and the victim had an air of mystery with her pen name. And then, there was the symbolism of being hung up in a redcoat jacket. His almost clinical assessment of the marketability of Charlotte's murder bordered on insensitive, but at the same time, I was excited at the prospect of getting a break as an author. Still, I couldn't help but feel that writing a book about my town, which exposed a not-so-nice side, might not endear me to my neighbors.

But I wasn't ready to rule it out altogether. There might be a way to write it and let the spirit of the community shine through.

I said, "Let me think about that. I've got some things to consider on my end."

And just like that, our conversation was done, "Well don't think too long. It's hot, really hot, and others are sniffing around," he warned me. "Got to dash, stay in touch."

He hung up before I could say goodbye.

Jack was throwing me a bone. A chance to sell a book, to be a published author like I'd wanted since high school, but it would require this murder being solved first. Even I knew that. Publishing companies wanted a resolution: a beginning, middle, and end. And in a real murder case, that meant finding the murderer and bringing closure to the family. I took Jack's phone call as a green light for me to double down on my efforts to find out who killed Charlotte and why. Forget about the police. I was now officially on duty.

But what to follow up on next? Jack's phone call had me thinking again about Charlotte's background, the thread I had followed to the newspaper in Rockport, which needed another look. Given that Jack had called while I was still half asleep, I would be able to swing by the Historical Society before anyone missed me at *The Exeter Independent.* If my suspicions were right, then Winnie had continued supplanting her murder file with the research on Charlotte's time in Rockport. I wondered what the trustees thought of Winnie's murder habit, or whether they even knew. They had so far not caught wind of that—or her poker habit—and I, for one, was not going to tell them.

I opted to walk to see Winnie. I knew the short window of summer would soon be over, and with New England weather, which bore the adage *"If you don't like the weather wait a minute,"* the prospect of snow and cold weather was closer than I liked. Plus, since I spent most of my day stuck behind a computer inside the newspaper building, I could always use the exercise.

As I passed the town hall, I found myself pondering the logistics of the murder yet again: not only how the killer had gotten her out onto the roof without being seen, but also how the killer had dressed her in the red jacket. It was authentic wool, I knew that much, but also, as Jack had indicated, the nature of the suit was clearly a symbolic gesture meant to send a message. Charlotte was a redcoat in a Revolutionary town, a traitor, but to whom? I had a feeling that once I found that answer, the identity of her killer would bubble to the surface.

The Historical Society was not open yet, but I spied Winnie's red cruiser bicycle out front, with the wicker basket she carried her cat, Buttercup, around town in. Buttercup was something of a local celebrity, occasionally appearing in promotional materials

164

on history as the town's "History Cat." The school kids loved him. I kept telling her she should write a children's picture book with him, but so far, she had not taken my suggestion.

Clearly, Winnie was here, but my raps on the heavy front doors did not get her attention. She was older, after all, and while her mind was sharp as ever, her hearing was not what it once had been. I walked around the side of the building and knocked on a window.

Buttercup appeared, looking down on me with silent disdain. Cats. I knew they were once revered as gods by the ancient Egyptians, but they had some issues. Just look at Oscar's determination to reclaim my carriage house. I never really understood why people loved cats, which liked you one day and turned up their nose at you the next.

I was more of a dog person at heart. We had yellow labs growing up, and my grandfather trained them well and took them duck hunting whenever he went down to the marshes around Plum Island in Massachusetts. They were great companions and loved the work, but they also required a lot of time and attention, which is why I was pet-less for the time being.

Winnie eventually spied me through the window. She pointed to the front door, where she met me and let me inside.

"Ooh, your ears must have been ringing," she said. "I just found some more information on that situation in Rockport."

I followed her back to her office-slash-kitchen and settled into her worn armchair as she perched behind her desk and giant computer monitor. She slid her glasses onto her nose and picked up a piece of paper with her trademark cursive notes.

"So, I talked to a colleague in Rockport and the Hank Tarr story doesn't end well," she told me, referring to the selectman that Charlotte had accused of embezzling from the town. Tarr, as he had feared, did end up losing his business. He mortgaged the building to pay for his legal fees to defend himself in a case that, as far as Winnie could deduce, never resulted in formal charges. But the damage was done, and Tarr left town—the town his family had lived in for generations—to find a fresh start. Tragedy followed him. He spiraled into alcoholism, and within a year, he took his own life. She couldn't find his obituary, but her counterpart had some details.

"And here's the worst part," Winnie went on. "He had two kids and a wife, and they also lost everything: the house, the business, not to mention Tarr."

I asked if she had any idea what had become of them. She did not.

"There's more," Winnie said. "The real clincher. In the end, the district attorney came out and said there wasn't any evidence that Tarr had actually stolen from the town. It turned out to be someone else."

Wow.

And Charlotte had been the one to accuse him of stealing in her big sensational stories in the *Rockport Report*. No wonder she had left town and changed her name. But how had she even gotten another job in journalism after that? Hap wasn't the type of person who would have hired her if he had caught wind of the background. Surely, she had given him a resume, writing samples, and references. Had she fabricated all of that?

"Were there any follow-up stories, anything that mentioned Charlotte's role in the mess?"

Winnie shook her head. "Nothing. It's like she just vanished into thin air."

Until she turned up at *The Portsmouth Clipper* five years later. Where had she been in the interim? And what became of those poor kids, the two children from Rockport who had lost their dad? Without an obituary, I didn't even know their names.

A horrifying realization hit me. One that made me instantly nauseous. I had just learned about two men who had a father who had a taste for alcohol. A father whose death had been a relief when it had happened. Could Hank Tarr have been that man? The last name was different, but Andy was about the right age. If he died when they were quite young, there was always the possibility that a relative had adopted them. It just seemed like too much of a coincidence that Andy's brother, Charlie, had told me about their father's affinity for drinking so recently. Still, I hoped it was just that—a strange coincidence—because it would be yet another reason for the police to keep Andy at the top of their list of suspects.

More than that, if I wanted to write a book about this case, take the bone that my former literary agent was throwing me, it could mean I'd have to finger Andy, someone who had always been kind to me. I wasn't sure I was ready to comprise myself like that.

But I couldn't stop thinking about those siblings from Rockport.

CHAPTER 24

The next morning, I settled in at the Morning Musket and felt a thrill as I held the hard copy of *The Exeter Independent* in my hand. It had my centerpiece story about Charlotte's work as a reporter in Rockport. Even though I'd written the story and knew every word by heart, I never tired of reading the hard copy of a piece like this. I paused only briefly to bite into the caramel croissant Jenny had given me, savoring the combination of buttery layers and warm and gooey filling.

Murdered Editor Used Alias

By Piper Greene

EXETER__Murdered newspaper editor Charlotte Campbell had been working under a pen name during her time in Exeter, according to newly revealed information.

Campbell, whose death at the annual Revolutionary War Festival is considered suspicious, was actually Carlotta Cabanovich.

"Of course, I knew she was using a pen name," said Exeter Independent *Owner and Publisher Hap Henderson. "I signed her paycheck all these years. But I never thought it was for any other reason than vanity purposes, a name she picked for writing."*

But a review of the editor's previous work, using her legal last name, brought to light an unfortunate incident early in her career. Cabanovich falsely accused a select board member in Rockport, Mass., of embezzling money from the town, a claim later proven to be untrue, but not before the man lost his business. He later died in what police believed was a suicide, according to newspaper reports.

Henderson said he was unaware of the situation in Rockport when he hired Cabanovich for the post at The Exeter Independent. *He called it concerning.*

Police Chief Frank Sinclair confirmed that police were aware of the murdered editor's past but declined to comment further pending the ongoing nature of the investigation into her death. He referred all other inquires to the State Police, who did not respond to a request for comment by press time.

"That's quite a scoop there," a familiar deep voice cut in, and I looked up to find Detective Richie Collins by my table. He was dressed in khakis and a deep-blue polo shirt and, I thought, looking rather attractive.

He gestured to the empty chair next to me. "Can I join you?"

"Absolutely," I said. I folded up the paper to make room for him.

He settled into the chair and sipped his coffee before continuing. "So, I'm glad I ran into you. Listen, the chief is worried about how it looks if I keep talking to you," he said, glancing at the paper between us. "The state cops hinted, or I guess more than hinted, that it was a bit unusual the local paper was getting so many good details. Especially since none of their guys have contacts here."

Inwardly, my heart sank. This wasn't news. He'd been building up to this since the last time we talked. But it still stunk when he confirmed my fears.

"So, you know, we go way back. I want to help you, but I've got to lay low for a while," he said, and I sensed he was truly apologetic. "The chief called me out, said he knew I liked you, and that I needed to be more careful."

Knew he liked me, what exactly did that mean? I wasn't bold enough to ask. Instead I responded, "It's okay, I know how it works. And I really don't want to get you in trouble."

He smiled at me, a real smile. Darn, those dimples got me every time. I fought back the warm flush that threatened to spread across my cheeks.

"I knew you would. And who knows? Maybe I can relax in a little while, slip something your way. But for now," he paused, looking disappointed. "I need to postpone having you over for dinner."

And here I'd been wondering when he was ever going to mention that invitation again. "Rain check?" I asked, surprised at my boldness.

"Absolutely," he said, then stood up. "I've got to get back to the station. Good luck, Scoop."

The loss of Richie's helpful tips was going to put a damper in my investigation. I drowned my disappointment in another caramel croissant. Jenny's baking could cure any problem, at least temporarily. At the same time, I couldn't help but feel a little twinge of excitement at his admission that the chief knew he liked me. In a way, it felt a bit like middle school. Did he like me, or did he *like me* like me?

I forced myself to focus on the investigation and what my next step might be. If Andy was still the top suspect, it would be nearly impossible to get updates. *Unless,* I thought somewhat conspiratorially, *Winnie pumped the police chief's secretary for nuggets during the women's walking club outings.*

In the meantime, I'd follow up on my hunch that there was more to learn from Charlotte's—or should I say Carlotta's—time in Rockport. Other than the former town official there, was there anyone else she had wronged so badly that they'd wanted her dead? The logical first step for police was often the significant other, but I had not made any headway there, even though I suspected that Kevin, the all-seeing bartender, knew who she was dating.

I waved to Jenny as I left, noting to myself that I needed to find time to catch up with her soon, and headed toward the newspaper. I decided to start with a closer look at what Charlotte had written in recent months. I headed to the rear of the newsroom, where past issues of the newspaper were stacked up in what was clearly a fire hazard. This always surprised me a bit because Hap Henderson was a longtime volunteer firefighter in town and very safety conscious. Just last year, he had helped the historic church, the same one started by the town's founder, get a sprinkler system installed.

I picked up copies of the last few months of *Exeter Independents* and headed back to my desk. I went back a month and skimmed the headlines and Charlotte's op-eds, trying to get a sense of something that was off or did not sit right.

June's editorials took on a raise for the town manager (unnecessary, she said), a warning about a proposal for a homeless day center to open in town (cops would end up needing more manpower to handle the clientele it brought, she said) and a piece that cautioned Exeter's old guard of getting so caught up in the past that they didn't look to the future with growth and incentives for young people to move to town. I bet Grayson had loved that one, though I had to admit it was a common sentiment among newcomers to town: there was not much to do if you were under the age of 40 and wanted to go out after dark. The town rolled up its sidewalks after dinner.

"Nice work on the story today," Jimmy said when he walked in.

"Thanks. Boy, it sure is different with Hap editing," I said. "He's old school, but it keeps you on your toes."

Hap was a stickler for accuracy, and I often found myself thankful for my early schooling, those grammar police who instilled the active-not-passive mantra in my brain, for getting through with fewer red marks than most.

As if his ears were ringing, Hap wandered over to our desks.

"So, I wanted to let both of you know where things stand," he began, looking toward Sheila's empty desk. "I was hoping all three of you would be around, but she called out sick today."

Hap crossed his arms, then sat on the corner of Jimmy's desk. "I'm going to continue to stand in as editor for the time being, while we get through the next few months."

It didn't make sense, he told us, to bring in a new editor while the case was ongoing and things were so fluid. He knew the cast of characters in town, Charlotte, and us. He also clarified why Andy's position had been cut. With advertising revenues diminishing thanks to free online sites, it was an unfortunate but necessary decision to try to keep the independent in the paper, rather than sell out.

"Charlotte could have handled that better," he said. "Honestly, I should have been the one to tell Andy, but it was a busy week with the festival, and I trusted Charlotte to be professional."

He told us that once the dust settled and the murder was not the only main news we were covering, he would begin a search for Charlotte's replacement. He also said it seemed insensitive to

172

hire someone too soon. I briefly entertained the idea of applying for the job, but I wanted to be a reporter, out on the beat, not stuck behind a desk. Plus, I wasn't sure how long I would stay in town. There might come a time I headed back to the city and my original career path if I felt like Gladys was okay on her own.

Hap continued, "I know it might be a stretch to encourage people with experience to apply here, with our salary and the size of the paper, but there are still journalists out there who value the role of an independent community paper, the kind that isn't beholden to shareholders."

Though, I added to myself, *there was often a lot of lobbying by people like Grayson for the paper to be beholden to the town boards and committees.*

Jimmy's phone rang, which ended the conversation, and Hap continued up front to chat with Clara. I checked my email, nothing exciting, and put in a call to Winnie.

"So, there's something that's been on my mind," I began. "Assuming that redcoat jacket was authentic, like the same as the reenactors at the festival, where might someone get such a uniform?"

It made sense that some of the local colonial reenactors had uniforms, but as of now, none had been reported missing. And so far, at least, there were no reenactors on my list of possible suspects.

Winnie chuckled. "Funny you should ask, because I was wondering too and put in a few calls."

It seemed, she told me, that there was only one place in New England that made that type of attire, out in western Connecticut. The others were all down near Williamsburg, Virginia, a much larger market for that type of clothing.

"I wonder if they'll share information with us about who

173

purchased a suit like this," I asked.

"I tried," she said, "and got the runaround. Customer privacy and all."

"Would the museum have any extras, you think?"

"Maybe, but you know how their curator is." She groaned.

Winnie was not a fan of the new curator over at the yellow clapboard museum that commemorated the town's role in the Revolutionary War. With her humor and wit, Winnie broke the stereotype of a historian, but he took it to the extreme the other way. He was much more interested in research and being scholarly than dealing with the public. He'd even declined my offer to interview him when he first arrived in town, saying he saw no need for it.

But I could always try. I told Winnie my idea. "Well maybe I can find an angle, some sort of follow-up to the festival, pitch it as a positive, and do a little snooping when I'm there."

Winnie giggled like a schoolgirl. "Who knew history could be such fun?"

Not her counterpart at the other museum. Despite my attempt to get him to take part in an interview about the museum and the festival, he declined.

"The museum doesn't want to be associated with all of that messiness with the murder," he told me. Good grief. Didn't he realize that they already were?

By the time I got done that day, I was bushed. Worried about Andy and the lack of another viable suspect, I stopped to say hello to Gladys. She was cloistered in her study, almost done with the biography of John McCain that she was reading.

"Oh, Piper darling," she said. "That story in the paper today was so very interesting."

"Yes, I thought so too."

"But it was more than that," she said, pausing dramatically as she was known to do. "You know what perked my interest? The Rockport connection."

Was she referring to my family trips to the tiny coastal town with Chester and my parents?

"Go on," I prompted.

"Yes, Rockport," she said. "You know, I knew it reminded me of something and then it came to me. Back when Grayson went off to college and then did his work in municipal government, that's where he interned for a summer, right there in their town hall."

CHAPTER 25

As I sat at my desk the next day, the bombshell from Gladys about Grayson Adams, Exeter's select board chairman, interning in Rockport had my conspiracy theory juices flowing.

Sure, I knew it was a longshot that he had worked in the town hall at the same time that Charlotte worked at the paper. But this meant he had a connection to Rockport, to the town where Charlotte's career almost ended. The town where a *really* horrible series of events transpired after she wrote her exposé on the selectman in that town who wasn't actually embezzling from the town as she suspected.

Was it possible that Grayson knew Charlotte before she arrived in Exeter? And if so, why hadn't either of them mentioned it? Unless they had not actually known each other before. There was always that possibility. But I did not necessarily believe in coincidences like this.

I kept my thoughts to myself as I mulled over the possibilities. Jimmy and I were the only ones in the newsroom, as Sheila was still out sick. *We've only got five sick days a year, so she must really be under the weather,* I thought. *That or she's finally been beamed up by the aliens at that support group.*

My main assignment that day was not until late afternoon, so I took a break midday, went home, and tidied up my carriage house before I headed down to take photos at the community concert by the river.

The music under an open-aired pavilion next to the river was a summer tradition in Exeter. Local musicians played for a few hours every week, and the town came out to catch up with each other and visit with neighbors. Everyone from families to retirees brought their chairs, blankets, and picnic baskets to the grassy area along the park to relax and enjoy the fleeting summer season in New England. I wondered how many of them knew they were sitting on an area that once housed a dump before it was donated to the town to become a park. The town's jewel on the river was a real trash-to-treasures story.

Some frazzled parents showed up with a takeout pizza and fountain soda, while the more ambitious arrived with carefully curated picnic baskets and hidden stashes of prosecco, which they sipped in coffee cups to avoid detection. It was an open secret at the concerts, but to me at least, another reminder of the town's Puritanical roots. "They'd be branded with the scarlet letter of Exeter if caught imbibing the spirits of alcohol," I often joked to Jenny.

It was like a "who's who" of town officials most weeks. The five members of the select board made sure not to sit together, lest they be accused of holding an illegal meeting, while the town department heads congregated and kept an eye on them.

The concert capped off a busy day along the waterfront park and walkway, where the road was blocked by early afternoon for the weekly farmer's market. Some people simply picked up a homemade dish from one of the vendors along the way, an empanada or authentic Indian food, then continued to the concert.

I set up my blanket at the rear of the lawn area, a spot where

I could watch the affair unfold without getting too immersed in the middle section, where young children ran wild, occasionally knocking over the food or drinks of their neighbors as they goofed around with their friends.

Pansy Bolton spotted me, and her expression was not unlike a bird of prey coming down for a helpless field mouse as she stalked toward me. Her bottle-blonde helmet head was looking much better than the last time I had seen her, held in place with enough hair spray that it didn't move as she came my way. I had to wonder if she had upped her hair-spray game after her wet-dog look in the paper last week.

"Really Piper," she sniffed. "The Rotary and the paper have always worked so well together—well, until recently. Did you really have to use that photo?"

I composed my face in what I hoped was a neutral, professional expression. "Sorry Pansy, I imagine it was embarrassing, but it was the news from the event," I said. "And someday, I suspect it will make a great story for you to tell your grandkids."

I wanted to say, "And maybe, just maybe, it made you appear a little more human and a little less robotic to the townspeople." But instead, I smiled politely and said, "Well, good to see you! I've got to get some photos of the band."

She wrinkled her nose, and headed toward her next victim, the vice chairman of the select board. I avoided them as I walked toward the front to get a photo of the band, this time a Beach Boys tribute group who looked like they had been wheeled there from the elderly housing at the end of the park. The drummer had propped his music on a walker next to him.

I got a few photos of the band and kids dancing with hula hoops, which I knew would be a great spot for the front of the

Community News section, then headed back to the empty newsroom to process the photos. It didn't take long to upload the digital images and adjust the color. The room was empty. Nate was on vacation, and Jimmy was covering a planning board meeting that night, an excruciating rite of passage for new reporters that was like watching paint dry.

I was still mulling over Grayson's connection to Rockport and decided to swing by the Tuck Tavern on the way home. Given that it was like his second living room, I thought I might find him there.

Stanley was in his regular seat when I arrived, and he gave me a little salute. He was dapper as always with a light blue bow tie with prints of tiny martini glasses. It was going to be a tough day for the tavern when he could no longer drive. They'd lose one of their most loyal customers—aside from Grayson, who, as I had suspected, was holding court on the other side of the bar with a man named Brian he'd graduated high school with. They were two of the town's most dependable drinking buddies.

I hopped onto a stool, caught Kevin's eye, and ordered a spritzer.

Grayson acknowledged me, then returned to chatting with his friend. Probably reliving their high school careers. The only history Grayson loved more than his ancestor's role in founding the town was his time as the starting quarterback for the high school football team. It was not unusual for him to wear his old varsity letter jacket to the Friday night games in Exeter during the fall season. Most people secretly rolled their eyes, while publicly telling him what a great show of school pride it was.

I edged my way closer to them.

"So, did you see the paper this week? I asked them, not getting much of a response. "Boy, that Rockport story with

179

Charlotte was really something, wasn't it?"

Brian shrugged. "Yep, I guess you never really know about people, do you," he said. Then he stood and threw a twenty-dollar bill on the counter next to Grayson. "Well, I'm off. You know how the wife gets when I'm late."

Brian's wife was often privately compared to a saint for putting up with his roving eye and late nights out at the tavern. To cap off her sainthood, she was also a Sunday school teacher.

"See you tomorrow," Grayson said.

Kevin walked by, looked pointedly at my still-full drink, and set to work unloading glasses from the mini-dishwasher behind the bar. Grayson called him back over and ordered another gin and tonic. Clearly, he was not worried about when he got home to his wife.

"So, any news on the computer thing I told you about?" he asked.

"Nope, other than that it's significant, some story she was working on. Something explosive, we heard," I said. "Any idea what it might be?"

He shook his head, but not very convincingly. If I were a betting person, I would wager money that he knew exactly what she was working on.

"Say," I continued. "I heard that you used to work in Rockport for a time, back in the day. Ever run into her there?"

Grayson glanced at me with an expression that looked almost impressed, if that was possible. "Boy, you do your homework, don't you?" he said. "But then, you and that brother of yours are always looking for an angle, aren't you?"

Wow, I knew that my brother Chester was holding onto his feud with Grayson, but until that moment, I did not know how strongly it went both ways.

"Just curious," I said, hoping to diffuse his paranoia. "I mean, I just wondered what she was like back then. Like, was she always as difficult as she was here?"

I sipped my drink and waited, but he did not respond.

"And, you know, also wondering . . . " I paused. "If you knew her before, then why didn't you ever mention that? Seems like something you might share, especially when she died."

Grayson finished his drink and held up his bar snack bowl for a refill. Maybe I was hitting a nerve.

"Listen," he said, "Is it possible, just possible, that maybe I was trying to be a good guy? That maybe, just maybe, I knew what a mess the situation was with that select board member down there and didn't want to bring it up again—you know, after she'd gone to all the trouble to reinvent herself and move on."

Kevin narrowed his eyes, very clearly disagreeing with that comment, but said nothing as he brought more of the salty snack that made people drink more drinks. A good bartender, never interjecting himself into the drama, but keeping tabs on all of it. What was it going to take for me to crack him?

"So," I said, "is that what you did, then?"

Grayson nodded. "Sure, when she first came to town, we acknowledged we'd known each other back then, but she asked me not to say anything, and I didn't."

Interesting, I thought, but that did not sound completely truthful. I had to wonder if Grayson's silence had come at a price for Charlotte. A price that involved her integrity, which was already damaged at best. But that didn't add up, especially since she had penned that scorching piece saying it was time for Grayson to relinquish his role as chair after two terms. Her actions hadn't seemed like he had too much hold over her.

I studied Grayson's face. He was looking away from me and

seemed perturbed. He was hiding something, that much was certain. But, I sensed, he wasn't going to volunteer any additional information to me. Time to cut my losses and try again another day.

"Well," I said, flagging Kevin down to get my bill. "I've got to get home; it's been a long day."

Grayson gave a half-hearted farewell then became focused on selecting his next nibble from the bar snacks, digging around looking for the perfect piece. I preferred the honey mustard pretzel chunks. It appeared he went for the sesame snacks.

I stopped to give Stanley, still genially sipping his martini and watching the show, a little hug. Then I made my way home. Moments later, as I walked along the sidewalk toward the bandstand, something kept niggling in the back of my mind. Something I had heard that night on the gundalow with the fireworks. Yes, it was when Emily Athens, the owner of the Tuck Tavern, told me the only person she had seen more than Charlotte recently at the bar was Grayson. My next thought was so farfetched, I couldn't believe it had entered my mind. *Was it possible that Grayson was the person with whom Charlotte was having an affair?*

CHAPTER 26

As I lay in my bed up in my carriage house loft that night, I could not get the possibility of Charlotte and Grayson being involved out of my mind. I had nothing but a hunch that they might have been romantically linked, but now it was all I could think about, even though they were the last people I wanted to imagine doing the horizontal mambo.

That aside, it would have been highly unethical for her, as editor of the paper, to be involved with the chairman of the select board. And yuck, I could not believe that Charlotte might have seen him as attractive. But they had kept their previous acquaintance a secret, so what else might they have been hiding? My mind drifted as I wondered if there was a way to confirm my suspicions.

No sooner had I dozed off when I woke up with a start. Something was wrong. Someone was knocking on my door, and they were not being quiet about it. Oh God, had something happened to Gladys? Was it the paramedics trying to rouse me to go to the hospital? I pulled on a pair of sweatpants and managed to scramble down from the loft in the dark without killing myself, no small feat given the angle of the stairs.

I peered at my side door, expecting to see the red lights of the ambulance next door, but only saw Kevin Daniels's face looking in.

What the heck was he doing here? I opened the door and got an instant whiff of liquor.

"Kevin, what's wrong?" I asked.

"Listen," he said, tilting sideways and propping himself on the doorframe. "I've got some things to say."

Wow! I had heard stories lately of his inebriated states, most notably the incident with him at the tennis courts when he hit Pansy Bolton with the ball. But seeing it for myself was shocking. I enjoyed a good cocktail, but this was well past the level of enjoyment. Kevin was drinking to forget. *Or perhaps*, I suddenly thought, *he is trying to summon some liquid courage to tell me something.*

"Why don't you come in?" I said, taking a step back and helping him inside. He stumbled across my entryway, and I managed to get him settled on the couch. I went to brew him a cup of coffee, glad I had invested in the Keurig for single cups.

Once he was settled with the coffee, I took a seat across from him in the old paisley armchair that Gladys had given me. "Kevin, so what's going on? Are you okay?"

He did not look good, like someone who was on the brink of emotional disaster.

"You know, at first it was fun, exciting, a little secret that made life back in this town tolerable," he began. "Char was older than me, but she made me feel good, you know."

Oh God, was that why his car was at the paper on the night of the murder? Romance? "Wait, you mean, Charlotte?"

He nodded, then put his head in his hands, and for a moment I worried he was about to pass out. But he rallied, leaned back into the couch, and went on, "And he's full of crap, just full of it," he spat out. "When I heard him lie like that to you tonight, I just lost it! I can't keep quiet about it any longer."

This was hard to follow. "You mean Grayson?"

"Who else? I see the guy five nights a week, listen to everything he's doing that he shouldn't be doing, and you think he tips well? Nope, nada, nothing. And then, when he told you that he was looking out for Charlotte, that he felt bad—well, I realized, you know, I don't owe him anything."

It took a while, but slowly, in disjointed bits and pieces, the story came out. According to Kevin, he and Charlotte had had a casual fling going on, nothing serious, just a bit of fun. He knew she was not a nice person, but something about the situation with Grayson, especially how he treated her, rubbed him the wrong way.

"She seemed kinda vulnerable," he said. "I let her cry on my shoulder one night, and it just sort of went on from there."

Kevin insisted that Grayson was not the charitable good guy he had tried to come across as earlier that night. "He was holding Charlotte's history in Rockport over her. He said he would not tell anyone in town about her past if she occasionally did him a favor on the editorial page.

"'You help me, I help you,' he told her. Lately, though, it was more than once in a while. Grayson was getting greedy. He'd started showing up at the Tuck Tavern whenever she was there, having backroom conversations—"

"But wait," I interrupted. "She slaughtered him in that editorial about his chairmanship on the board."

Kevin shook his head. "They planned it. Charlotte insisted it would look suspicious if she never called him out for anything."

"So, they were working together?" I said, doubtfully. It was getting hard to keep up.

"No; they weren't friendly talks, not at all," Kevin said. "He was bordering on threatening, almost blackmail if you ask me."

Then Kevin went back to talking about his dalliance with Charlotte. He realized fairly early on that she was also using him for other things besides sex, like information he overheard at the tavern. Who was meeting up? What were they talking about? What did he know about certain business dealings that played out in the corners of the tavern?

"I knew what it was," he told me. "I'm not stupid, but no one likes to be used like that, you know what I mean?"

Usually, it was the woman who felt used in these types of scenarios, not the man. This was a classic example of the kind of person Charlotte was. But despite that, it sounded like they had agreed on their mutual dislike of Grayson.

"That guy, he's just out of control, really. His arrogance is just beyond compare," Kevin said. "I wish I'd never come back here, you know what I mean?"

Perhaps Kevin thought we were kindred spirits. Both of us had left the area after college and both of us were now back in Exeter. The difference was I didn't mind being back home, helping Gladys and having the freedom at the smaller paper to investigate the case on my own.

Kevin leaned back again, resting his head in the soft upholstery of the sofa, then closed his eyes. I waited for him to go on, but as I watched, his mouth opened and he began snoring. I covered him with an afghan and went back to the loft. I had a lot to take in.

Kevin was the mystery lover, the one who, in a typical investigation, the police look at first. However, he genuinely seemed upset about her murder, about how she was treated before her death, not a jilted lover bent on revenge. What if someone else knew about their relationship, someone like

Grayson? The select board chairman was certainly in the right place—the tavern—at the right time, every night, to see the two of them together. What could he do with that information? It might be embarrassing for Charlotte to be dating a man so much younger, but it wasn't like that hadn't happened in other affairs.

The last thought I had before I drifted off again was about Richie Collins. Did he know about this? And if I told him, would I be back in his information pipeline?

When I awoke the next time, it was light out, and someone was once again knocking on my door. This time it was Gladys. Oh boy, this was going to be interesting. I tiptoed past Kevin, still asleep on the couch, and cracked the door.

Gladys peered around me. "Well, now Piper dear, that's not what I would have expected from you," she said. "And he parked on top of my hydrangeas."

I closed the door and stepped outside. "It's not what you think, Gladys," I began. "He showed up here, in the middle of the night, inebriated, and confessed to having an affair with Charlotte."

"Oh my!" Gladys said, her penciled eyebrows arching in surprise. "Now, that's an interesting development."

I filled her in quickly and promised to fix her hydrangeas that afternoon.

"Oh, don't worry about that, dear; they already passed their bloom time anyway," she said. "But you know, Carson is still here for a few more days, and it would be so nice if you took him around town."

I knew she was trying to help Stanley, but dear God, Carson was a bore. I smiled but did not commit to anything. "We'll see," I said.

She turned to leave. "I can't wait to tell Stanley about this development!" she said. "How did he miss seeing those sparks flying between Charlotte and Kevin? He was probably there when this whole liaison began."

I loved how much faith Gladys put in Stanley's powers of observation. Too bad it was more optimistic than accurate. Though, I had to admit, Stanley was a wildcard, and every so often, like with Andy's truck being searched, he came through.

Kevin was stirring on the couch when I returned. He squinted at the light coming through the old carriage door windows, saw me, and groaned. "You're not going to tell anyone about this, are you?"

"Well, that depends," I said. "Can we make a deal?"

He did not respond, so I went on. "So, you tell me what you know that might be helpful to finding out who killed Charlotte . . . " I paused to cross my fingers behind my back, "and I don't tell anyone about you and Charlotte."

He sighed, resigned, it seemed, to the situation he found himself in. "Fine, but it's just between us, right?"

"Absolutely," I said, with my fingers still crossed.

I got us both coffees and sat down. "So, one thing I was wondering, with Grayson and his borderline blackmail of Charlotte," I said. "Do you think that had anything to do with her death?"

Kevin shook his head. "Well, at one point, yes, it could have been an issue," he said, "but Charlotte had something she was working on too, something that was going to put a stop to him."

I almost spit out my coffee. "Wait, like what?"

"I know we have a deal, but this is something I'm not quite ready to share. If it ever got back to me, I'd be done in this town, like really done for good."

With a tease like that, there was no way I was letting that drop.

I needed to find out what Kevin was holding back, but how?

CHAPTER 27

Sheila was finally back at the office the next day after being out sick for two days. I gave her wide berth, not wanting to catch whatever she had, especially since I could not afford to slow down on my snooping.

"What do you make of her?" Clara whispered, looking at Sheila as she wandered from desk to window at the rear of the newsroom. "Think she faked being sick to get some time off?"

"Really, Clara," I responded. "First of all, what would make you think that? It was a stomach bug, I think."

"Keep telling yourself that, but mark my words, those people she's been hanging around with!" She sniggered. "Something's up with them. Trust me; they're nuttier than a five-pound fruitcake."

I did not want to encourage Clara, but I tended to agree.

"Stop," I said to Clara with a pointed look. Then I walked back to my desk.

"Feeling better, Sheila?" I asked, again shooting Clara a quick keep-your-mouth-shut kind of look before returning my gaze to the slight young woman.

Sheila was clad, as usual, in a long billowy skirt and an almost translucent button-down shirt, the type of outfit I envisioned a gypsy might wear on a caravan trip. She looked tired.

"Oh yes, thanks for asking. Clyde got a little out of control and scratched my arm recently. I didn't think much of it, but it got infected," she said, pushing up her sleeve, where I could see a bandage. "And my doctor said I shouldn't type for a few days given how sore it was."

As if I needed further proof that keeping a bird as a pet was a bad idea. This story pretty much solidified my opinion on the matter.

"How's the homeless story coming along?" I asked. "I saw that woman again, that one I mentioned, but she was super skittish, just about bolted when I told her I worked at the newspaper."

I briefly wondered if Sheila would have been given the go-ahead to write this story when Charlotte was still here, given the stance she took in that editorial about the town's role in helping the homeless.

"Yeah," I went on. "I bet Charlotte wasn't on board with this angle, given her opinion on crime following the homeless to town."

Sheila shook her head. "Well," she said. "You know and I know what she was like, but between you and me, it really bothered me that she was so unkind to people who found themselves in that position."

She stopped for a minute, clearly becoming emotional, as she was known to do when talking about her subjects. "And really, Piper, you know anyone could find themselves down on their luck, anyone, and who is she to be judge, jury, and executioner?"

Wow, that was a strong position coming from Sheila, who usually too mousy to spit out a question. But in this instance, I could understand how she felt.

"Well, I've got to get back to my list," I said, gesturing to a pile of papers on my desk, submissions for the newspaper-sponsored coloring contest. I needed to sift through the pile and find the top five to publish in the community page next week before I could get back to my next murder story update.

Calgon, take me away, I thought as I looked at the stack of drawings. Or more likely, Jack Harper, take me away. I reread the email I'd received from him that morning.

Piper,

Just touching base on that case up in Exeter. My true crime editor contact is REALLY!!! hot to acquire some titles that he sees as everyday-America type of stories. Small-town crimes, like yours. So let me know as soon as there are developments. We need to move fast when the time comes.

Best,

Jack

Well, that was a bit of a stretch. I didn't think that being hung from a historic town hall in a redcoat jacket could happen to everyone. But Jack clearly seemed to think the Exeter connection was going to be a draw for readers.

I tried to look at the town with objective eyes as I walked home that afternoon. I knew it was quaint. Heck, I just had to look at the paintings inside the window displays along Water Street to see that. Countless scenes of the downtown area—complete with the brick facades of buildings that were several hundred years old, mixed with updates to old clapboard colonials with black shutters and old chimneys—were strategically arranged for sale. More often than not, these pictures included the historic town hall, the center of the town, which ironically was no longer used for town business except when it was opened once a year in March for Town Meeting, the annual ritual where the whole town gathered to hash out the annual budget and business.

I knew Jack had a point, but I was still protective of the town I'd grown up in and not sure I was ready to expose the community just to get a book contract. But the murder had yet to be solved, so I still had time to mull over my decision.

Which brought me back to Grayson, who was starting to seem like someone the police should talk to a little more. He had known Charlotte before, during their mutual time in Rockport, and, according to Kevin, he had been holding that over her for favorable coverage in the paper—until she found something that was going to put a stop to his control over her. But what that was, and if it involved the explosive information on her laptop, remained a mystery. Short of the police leaking me information, I wasn't sure how I could find out.

I finished up the coloring contest and headed back to my carriage house. I knew I needed to take a breather, give my brain a little break from my pondering, but it was hard. I decided to take a hand at resurrecting Gladys's purple hydrangeas, maybe salvage them after Kevin's car had flattened them.

Thankfully, I realized when I looked at the bushes, the blooms had already been cut by Gladys, so what was left was a somewhat mangled plant. My mother had hydrangeas at the family home where my brother Chester now lived, and I knew a thing or two about pruning them. I set to work like a surgeon, knowing it was a bit early in the year to prune but also that it might be the only way to bring them back next summer.

As I dug around the outside of the bed in a shady spot next to my carriage house, something caught my eye by the edge of the lawn. Something that had fallen out of Kevin's pocket or car last night? I wandered over. This was getting stranger by the day. This was the second Zagnut wrapper I had found near my place. My heart leapt as I thought of that mysterious woman and my feeling that she had been watching me. This seemed like more confirmation that she had been here more than once. I knew Richie was laying low, but this gave me one more reason to call him. I already needed to fill him in on what I'd learned about Kevin and Charlotte, and I'd forgotten to tell him about this woman the last time we talked. Who knows? Maybe he would rush over to play bodyguard!

Gladys's voice brought me back to reality, though my sense of unease wasn't going to fade.

"Now darling," Gladys called. "I told you that you didn't need to fix that bush. Really! I was going to have the man do it."

"The man" was a blanket term Gladys used to describe any number of people of any gender she hired to help her around the property, from the landscaper to the handyman to the man from *Antiques Roadshow* who found the Revolutionary War-era pistol in the carriage house, which helped fund my apartment. Gladys had a lot of uses for "the man."

"Oh, it was no trouble, really," I said. "I wanted to do it, get my mind off things for a bit."

"Well now, why don't you clean up and come over for a drink. Stanley and Carson are coming by, a farewell dinner, and it would be nice for some additional company."

I knew my face gave away how I felt about Carson.

"I know, Piper—I know he's a bit of a stodge—but he'll be gone tomorrow, so come over for some nibbles, won't you?"

After a few years of living alone and being single in the city, I had to admit that Gladys's dinner offers had grown on me. Just a few months ago, my diet had consisted of a box of crackers and cheese for dinner. Now it could be crab imperial or handmade pasta from the new Italian restaurant Gladys was enamored with.

I cleaned up from my gardening and headed over, whereas

per usual they were on the patio on the white wrought-iron chairs.

"Oh, Piper," she said, "Welcome. I was just telling Stanley and Carson about the biography of John McCain I just finished. They say he had a very bad potty mouth."

For someone as cosmopolitan as Gladys, the use of *potty mouth* seemed a bit beneath her, but I knew how she disliked crass language. She was civilized, after all. She handed me a glass of wine and offered me a platter of crackers with a mystery dip in the middle, which I peered at in confusion.

"Oh, it's one of my specialties: cream cheese with crab cocktail. It's delicious, trust me," she said. "It was all the rage on this street back in the seventies."

And here we went. She did love to talk about that period: the "golden age of Exeter," she called it.

"You would not believe the things I saw back then," she began, stopping only to sip her martini as she settled in for another tale of the Exeter she remembered.

Stanley looked delighted to take a stroll down memory lane, while Carson checked his phone, clearly not interested. Gladys picked up the framed photo she kept of herself in a black velour cape and fox stole and held it out for Carson to see.

"They didn't know what to make of me when I wore that around town," she said. "But my clothing seemed simply overdressed, really dear, compared to what I saw in town back in the day."

To hear her tell it, a wealthy man's wife wore a long white dress sans undergarments, while others caught up in the spirit of the decade attended key parties, where they went home with the person whose keys they plucked out of a fishbowl. Gladys made it clear that she would never have attended a key party herself but that she had certainly heard stories about those who did.

She missed Carson's stricken look of dismay and ploughed on. "Those Adams, they come across as so pious and Puritan! Well, I can tell you I heard some stories about them, oh my, oh my!" Then she finally glanced at Carson and said, "But enough of that." She stood up with a flourish and tried to pawn some more of the vintage crab appetizer off on him. Then she turned her full attention to me.

"How's that Kevin making out today, Piper dear?"

"Not sure," I said. "I haven't talked to him again."

"Well, the timing was just so interesting," Gladys went on. "You know, I saw him this morning, and then I had lunch with a friend today, and she was talking about him too."

She chewed another cracker with crab before she continued, lowering her voice. "Well, she thinks that Kevin's star power, from his time on the circuit, has run its course with the ladies at the town tennis courts," she said. "He's missed lessons and then Pansy's friend Margie saw his car over in New Castle, and when she asked him about what he was doing there, he denied it was him."

I thought it was probably nothing more than Kevin's desire to avoid the microscope of small-town life. Or was it?

CHAPTER 28

I arrived in the newsroom the next day to learn of another death in Exeter. Leonard Simpson, the current holder of Exeter's *Boston Post* Cane, had died in his sleep at 104.

The owner of the funeral home was on the phone to Clara first thing that morning to let her know we'd had another "very prominent" death in town. *By "very prominent," he also meant "very old,"* I thought.

Word of Leonard's death spread faster than last winter's news that Billy McKinley had pulled in a 20-pound eel in his smelt shack. I had no sooner sat down when I got a call from Olive, the head of the Council on Aging.

"Listen, Piper," she began. "So, we will need to find the new oldest resident. Can I count on you to get the word out?"

I imagined the headline I could write in an alternate universe, *"Oldest Resident Sought to Receive Town's* Post *Cane, Death Guaranteed."* But I pushed that aside and reminded myself that the tradition was a longstanding one in Exeter, one that people seemed to have no plans to give up anytime soon. It was an honor—a *real honor*—to get the cane, or so Olive had told me more than once.

"Well, sure," I responded. "But I should probably also have some sort of story in the paper about Leonard, his life and long reign as the town's oldest citizen."

"Oh yes, yes," she said. "You will want to talk to his daughter, Genevieve. She lives down at the elderly housing."

Of course, she did. When you were 104, even your children were elderly.

"Do you have a number for her?"

"Oh, yes, right here," she said, rattling off the digits. "I spoke to her this morning, expressed my condolences, and arranged to pick up the cane when she has time."

No grass was going to grow under that cane. I had to admire Olive's dedication to keeping the tradition alive and moving along at a prompt pace. I thanked her and began looking in the archives for the article done on Leonard when he became the town's oldest citizen. This had occurred before I returned to town. The original reporter was now at *The Portsmouth Clipper.*

According to the article, Leonard was born in Exeter, had 10 siblings, and attended the St. Michael's School growing up, before going off to serve in World War II. Upon return to Exeter, he got a job in the shoe factory, where he became a foreman. He attributed his longevity to his diet of fried eggs for breakfast each morning (in bacon grease), and one can of Old Milwaukee each evening, which, the article revealed, he got special permission to drink at the nursing home.

I decided to see if the Historical Society had anything in their archives about his time in the war or any mention of his work at the shoe factory. While the newspaper had recent files, for anything back more than 20 years, I needed to go to the town's archives at the Historical Society. Knowing Winnie, she already had the file on *Boston Post* Cane recipients out in her office. She liked to stay current with "the first draft of history in town," as she called the news.

I walked the back way to the Historical Society from the newspaper, up Spring Street and past the red brick building that housed the First Baptist Church, one of the town's oldest houses of worship. Newcomers often stopped to appreciate the stained-glass window on the church.

I found Winnie next door at the Historical Society, already updating her weathered manilla folder for the *Boston Post* Cane.

"Wow, word travels fast," I remarked.

She looked at me and winked. "Well, you know the women's walking club met this morning, and nothing gets by them."

Or by you, I thought, but I kept that opinion to myself.

"So, what do you have on old Leonard?" I asked.

She opened the folder and shuffled the papers inside, which included a hard copy of the article I had already read about when he received the cane. She also had clippings from old issues of *The Exeter Independent* from the 1940s, which described his time in the war, including receiving a Purple Heart after he was wounded while pulling another Exeter boy, Tommy Sinclair, a relative of the police chief, to safety after their unit was ambushed. Tommy lost a leg but lived, while Leonard was hit in the arm, which he kept, although he never regained full function.

"This is great information," I told her. I made notes of the details and looked at a few other photos from later years, with Leonard pictured at the now-defunct shoe factory. I had a few friends who lived in the loft apartments now housed in the old factory. They were small, but the high ceilings with industrial ductwork and wooden beams were a nice touch.

Winnie nodded. Then she said, "Oh, while you're here, I found something else you might want to see." She held up her infamous Murder File, which was a good deal thicker than the last time I'd seen it.

"Yes," I said, looking eagerly at her folder.

Winnie sat down at a solid wooden table, opened the folder, and began flipping through papers. "Yes, here it is," she said, holding up the copy of *The Exeter Independent* from the week before Charlotte's murder. It was the copy with the interview in which Grayson talked about the history of the town, which I had started reading at Gladys's but had not finished.

She said, "Remember how that company in Connecticut wouldn't tell me who bought redcoat uniforms?"

I nodded.

"Well," she said with a flourish, as she flipped to the back page of the paper. "It turns out, we didn't need them."

She held the paper up for me to see, like treasure found within the trash. And there, looking back at me, was a picture of Grayson Adams, decked out in the navy-blue-and-red coat of a Colonist soldier in the Continental army. Behind him, hanging from the door, was the redcoat suit of a British soldier. Bingo.

"What?" I sputtered, with a sudden rush of excitement.

Winnie raised her eyebrows in response. "I'll eat my hat if that's not the same jacket they found poor Charlotte in when she died," she said.

I'd not only eat my hat, but her hat too, I thought. Did the police know about this? I could not imagine they had not seen it in the paper, but had they put two and two together yet? I peered at the photo caption, unsure if Sheila, who had written the article, had also taken the picture. No, the photographer was Andy. One of his last assignments for the paper before he was let go.

Grayson was starting to come up an awful lot in my snooping, and while it could be coincidence, it was starting to feel like I was on to something. The way he kept his history with Charlotte secret really rubbed me the wrong way. If he had nothing to hide, why wouldn't he have shared that with us when we talked to him, got a quote about her, after her murder?

"Winnie," I said, barely able to contain myself, "thank you. I'm going to follow up on this. I've got an idea."

She gave a little wave and teetered back toward her historical hovel, with Buttercup right behind her. I practically skipped down the steps and headed back toward the newspaper office, praying Jimmy would be there when I arrived. I couldn't wait to tell someone else the news.

Both he and Sheila were at the desks when I came barreling in.

"You guys are not going to believe this," I blurted out, as I continued toward the stack of past issues at the rear of the office.

"Here," I said, holding up the same paper that Winnie had just shown me. "Look, here. What do you see?"

Jimmy's eyes opened as wide as flying saucers. "Wait, what?" he stammered. "But that means—"

"I know!" I cut him off.

I turned to Sheila, who didn't look enthusiastic. Probably working on one of her feel-good stories. I had to ask her the question at the tip of my tongue: "Didn't you think anything of that, especially after, you know, the way Charlotte died?"

She shrugged. "Well, no, honestly, I didn't. I imagined in a town like this that there was more than one person who had a suit like that."

She was not wrong, but there was not more than one person who had a suit like that and had a mysterious past connection to a murder victim.

I decided to break the rules and call Richie Collins. He picked up on the first ring.

"What's going on, Scoop?"

I couldn't hold back. "So, I'm just sharing some information," I said. "I don't want to get you in trouble."

"Y-e-sssss?" he said, drawing out the word in such a way that I knew he was curious.

"So, did you know that Grayson had a redcoat soldier uniform? It's in the photo of him in the paper the week before the festival."

Silence. Then he let out his breath so loudly I could hear it like he was sitting next to me. He lowered his voice.

"You're killing me, you know that?" he said. Then he grumbled, "You didn't hear this from me, but the suit in question was reported stolen the day before Charlotte was killed."

I gasped so loudly that Clara turned around to look at me. Just when I thought pieces were falling into place, the case got a lot more complicated. Winnie was not going to believe this.

CHAPTER 29

The next day, I brought Gladys and Stanley downtown to hear some music at the historic bandstand next to the town hall. Unfortunately, I hadn't paid attention to the description of the music ahead of time. Andy's roommate, the aspiring rapper A-Train, was the opening act, and Gladys was not impressed.

"Oh, Piper dear, I hate to admit it, but I'm showing my age. What exactly is this?" Gladys asked, as she tilted her head to listen. "It sounds like a car with bad brakes, or perhaps a wounded animal."

She paused for a moment and then went on, "And good heavens, what is he wearing?"

The wannabe rapper had a bandana tied around his head and wore loose, ripped jeans as he belted out lyrics. I don't think Gladys even owned a pair of jeans, let alone ripped pants. If she did have jeans, I was certain she would refer to them as dungarees.

"Yo, yo, yo, welcome to the partay," A-Train called out to the crowd, most of them, like Gladys, looking completely perplexed by his performance. "Come on Ex-Town, let's shake it up!"

A-Train was the opening act for a new weekly event downtown that coincided with the end-of-summer sidewalk sales promotion. The downtown merchants had banded together to pay for music to encourage people to get out, go downtown, make a night of it, and shop. Unfortunately, the opening act was falling flat.

"Nothing like the brass band, that's for sure," Stanley piped up from his seat next to Gladys.

The Exeter Brass Band was a throwback to an era of civility that Gladys and Stanley enjoyed. Unlike A-Train's more modern expression of attire, the brass band stuck to tradition with black pants and collared white shirts. They also performed the music Gladys and Stanley enjoyed: the old standards from the 1940s and 1950s. One man had been playing drums in the band for close to 70 years.

We had pitched folding lawn chairs in front of a brick building across from the bandstand to watch the show. I was there to take photos for the community page, once again, because we were *sans* a photographer.

And speaking of photographers, there in front of A-Train was Andy Hathaway, snapping away. He was probably doing it as a favor for his roommate, a way to boost A-Train's morale as he attempted to launch his music career from his nana's garage. I had not seen Andy since the day I trailed him to Hampton Beach and discovered his twin brother, Charlie.

I edged over closer to the bandstand and caught his eye.

"Hey," I said, then smiled apologetically as I held up my cheap digital camera. "We really miss having a real photographer."

For the first time since I'd known him, Andy didn't smile in return. *Oh boy*, I thought with a sinking heart. *I guess word of my prying reached him.*

"You know Piper, I get it, I understand you want to help," he said. "But you really invaded my privacy, you know."

I felt a wave of red shame spread up my cheeks. It felt like the time my fourth-grade teacher caught me reading her grading book. During recess, she had made me stand in the corner with my nose on the wall.

"I know," I said hastily. "I'm so sorry! I didn't mean to pry, but you were being so close-mouthed, and I was just so worried that the police weren't going to follow up like I did." When he didn't reply, I pressed on. "I meant well, really, you've got to know that."

"Well, there are some things I prefer to keep private," he finally said. "And anyway, Darby is taking care of things."

I was sure Darby was taking care of things, and I still could not figure out how Andy was paying him. But given the way the conversation was going, I did not think I would find out that day.

Still, I could not resist prodding a little. "I know about the wire they found in your truck. You've got to know that doesn't look good."

Andy's eyes widened in surprise, then irritation. "Well, then you should also know that I told the cops it was from the downtown webcam I helped the chamber of commerce install in the top of the town hall."

Huh, well, that made sense, but funny that Richie hadn't told me about it. Andy didn't look ready to tell me to leave yet, so I decided to forge ahead with more questions. I might not get another chance like this. Ever since I had learned that Andy and Charlie's father had struggled with alcoholism and had died when they were young, I couldn't help wondering if there was a connection to the case in Rockport.

"So, Andy," I started. "I know I'm already being way too nosy, and I get that you don't want to talk about it, but there's something that's been on my mind." I paused and looked at his face, which was still hard to read, then asked, "Does the name Hank Tarr mean anything to you?"

He looked like I had just asked him if he had ever seen a spaceship. "Who?"

Either he was an incredibly good actor, or he had never heard of Hank Tarr.

"Never mind," I told him. "It was nothing."

He turned back toward A-Train, still rapping his heart out, and started snapping photos again. Clearly, our time was up. I had hoped to ask him about photographing that redcoat uniform at Grayson's house, but I sensed by the view I had of his back that I would not get the chance today.

"Well, see you around," I said.

He looked back for a moment but did not say anything further. I wandered back over to Gladys and Stanley, who were still carrying on a lively discussion about the scene in the bandstand, and surveyed the crowd. It was a microcosm of new Exeter vs. old Exeter, with a handful of teenagers, some dressed like A-Train, watching the music, and the predictable smattering of town officials and business owners, who made a point to be seen at events like this to support the downtown businesses.

Then I stopped in my tracks. God, my brother Chester was among the representatives of old Exeter, and he had spotted me. He wandered over and stood next to me and Gladys, giving her a brief smile before he started in on me.

"Well, well, I guess that answers my question. You *are* alive," he said. "You've missed the weekly dinner for a few weeks now. Don't you think it would behoove you to show your face now and then?"

So, he had time for dinners with his local business friends, but not time to help our aunt? I held my tongue.

"Sorry, just really busy with everything that's going on, you know," I said, gesturing vaguely toward the town hall and hoping he would carry on and leave me alone.

"Well, I'm glad I saw you," he said. "There's a program at the Gilman Garrison House next month, and they asked me to see if you could get something in the paper."

Chester was on the board of directors for the 1709 house, which was now a museum. The red clapboard house was a classic example of a garrison, or fortified structure, built to protect its inhabitants from Native American attacks.

"They are going to have an expert in early New England architecture there to talk about the use of sawn logs and the pulley at the main entrance," he explained. "Should be a good program."

Oh yes, I knew all about the pulley that was used to open the reinforced door. I had gone on a field trip there when I was in Girl Scouts to earn my local history badge.

"Have them send me the information," I told him, knowing this was a legitimate piece of news for the community page and not his usual type of attempt to get free publicity for his friends.

"Well, very good then," he said, turning to go. "I'm off to The Terrace."

Of course he was going to The Terrace, the upscale option in town for dinner for those like Chester who were impressed with their status.

"He'll never change," Gladys said after he left. "Still as self-important as he was as a boy."

I spied Chief Sinclair up the way with Grayson Adams, so I gave Gladys a quick wave and headed that way. The chief saw me and immediately crossed the street to stand in front of the town hall. Guess he was still under orders by the state cops not to talk to the local press, at least in public.

Grayson, the consummate small-town politician, smiled at me in greeting.

"Hey, what do you think of this entertainment?" I asked, slightly tilting my head toward A-Train, who was now rapping a song about a boy from a small town who makes it to Music City.

"Well, it's not my thing, but you know the merchants are working really hard to change the image of the downtown area, make it more inviting toward the young people," he said. "But you know, I think the young people just go to the cities with oceanfront deck-dining, to be honest."

He wasn't wrong.

I knew that the police had already been in touch with Grayson about the stolen suit. I didn't want to get Richie in trouble for confirming that detail, but I couldn't resist asking about it.

"So," I began, "I got an anonymous tip that the redcoat general suit you were photographed with recently was stolen."

He looked around before responding. "Well, once again, you're doing your homework, but I'd rather not say anything right now. The police are doing their job, and they asked me to keep it quiet."

I was not deterred and decided to push him a bit.

"Oh, I know, but Grayson . . . " I lowered my voice so only he could hear me. "Can you imagine if it was your jacket that the killer put Charlotte's body in? I mean, my God, that's a little too close to home, right?"

"Well, it wasn't like I ever wore that one," he said. "I stuck with the Continental Army uniform, more in line with our history here in town."

"Still," I went on, "what do you think it meant? I mean, clearly, whoever killed her was sending a message, don't you think?"

He looked uncomfortable, like this conversation had been going on a little too long and a little too deep for his taste.

"Well, I think that's obvious, isn't it?" he said. "Someone viewed her as disloyal, a redcoat in a town of patriots."

Someone disloyal who planned to expose something in town, something on her laptop, which was now in police custody. Was it a story that someone might see as treasonous? I wondered. I flashed back to Kevin's comment about Charlotte's mysterious preparations to "take care" of Grayson's blackmail attempts. That certainly sounded like she had the goods on him, but what could it be?

It appeared my time was up. Grayson said, "Well, I'd love to stay and play Nancy Drew some more, but I've got plans." As he turned to go, he added, "Maybe you should leave this to the professionals."

I watched him walk up the street, toward the Major Blake Hotel, famous as the spot where Amos Tuck and his followers had founded the Republican party. It was now an impressive office building, with a high rent to match.

As Grayson disappeared from my view, something caught my eye. That potentially homeless woman was standing at the edge of the park before the hotel, backpack on. Not only was she watching me, but she was also eating a Zagnut bar. Two things came to mind. First, how many Zagnut bars could one person eat? But more important, enough was enough. I was going to find out what she wanted.

CHAPTER 30

I started walking at a good clip, determined to catch up to the Zagnut woman. For someone who looked a few decades older than me, she was remarkably zippy. I followed her up Front Street, past the large open lawn of the prep school, and then down a left-hand side street, which connected to the two-lane road that many used as a more scenic route to get to Massachusetts.

I was now more convinced than ever that there was something very suspicious about this woman. She seemed to flit in and out of the downtown area like a ghost, and she had only appeared after Charlotte's murder.

I eyed her backpack. It looked heavy, and I wondered what she carried in there. Likely, her most precious belongings. Then I thought about it more and wondered, *Or loot from breaking into cars?* The police still were leaning toward teenage vandals, but maybe it wasn't that simple.

Before I could get any closer, she stopped abruptly, turned around, and faced me.

"Stop following me," she said, looking me in the eye. "I don't want any trouble."

I backed up a few steps and held up my hands.

"I didn't mean to frighten you," I said. "I noticed you like the

Zagnut bars. Haven't seen them around since I was little."

She relaxed ever so slightly. "My old boss loved them," she said, her eyes taking on a wistful look. "I eat them now to remember him."

She must really want to remember him, I thought. *She's practically turned them into one of the main food groups.*

I looked at her more closely now. She had let herself go: her grey hair was long, pulled back in a braid that reached halfway down her back, and her hands were dirty. But her face, and her manner of speaking, reflected someone with an education, someone who hadn't always been down on their luck. She didn't look like someone I should be afraid of, but what had she been doing behind my carriage house?

"I'm Piper," I said. I hoped she wouldn't flee like the last time.

"Katherine," she said.

"Are you staying around here?" I asked.

She pointed up the street, "At the campground."

I knew exactly what she meant by the campground. When I was a kid, it had been the type of place that families had gone to for a legitimate summer vacation, but over the years, as it had changed owners, the campground had become a common spot for the local transient population to live. People who went to neighboring Hampton Beach in the winter, where they found dirt-cheap off-season rentals, returned to the campground for the summer when they could avoid tourist prices at the beach.

"So, what brought you to town?" I asked.

"I'd rather not say," she said, a bit too quickly. "Listen, I've got to get back."

"Wait," I said. "Did I see you recently behind my carriage house?"

But she was already marching off down the street toward the campground. *Katherine*, I wondered, *what is your story?*

I was still puzzling over the woman when I walked into work the next day.

"Sheila," I called across the newsroom. "Are you still following up on that story about the homeless population in town? I saw that woman again last night."

Sheila walked over to my desk, her long purple skirt making a whooshing sound as she moved. "I'm almost done," she said. "I found someone who was willing to be interviewed through the social worker I know."

There was something to be said for an interview subject who was willing to talk with you, as opposed to Katherine, who clearly did not want to be pinned down too long in conversation.

"Well, that's probably for the best," I responded. "This woman is cagey—doesn't want to talk much."

Sheila lingered by my desk, and I wondered what past-life story she was going to share with me that day. So far, she had mentioned being in the French Revolution and a strong sense that she had a connection to Joan of Arc.

"Listen, Piper," she said, an edge of excitement creeping into her voice. "I'm applying for a journalism fellowship, a yearlong immersion in a social justice writing program in California."

I hated to stereotype, but she would fit right in out there.

"And the thing is, I need some references to put down, people who can attest to my dedication to that kind of work," she said. "Can I use your name?"

"Sure," I said. "And good for you; that's great! But why now?"

Sheila looked around the newsroom, almost nostalgically.

"You know, it's just time," she said. "I feel like I've accomplished what I wanted to do here, and it's time for a change."

I turned to Jimmy, who had just arrived in the newsroom. He was digging around on his desk like a dog looking for a bone. I said, "And once summer vacation is over, Jimmy, you're going to leave me too."

Jimmy nodded, clearly distracted by his excavation through the paper pile.

"Darn it," he muttered. "I lost my notebook from that historic district commission meeting last night, and I am literally going to die if I have to watch the tape of the meeting again to get the information I need."

I knew the horrible feeling that went along with losing your reporter's notebook. "Do you want some help?"

"No, it's got to be here somewhere," he said, throwing notebooks left and right, then stopping abruptly. "Wait, you know what? I bet I left it at Amelia's place last night."

Amelia was his adorable—and very smart—new love interest. She worked as a bookseller at the independent bookstore downtown. Jimmy was up and out the door before I could respond.

"Piper, do you need a hug?" Clara said, in what I could only imagine was the same way she approached her many grandchildren.

"Oh, Clara," I said, accepting her soft bosom as she approached me. "Pretty soon it's going to be just you and me living out our days here."

"Well, better here than the nursing home," she said. "Though they do have three squares a day there, and I heard they have a lady who teaches chair Zumba once a week too."

Well, that was uplifting. Someday I could look forward to chair Zumba and regular meals.

Jimmy barreled back into the paper a short time later, brandishing his notebook like a prize. "Found it!" he exclaimed. "God, I can't imagine if I had to sit through that awful meeting again."

I knew from what I'd heard at the Morning Musket that day that the meeting was a long one. The historic commission was taking up renovations to an old building that was being converted to a restaurant. The new owner, citing weather damage, wanted to replace the old shingles with vinyl, to save on maintenance. The commission was having none of that and wanted him to restore the original wooden clapboards, at a price four times more than vinyl. From what Jenny had overheard that morning, the commission at the meeting went back and forth looking at samples of vinyl siding for three solid hours. Talk about a cure for insomnia.

"Any news on the investigation?" Jimmy asked. After the planning board, he clearly wanted something more exciting to think about.

I shook my head.

"A big fat zero," I told him. "I call the state cops every day, just to check in, get them used to hearing from me, but nothing. They said no further information will be released now because they don't want to compromise the investigation. So, the official statement I got was something like, 'We continue to follow all leads and investigate the case to the fullest extent of our abilities.'"

It was public information officer language times ten: saying something without saying anything.

My email dinged to indicate I had an incoming message. Jack Harper again.

Piper,

What's the status of the case up there? I am sending you some samples of other recent books like this for you to familiarize yourself with the style. Let me know the minute (!!!) you hear about an arrest. And keep notes of everything that happens. Local color!!!!

Tata, Jack

I had been keeping notes, and I wrote down anything I thought was a clue or something that should be remembered for posterity. But one area I was woefully slim in was anything nice about Charlotte, her life, and her friends. Did she even have any friends? I mean, there was Kevin, her "friend with benefits," but what about childhood friends? True crime stories often followed a predictable formula with a chapter devoted to the person's upbringing and childhood.

I pulled up her online obituary, knowing people often left comments of sympathy or memories on the online page, regardless of whether they attended a funeral or not. With no public services for Charlotte, this seemed like my only chance to find people grieving her death. I scrolled through the comments, mostly notes to her parents remembering what a bright and ambitious young woman she was in high school. "We always knew she was going places," another said. It was still strange to see her real name in the obituary.

And then, someone named Krystal Murphy sounded in. "I hadn't seen Char since college. We lost touch after graduation, and now that I see she changed her name it makes sense why I couldn't find her. I wish I'd had a chance to see her again, but now I'll never get the chance."

I wondered who Krystal Murphy was and what she was suggesting. It seemed like she knew Charlotte well—very well, judging by her comments. But why hadn't Charlotte stayed in touch with her? I wondered if Charlotte had ever talked about this with Kevin, a little pillow talk, when they were sharing secrets.

After I finished up that afternoon, I headed over to the Tuck Tavern to find out what he knew. We did have a deal after all: I had pledged to stay quiet about his relationship and the incident at my carriage house, and he had agreed to share information with me as he found it out.

Stanley was in his regular stool when I arrived, but Emily Athens, the owner of the Tavern, was behind the bar, not Kevin.

"Where's Kevin?" I inquired.

"Your guess is as good as mine," Emily said. "He didn't show up today, and he hasn't answered my phone calls."

She looked angry, and I did not blame her. But I was more curious about Kevin. He'd denied being in New Castle after Pansy's friend Margie spotted him there. And, I knew he had been drinking a lot lately, even when teaching his tennis lessons. Was he just home, hung over, maybe on a bender? Or was he more upset about Charlotte's death than he had let on?

CHAPTER 31

Kevin was not at the Tuck Tavern for the next three days, and no one had seen or heard from him. His boss, Emily, became more irritated by the minute as he did not respond to her messages. Honestly, I wondered if he would have a job to come back to if he did reappear.

When I tried his phone, it went straight to voicemail. He did not answer my text messages either. I knew he had not been super dependable lately, missing his tennis lessons and then showing up at my place in the middle of the night, but I had a bad feeling.

I kept thinking about Charlotte's mystery story—the one that was so explosive that it would shake up the status quo in the town. The story that was never published before she was killed. And now Kevin, the only other person besides the police who knew about the story, was also missing. I hated to think it, but what if he was in danger, actual danger, because he knew about this story?

"Jimmy," I said that afternoon in the newsroom, "I can't take it anymore. I've got to call the cops about this."

He didn't look optimistic. "I thought you said they won't talk anymore?"

He was right, but I was too riled up to care.

"That's true," I said, "but something tells me that with Kevin going MIA, it might be time."

I dialed the direct line to Chief Sinclair. I wasn't going to put Richie on the spot, and given Kevin's potential disappearance, it did feel like a legitimate police issue.

The chief sounded tired when he answered.

"Chief, it's Piper at the paper," I began. I decided to come out of the gate strong and put all my cards on the table up front. "Listen, I'm calling because Kevin Daniels hasn't been seen for a few days. I know he was dating Charlotte before she died, and he knew about a big story she was working on, and now he's just vanished. No one can find him."

I stopped to catch my breath, before adding, "And I just don't have a good feeling."

There was a moment of silence, and I worried I'd come on too fast. The chief cleared his throat.

"Well, he's not been reported as a missing person," he began. "So, from my side of things, it's not something we are following up yet. And quite honestly, there wouldn't be a lot I could tell you even if we were."

Ugh, it could be so frustrating to get information from the police, but I forged ahead. "But Chief, come on! Don't you think it's suspicious that he knew what Charlotte was working on, some big sensational story about this town? She's dead and now he's nowhere to be found!"

He didn't respond. I tried once more. "Any chance you might give me a clue about what she was working on?"

He lowered his voice. "If I tell you about that, it won't just be my job on the line, but my time in town," he said.

Wow, that was extreme. And it only made me want to know even more what the story was about.

"So, sorry to disappoint," he said, right before hanging up, "but you won't get anything out of me today."

So, I was right where I started. No news on Kevin. No news on what Charlotte was writing about. And no news on who the murderer was. Jimmy didn't look surprised in the least when I told him about the call.

He stood up and groaned. Then he explained his next assignment. "I've got to head over to the water treatment plant, learn all about their new filtration system."

Now that sounded about as exciting as organizing my sock drawer. By comparison, my own assignment that afternoon, to head to the local animal shelter and photograph their cat of the week, sounded a lot more interesting. As a community service, each week we ran a photo of a cat that was usually less adoptable or had been at the shelter for a while, with a little story about it. I still preferred dogs, but I did believe every pet should have a good home.

At the shelter, I was ushered into their cat pavilion, where the shelter worker pulled out a giant black and white cat the size of a Pug.

"This is Paddy, as in well padded," she told me. "He was brought in after his owner died."

God, did he eat his owner? I wondered, marveling at his size.

"The poor thing is a tough sell, diabetic and on special food, but just look at him," she said. "I mean, that face."

I looked at his face. All I saw was a cat looking for his next meal. I snapped a few photos while she crinkled a cat toy behind me to get a more alert expression from Paddy. Surely some crazy cat person would take him home. I knew I would have to hold back from writing a headline about how there was *more to love* with this cat.

I signed off, told them I would see them next week, and headed back toward the newspaper, making a pit stop at the Morning Musket for lunch. I hadn't seen Jenny in a few days and wanted to try the homemade pizza she'd started serving this week. Two big square slices remained in the display case when I arrived. They looked like a tomato-basil combination, which was not my favorite, but I knew her homemade dough would make anything taste good. Jenny spotted me and came out to the counter.

"Want to try some?"

I nodded eagerly. She plated them up for me while I filled her in on Kevin, sharing my growing sense of dread that something bad had happened.

"Well, that sure is puzzling now, isn't it?" she said.

"Not *that* puzzling," a voice behind me chimed in, and I turned to find Pansy Bolton standing in line. "He's been missing his lessons for weeks, and I'm sure you heard how he behaved when he did show up."

She sniffed as if she had seen dirt on the clean white counter. "If you ask me, he probably checked himself into rehab."

I can't say I hadn't considered that possibility, but if that was the case, wouldn't he have told his boss before he left?

"It's really just terribly inconvenient," she continued. "And completely selfish for him to do this to Kitty and me before our big doubles tournament next weekend."

Funny, I hadn't known that Kitty, Grayson's wife, played tennis, but then I didn't know much about her.

Pansy wasn't done airing her grievances about Kevin. "My friend Margie did see him in New Castle last week, and none of us could figure out what he might be doing there," she said. "We wondered if he might be moonlighting, teaching over there where he could make more money than here at the town's tennis courts."

As interesting as Pansy's scuttlebutt about Kevin was, my stomach was growling. I needed to eat, so I turned to find a place to sit down.

"Well, see you around," I said to Pansy, hoping that her willingness to chat with me meant she had gotten over the humiliation of that photo from the duck race. I had mentioned her prize-winning roses in that adopt-a-spot article. Perhaps that had made up a bit for the embarrassing episode in the river?

I found a seat by the window and dug into the pizza. Jenny had outdone herself once again. The dough was thick but fluffy, and each slice had a nicely caramelized crust on the bottom. As I chewed, I thought about what Pansy had said. She might be onto something there with her New Castle comment. The island community past Portsmouth was an old-money type of place with a fancy country club and the restored Wentworth by the Sea Hotel and Spa, which brought in the type of clientele who would pay to take lessons with a former tennis circuit pro like Kevin. Maybe he was just taking a few days off to recharge.

I decided to take a drive over there and nose around a bit after I uploaded the photo of Paddy the well-padded cat. It was, after all, summer, and the route to New Castle was one of those drives that reminded me why the Seacoast was an exceptional place to live.

I took the back way over to New Castle, cutting through North Hampton by their gazebo, which also played host to a series of summer concerts, then crossed over Route 1 and continued until I got to the coastal route, which wound along the state's scant eighteen miles of coastline on the Atlantic Ocean. Just before the city limit sign for Portsmouth, I took a right and drove toward

New Castle, a picturesque spot that was both the state's smallest town and the only town entirely located on an island.

The grand-looking Wentworth by the Sea Hotel was an example of the classic Second Empire style of architecture, with tall towers and a flat roof. It was certainly magnificent, but it was also a spot I would never be able to stay at overnight based on my meager salary at the newspaper. It was the type of posh place I wasn't likely to feel comfortable, but where Chester occasionally attended charity events in the off-season.

I did a drive-by of the hotel, looking at the parking lot, which was rife with BMWs, Volvo SUVs that were much pricier than Walter the Wagon, and Mercedes with out-of-state plates. And there at the end of the lot, parked between a red convertible and a black Lexus, was an antique silver-blue convertible with a vanity plate.

Kevin's car.

I thought, *You have got to be kidding me. So, he is in New Castle, but what is he doing inside?*

There was no time like the present to find out.

CHAPTER 32

Before I could choose my next move, my phone rang.

"Piper, you're not going to believe this," Jimmy blurted, the moment I answered his call. "*Tennis Today* just posted a picture of Kevin with Maria Elsinger. Apparently, they are holed up at the Wentworth."

And I was right outside.

Maria Elsinger—now that was interesting, and not the possible deadly fate I had imagined for Kevin when he went off the grid three days before. Though on some level, this fate was maybe worse than death, given their history. The Swiss-born tennis phenomenon had topped the field at Wimbledon a record number of times before becoming a sought-after women's coach; she had also become Kevin's very public romantic interest on the tennis circuit when she had started coaching both women and men.

Most notably, Maria Elsinger had shown up at the U.S. Open last year during Kevin's final match with his rival on her arm. Kevin's subsequent public tantrum, including breaking his racket, had ended his hopes of getting to Wimbledon after he lost the match in a landslide. Now Maria was ensconced in the hotel in front of me with Kevin. After his fling with Charlotte, it was clear that he didn't have good judgement when it came to women, but what would possess Kevin to reconcile with Maria? I was going to try to find out.

I smoothed my hair, added a touch of lipstick, and walked into the Wentworth like I belonged there. The lobby oozed elegance, with ornate white wooden columns and a brass chandelier hanging over an antique claw-footed table. The tabletop was polished to such a sheen I could see my face in it. I approached the registration desk, where a woman wearing a neat white button-down shirt looked up.

"Are you checking in?" she asked.

"No, actually I'm meeting a friend who's staying here, Kevin Daniels," I began, "but he forgot to give me his room number, and I don't have my phone with me to call him."

Her brows arched ever so slightly, and I realized she must have known about the media report. She immediately shook her head. "I'm sorry, but we can't give out guest information," she said. "You're welcome to wait in the lobby for him, but I can't help you."

I should not have expected anything different, but you never know unless you try. I looked around the lobby, which was a throwback to another generation. The design and the furnishings reflected the style of the other grand hotels of the state, some of which, like the Wentworth and the Mount Washington, had been restored while others, like the Balsams in the far-northern reaches of the state, sat waiting for investors with deep pockets willing to take a risk.

Given that the report was out on Kevin and Maria, I did not expect to see them just wandering around the lobby. But on the off chance I got lucky, I waited a few minutes before returning to the parking lot. Outside, I walked over to Kevin's old silver-blue convertible and slid my business card under his windshield wipers. Subtle, but effective.

Back in Exeter, I made a stop at the Tuck Tavern, where the report on the celebrity tennis news site was all anyone was talking about. The story was viral at the tavern or at least as viral as something could go in Exeter, where the last news to spread this fast was the time the Planning Board chairman was chased down the street on his Huffy bicycle by an irate peacock. A bird expert surmised the blue of the bicycle was seen as competition for the ladies by the male peacock.

The regulars were in their usual spots. Stanley sat on his corner, sporting a simple blue bowtie with red dots and a perfectly pressed white shirt. Grayson was across the way with his high school friend, Brian. Pansy Bolton and Myrna Smith sat sequestered at a side table, heads bent close together and deep in conversation. Pansy's head popped up when she saw me.

"Piper," she called, waving her arm toward their table in invitation. It was the last thing I wanted to do, but I edged toward them. She said, "So, tell us! What have you heard about this scandalous situation with Kevin, any updates?"

I shook my head. "Sorry, I'm relying on that celebrity tennis site the same as the rest of you."

She wrinkled her nose in irritation before responding.

"Well, it's just unprofessional, that's what it is. I mean really, does he expect that Kitty and I are just going to get by with that high school kid they've pushed us off onto for our lesson this week?"

Myrna sat upright, her shirt buttoned as far as possible, and listened, showing no sign of emotion or reaction. Typical New England Yankee who kept her opinions to herself, unless of course, she was scolding the rest of us for our behavior. Not one to imbibe alcohol, she had a cranberry juice cocktail in front of her. She would have been right at home as an early Puritan resident of Exeter.

I wanted to ask Pansy what she had done for lessons before Kevin returned to town and started teaching at the recreation department courts. It was not like they had a huge pool of tennis professionals to choose from in the area, though I knew the program they relied on was known for instilling solid basics in new players.

"I'm sure you two are better equipped than you think," I told her, as I began to edge away from their table.

Pansy sniffed again. "Well, I hope so, because it certainly doesn't seem like he's going to help us now, does it?"

I spotted my brother, Chester, and his business partner, Teddy, on the other side of the room, eating at a table in the restaurant section just off the bar area. Teddy waved me over.

"Want to join us? I'm dying to hear about this situation with Kevin Daniels."

Chester looked less enthralled by the prospect, but I slid into a seat at the table, caught the eye of their server, and put in a drink order.

"There's not much more to tell than what you probably already know," I responded. "Kevin hasn't been at work here for the past four days, he isn't answering anyone's calls, and he has apparently been at the Wentworth with Maria Elsinger."

"She's a hot ticket," Teddy said. "I followed her antics on the circuit last year. That leopard-print tennis skirt was really something."

"Well, it's kind of a relief," I said. "I was starting to wonder if something bad had happened to him."

Teddy and my brother both looked perplexed, and I decided the time for keeping my cards close to my vest was over.

"So, he was having an affair with Charlotte before she was killed," I began. "And, apparently, he knew about a big story she was working on that was really scandalous—the type, I heard, that would blow up the status quo in this town."

Teddy's eyes widened in interest, while Chester took the opportunity to get on his favorite soapbox.

"Hopefully, something about that bloviating Grayson Adams," Chester said. "He's just impossible to be around with his constant need to find new ways to get the family name up on more buildings in town."

Nothing like the pot calling the kettle black, I thought, as I mentally counted the number of buildings around town with the Greene name on them.

"I really don't know," I said. "The police won't reveal anything, and the only other person who knows is Kevin. He's not saying anything."

Our server returned, placing a large—and very rare—slab of prime rib in front of Chester, a healthier-looking salmon by Teddy, and a white wine by me.

"Can I get you anything else?" she asked them. Then she turned to me. "Will you be ordering dinner as well?

Well, if Chester or Teddy is buying, I thought.

"Yes, I'll have the haddock special," I said.

"So, what's this I hear that you are in talks to write a book?" Teddy said. Then, noting my confusion, he added, "I talked to Jack Harper the other day."

I always forgot the two of them graduated from the prep school together. "Well, nothing as long as this murder remains unsolved," I said. "Just something I'm considering."

While Teddy looked intrigued, my brother looked anything but impressed. Thankfully, my phone vibrated with an incoming call, which gave me an excuse to get up before Chester voiced his opinions. I glanced down at the incoming number as I stood up. It was Kevin. I answered and put the phone to my ear as I looked for a quiet spot to take the call. I slipped into one of the dim hallways off the dining room.

"Nice move," he began. I could only imagine he was talking about my business card on his windshield.

"Kevin," I whispered his name, not wanting to alert anyone nearby, "what the heck are you doing?"

"I don't know Piper; I really don't," he said. "I just can't take being back in Exeter anymore. I need to get back out there, and Maria and I, well, I think we've worked things out."

Three days in bed would give you that idea, I thought, but I was not holding out hope for the long-term viability of their romance.

"So, I'm going to go back to California with her, get back into the circuit, see if I can stage a comeback."

I can't say I was surprised. I had not expected him to last long in town, and while he had been a good bartender, a discreet person with his regulars, he had never really looked happy. But he and I had some unfinished business.

"So, does that mean you're going to finally tell me what Charlotte was working on before you leave? I mean, what do you have to lose at this point, right?"

"I don't know; let me think on it," he said. "Listen, I've got to go."

He hung up and I stood there for a minute in the dark-paneled hallway of the Tuck Tavern where he and Charlotte first got together, hoping the secret they shared was not going to stay with him when he left town.

CHAPTER 33

Kevin was on my mind as I walked to *The Exeter Independent* the next morning. I knew it was a long shot that he would tell me what Charlotte was working on, but I hoped that if I wished hard enough, maybe he would cave before he left town. Short of the police leaking details, he was my best chance to find out what was really happening with Charlotte before she died.

I stopped a minute on the Great Bridge, the official entryway to the town's downtown business district, and looked down the Squamscott River. Further out, a sleek rowing scull cut through the water, headed away from the downtown area and out with the tide toward Newfields. Come fall, the river would be busier when the rowing teams from the prep school made their daily practice runs up and down, followed by their coach shouting out instructions from a megaphone in her tiny Boston Whaler motorboat. It made a nice visual from the shore, but I had never had the motivation to get up at the predawn hour the crew team rigidly adhered to for their competitions.

At the Morning Musket, I stopped only long enough to get a coffee and a cherry and dark chocolate scone to go. Before I continued on my way to the newspaper offices, I waved to Jenny and signaled that I'd call her soon. I was too distracted thinking about Kevin to stay and make small talk.

"Some guy has been looking for you," Clara told me as I walked in the front door. "He's called twice, all official sounding, Jack someone."

Jack Harper. That was unusual. He had my cell phone. Why would he call the paper directly? It did not make any sense. I glanced at my phone to make sure it was working and realized I'd left it on *do not disturb* when I went to bed the night before. I could see three missed calls and a text message beckoning to me, but I didn't have time to investigate further because Hap was trying to get my attention.

"Got a minute?" he called from his office at the back.

I dropped my scone on my desk and brought my coffee with me to his office.

"Sure, what's going on?" I asked. He walked around his desk, shut the door, and returned to his seat.

"Well, I got a call from an old reporter friend who is on the board at the New Generation Media Institute. The place where Sheila applied for that fellowship."

Boy, that was fast, I thought. She had just sent in her application. "So, this is between you and me, okay," he said, looking up at me.

I nodded.

"Well, nothing is definite, he was just calling to talk to me because I was one of her references, but it sounds like the board is eager to pull some people from smaller, independent papers this time around, so she's got a good shot."

I paused to take a long sip of my coffee. "Okay," I said, not quite sure why he was telling me this now.

He seemed to pick up on my puzzled expression. "So, I may need you to take on some extra duties if she gets it," he said. "Like the special sections she was in charge of, mostly the

Seacoast Seniors, which comes out quarterly."

God, so this is what it had come to: single, wannabe mystery author and early recipient of my own membership to the AARP.

"Sure, no problem," I said. It wasn't glamorous, but it would mean a few more hours added to my part-time schedule, which was fine by me. Gladys was doing a lot better, and she certainly didn't need as much help as she had required when I first returned.

"Thanks for being such a team player," he said. "It's good to have someone who knows what they're doing that I can depend on."

Well, that made me feel a little better, but not much. Back at my desk, I stuffed the scone in my mouth, wishing I'd gotten a second one, and remembered Clara's alert about Jack calling several times.

I tapped into my voicemail and took a long sip of coffee.

Piper, Jack Harper here. Listen, I tried your cell, and you didn't answer. I have some unfortunate news. That editor, he's young, he's impulsive, and apparently, he just made an offer for a book deal on a case out of Utah, something really splashy with the Mormons. Now, I'm not saying yours isn't possible, but this definitely doesn't help, because from what I heard, he spent his yearly budget on the advance for this one. So, give me a call. If that case isn't moving ahead, maybe there's another historical one that might work. Got to dash.

Nothing like being kicked while you were down. I hadn't heard from Kevin that afternoon, and given the way my luck was going, it seemed like he was going to leave town without revealing anything else.

I was more upset about Jack's phone call than I expected. While I liked being back in Exeter, the prospect of editing a senior citizen section had me feeling down. I spent the afternoon slogging through calendar listings for the next issue, which included such scintillating events as the end-of-summer church tag sale, a lecture at the library on river ecology, and a free seminar for seniors on estate planning. God, at the rate I was going, before long I'd be writing my own obituary like Winnie. Piper Greene, the longest-serving employee of *The Exeter Independent*, died at her desk and was later found buried beneath old issues of the paper.

Well, if nothing else, I have a nice place to live rent free and an aunt who loves having me there, I thought, as I stepped into my carriage house home that evening. I did not even have time to sit down before Gladys came rapping on my door.

"Oh, Piper, do come over for dinner, would you?" she began. "I ordered from that new Italian place downtown, and the portion is enough for a week of meals."

After the day I had just completed, the appeal of a nice dinner with Gladys from what she simply called "the new Italian place" but was, in reality, a trendy Italian bistro sounded wonderful.

"Give me a few minutes and I'll be on my way," I said. "It's been one of those days."

She paused and looked at me for a minute. "Oh, Piper darling, it sounds like I should chill the good wine for you."

A short time later, I was ensconced in Gladys's large kitchen in her built-in eating nook. A heavenly aroma of garlic and spices filled the space as she flitted around arranging some antipasto on a plate. Now, if it were me, I would have just brought the takeaway container to the table, but Gladys always served her food artfully arranged on a platter.

"Now, Piper," she said, pouring me a large glass of a rather expensive French wine. "Do tell me what happened today to put you in such a state. Honestly, I could tell the moment I saw you that you weren't quite yourself."

I took a long sip and decided it was time to confide in her about my possible book deal. "Well, it seems," I said, looking over at her mournfully, "that my chance of getting a book contract is doomed."

She raised her eyebrows in surprise but didn't say anything. I filled her in on Kevin leaving town, Sheila being in the running for the fellowship, my new job doing Seacoast Seniors, and lastly, the worst news, Jack Harper's phone call.

"So basically, my book deal is dead in the water," I said, pausing to pick up a piece of melon wrapped in prosciutto.

Gladys stood up with a flourish and arranged her scarf over her neck before opening the oven to check the main meal. For someone of her age, she really did move both quickly and gracefully. I had to remind myself that I had returned home to look after her, not the other way around.

"Now, my dear, it's not the end of the world. You know, your writing is really spectacular, really, better than anyone they've had at that place." She stopped as she put on some oven mitts and pulled a large aluminum tray from the oven. Then she turned and said, "I got the chicken marsala. I know, it's summer and hot weather outside, but I heard the marsala is imported from Italy and the mushrooms were hand-foraged locally."

She spooned some of the chicken into low soup bowls over a base of linguine. Then she placed one before me before sitting down again.

"Now eat up, my dear. There's nothing a good meal, some wine, and a little perspective can't fix!"

Gladys was always the optimist, but I was having a hard time embracing her outlook. Still, I would eat well living in Gladys's carriage house the rest of my days.

I tried a bite of the chicken. "Oh, this is amazing," I said, before going back for a second taste. "I mean, this isn't the type of Italian fare we usually find in this town."

She winked at me. "I know, but you know how that restaurant's landlord is about good food. He hand-picked this chef and brought him in."

"Well, it was worth it. Wow!" I responded.

"So, about your day?" she prompted again.

"I don't know, Gladys," I said. "I mean, unless I can find another good case to write about—something historical, Jack Harper suggested—it's a lost cause."

Gladys peered over at me and smiled mischievously. "Well, Piper dear, if you really need some dirt for a book, I've been here a long time, and you wouldn't believe the things that happened back in the day. Those key parties were just one example." She stopped to take another bite. "I mean, really, there are all sorts of secrets in this little Puritan village that would make a good novel."

I was skeptical, but I'd started to relax in the familiar kitchen with the good food and wine; I was feeling a bit less hopeless even. Maybe she knew what she was talking about. I took the bait and said, "Like what?"

Gladys shrugged, took a long sip of her martini, and winked at me. "Well, now, Piper dear, there are many juicy stories. Winnie Smart knows about a ton of secrets—a little interest of hers, I hear."

She continued, "If I were you, I'd make a little visit down there tomorrow and ask her what other scandals she has in her files. You never know what you might find out."

I wasn't overly confident, but I agreed to think about it.

"Promise me you'll do it, and I'll give you some of this tiramisu," she said.

Who could refuse tiramisu? I savored a generous portion with another glass of the fancy wine. Winnie had helped me tremendously with the murder files so far. But could she come through one more time?

CHAPTER 34

My evening with Gladys left me feeling a little less discouraged. After all, Exeter was a historical town. Lots of significant events had transpired in the quaint colonial enclave over the years, and if anyone knew if any of those events were criminal, it would be Winnie. Given that she kept an actual murder file in her possession, I could not rule out that she had something in that file that would make for a compelling historical crime piece. If nothing else, maybe there would be enough material for a magazine-length feature article, something to give my mood—and my writing career—a boost.

Though the Revolutionary reenactors had left town since the festival, the vintage Fourth of July flags put up for the event still hung outside the Historical Society building. The society wasn't officially open, but I found the front door unlocked when I tried the handle.

I did not find Winnie when I walked into the old building, just her cat, Buttercup, who was sprawled on top of the heavy wooden table in the front room like she owned the place. She lifted her head and stared, almost haughtily, like she was questioning my presence in her kingdom.

"Winnie," I called, then waited and called again, "Winnie, are you here?"

The door to the dungeon of the building was open, and I began the trek down into the dark depths of history, prepared this time for the broken Lady Justice at the bottom of the stairs.

"Winnie," I called again.

"Back here," she answered, and I followed her voice through a heavy metal door into a room of file cabinets and newspapers, where I found both her and Grayson Adams bent over a stack of papers on the table. Grayson's normally tidy hair was poking in several directions, and he had not shaved. I'd never seen him this disheveled. Something told me not to say anything, so I turned toward Winnie.

"Listen, I just wanted to take a look at that murder file of yours for some other research I'm doing," I said.

She stood up and followed me back upstairs to the front room. I managed to wait until we were alone before blurting out the thought I had held back downstairs. Maybe there was hope for me yet.

"Okay," I said. "I have to ask. Is it just me or does Grayson look really bad?"

"You are a keen observer of human nature, my dear," she responded.

"What's he doing down there?" I asked.

"I wish I knew," she said, and sighed. "He's been pulling all sorts of records on the Beddington family and Reverend Samuel Beddington, and quite frankly, it's making it impossible for me to get anything else done in here."

Hmm, I thought. Samuel Beddington was the minister who was credited with bringing the church in town back on track after Grayson's relative left. Perhaps it was just curiosity or another attempt by Grayson to cement his legacy in town.

"So, sorry I can't keep you company," she said, as she handed another manilla folder, this one titled *Murder File #1*, to me.

I sat down and started flipping through the old newspaper clippings in the folder. I already knew about the disappearance of a girl about my age on her way to school. The fear we all felt after she vanished had stayed with me for years. We were not allowed to walk alone, and the school began calling home if one of us was absent, something they had never done before. But that case was not one to publicize any further, I knew. The police officers who investigated still had a hard time talking about the situation, which remained unsolved, and it was something the entire community collectively grieved. The community was also incredibly protective of her family.

Next up, an even older newspaper, *The Exeter Gazette*, from 1924.

Police Officer and Friend Slayed

EXETER__Police Officer Albert Colson and his friend Arthur Bennett were shot to death on Franklin Street while Colson was making his rounds on July 3.

The two encountered a man on his porch who was holding a shotgun. The man had been annoyed the prior Fourth of July by boys in the neighborhood that he felt were "acting up." He had made it known that he was going to protect himself.

Colson tried to talk to him, did not get anywhere, and attempted to get the shotgun away from the man, who shot him in the stomach. Colson died instantly. His friend, Bennett, then tried to get the gun and was also shot, later dying at the hospital.

The suspect was sent to the hospital for the criminally insane until further notice.

I looked at Colson's picture and realized where I had seen it: in the lobby of the police department, with a plaque honoring his service and noting that he died in the line of duty. It was an interesting case, but not one that could carry a whole book.

Another series of clippings, with a man who looked a lot like Ted Bundy with an attractive hairstyle, related a 1981 murder. The handsome criminal had shot and killed the night clerk at a local variety store with a stolen gun. The site of the shooting was the first store many of us had gone to alone growing up, when our parents let us bike to pick up a soda or ice cream on our own. It was also the place where I had tried to buy my first bottle of Boone's Farm wine with a fake ID when I was in high school. My plan was quickly thwarted by the clerk, who raised his eyebrows at me, told me he knew my aunt, and reminded me that I most certainly wasn't of age. I hadn't heard about this case before.

I peered at the photo of the store, which aside from the vintage of the cars, looked exactly as it did today. That was the thing about small towns: the more things changed, the more they stayed the same. I flipped through the file some more. The next article revealed that the shooting suspect was later shot and killed during a traffic stop in another town. This also seemed like a dead end for a true crime bestseller.

Winnie joined me, and I couldn't resist quizzing her about the case.

"Hey, did you know about this crazy scene at the variety store?" I asked her.

Her eyebrows arched. "Well, *I knew that*," she said.

Of course, she knew. She knew everything that happened in this town.

Grayson lumbered up the stairs behind her, saw me, and stopped. I could not resist. "What are you working on?" I asked.

He kept his head down and shuffled from foot to foot. "Just a little research on town history, nothing big," he said. Then he exited the room.

Winnie and I looked at each other with raised eyebrows but we did not say anything.

"Well, thanks for this," I finally said, handing the Murder File #1 back to her.

"Oh, any time," she said. She bent down to give Buttercup a scratch under her chin. In an instant, the cat went from looking like a threat that wanted to kill me to a gentle kitten.

"And I hope you get a break from you know who," I said.

"You and me both."

I gathered my things and headed out, stopping on the front steps. I was not any further ahead than when I started. No interesting case to replace the one I was working on, which had not yet been solved. My phone pinged and I glanced down to see an incoming text message.

It was from Kevin. "I'm leaving town tomorrow, so if you want to talk, meet me tonight at the cannons at Gilman Park at nine."

Things were looking up.

CHAPTER 35

I paced around my carriage house for the next few hours. I couldn't wait to find out the real story Charlotte had been working on, and I really hoped Kevin's text message meant he was ready to spill all the details.

When I could no longer stand looking at the same four walls in limbo, I fired up Walter, glad for the steady presence of the old Volvo, and headed toward the rendezvous spot. I was early, but so be it. From a quiet residential neighborhood street, I made a turn onto a bumpy dirt road and arrived at Gilman Park. I ignored the sign about the park being closed from dusk until dawn. I'd feign ignorance if anyone caught me.

I was the only one there. The park was small but well used by locals, especially dog walkers and kayakers, who put in at the public boat launch. Nestled along the banks of the river sat the infamous cannons, the spot where Kevin had told me to meet him. When I was a teenager, people used the cannons as a meeting spot to hook up or drink up. Tonight, I was the only one there, and I had no plans to do either.

I locked my car and headed toward the cannons. The only light came from a lamppost on the field, and the secluded spot by the cannons had an ominous feeling. The graffiti and empty beer cans did not help my nerves.

The natural light was fading fast, and I wondered if I should have brought a flashlight. I was completely alone. The trail on the other side of the field, which wound through the trees on the side of the river, was rumored to be home to the Exeter hermit. Local teenagers claimed he was like the hermit discovered in Maine a few years back, who lived alone in the woods for years without seeing another person. I had always chalked it up to urban legend—in fact, the only activity I had heard about in the woods this summer was a group of teenagers who got busted smoking dope in a makeshift tent—but now I wasn't so sure.

I jumped at a rustling in the bushes on the side of the park. Thankfully, it was just a wild bunny hopping out for a snack. God, I was getting a bit anxious in my old age.

Where was Kevin?

I checked my phone to make sure I had not missed a message. But the last one said he would be there at nine, and it was only a few minutes past, so not time to throw in the towel yet. But, boy, it was a little eerie out there alone, especially knowing that someone in our town had carried out a murder. Had I lost all common sense agreeing to an isolated meeting at a time like this?

Just then, a set of headlines poked through the twilight, and I watched the now-familiar silver-blue convertible park next to my car. Kevin did not waste any time, turning it off and walking over to me. He looked around, clearly edgy, and leaned against one of the cannons.

"I'm going to make this quick," he began. "I can't believe I'm even telling you all of this, but I'm out of here tomorrow, so what does it matter."

"If it helps, I didn't hear it from you. Off-the-record background," I told him.

"It doesn't really matter anymore," he said. "Once this gets out, it's going to be obvious it came from me, but like I said, I'm out of here, so whatever."

I waited, trying not to pounce and ask him questions, but I was crawling out of my skin with the anticipation that comes from getting a juicy piece of gossip. To me, there was nothing so exquisite as that feeling.

I decided to give him a nudge. "Okay, so, can you tell me what she was working on then?" I tried to sound as nonchalant as possible but knew that I was failing.

"So, Grayson, you know he comes into the Tuck Tavern almost every night, right? That's not a secret. Often has a few too many cocktails with his buddy, Brian, but he can usually walk himself home when he leaves."

He paused, as if he had one last-ditch moment of doubt, and then forged ahead. "So, this one night last spring, he was like I'd never seen him. His buddy, Brian, left, but Grayson just kept ordering more drinks. The guy was in rough shape, like something was really bothering him."

Kevin went on to tell me that Grayson had stayed until closing time, again an unusual event. He was in such a sorry state that Kevin called one of Exeter's few cabs to bring him home.

"I basically had to help him walk out and physically slide him into the back seat," he said. "And then, when the cab drove away, I saw a slip of paper on the ground. It looked like he might have dropped it."

Kevin had picked it up and, out of curiosity, unfolded it and looked. "And this is the part I don't want coming back to me, understand," he said, giving me a long stare.

I nodded. My heart was thumping. "Absolutely."

"So, I opened it up, and it was the paperwork from one of

those DNA-testing kits, the ones where you find your long-lost relatives. Only the names on his results weren't Adams relatives. They were Beddington names."

I heard what he was saying but I almost couldn't process it. I drew in a shaky breath. "So, are you saying what I think you're saying?"

Kevin nodded. "Exactly. He's not actually an Adams."

Jesus, Mary, and Joseph. I leaned against one of the cannons to steady myself. That was scandalous, and as I'd heard from the police, something that would change the course of the town on a massive level.

"But, so, who is he then?" I asked. "There are countless Beddingtons around here these days. It could be anyone."

Kevin put his hands up. "That's where my input ends. I gave Charlotte the paperwork, and she was working on that. I know she had some leads, but she didn't tell me anything more."

Kevin admitted that, almost immediately, he had regretted sharing the information with Charlotte. He had known she was using him, and he had been terrified that she was going to reveal that he was the one who had leaked the information. But by that point, it was too late. She had been off and running with it, determined to use the ancestry results to get Grayson off her back.

"I think he knew what we were up to on some level," Kevin said. "The next day he came into the Tavern frantically looking for the paper, but I lied and told him I hadn't found anything. I think Charlotte got a little too bold with her general questioning in town. Word got back to him, and he must have figured out that she had the information."

That was huge. And I hated to even think it, but it was so gigantic, someone might have killed her to keep the story quiet.

Especially someone whose entire identity revolved around his birthright in the town. Someone eager to plan the first annual Adams Day celebration with himself at the helm.

"Well, I'm out of here," Kevin said. He took his keys out of his pocket and started to back away from me "I hope this wasn't a mistake."

"Thank you. I promise I'll protect you as my source," I said. "Good luck with Maria and the tennis thing."

"Yeah, we'll see," he said. "If nothing else, it gets me out of here. I never thought I'd be back in this town after I left for college. I'm going to try my best not to make that mistake again."

I walked with him to the parking lot, gave him a little wave, and got into Walter. I leaned against the familiar, sturdy driver seat and took a long breath. I did not know whether to rush back to the newsroom and call Hap, or just head home to decide my next move. In the end, I opted for home. It was late.

I sorted my mail, got a snack, and headed over to the main house to talk with Gladys. It was a bit late, but the back light was still on, our signal that calling hours were still acceptable. Like the Motel 6, she left the light on for me. I gave a little rap, and she greeted me in a floral silk kimono.

"Oh, sweetheart, I was hoping you'd stop by," she said, as she ushered me into her library. "Did you have a better day?

I nodded enthusiastically and she continued, "So, does that mean you have a new story, something from Winnie's files?"

"Not exactly," I said, amazed at my ability to hold back this juicy information so long already.

She had a martini in hand and asked if I wanted one.

"Yes," I said. "I'm going to need one to tell you this story."

I filled her in on what Kevin had told me about Grayson, the DNA results, his paranoia that Charlotte was asking questions about the Adams and the Beddingtons, and the uncomfortable feeling I had about what Grayson would do to keep this information quiet. I sipped the martini and tried to keep my expression neutral as I realized it was one of her high-test vodka nights.

Then I asked her, "So, what do you think? Is it possible that this is true—that Grayson isn't an Adams?"

Gladys tipped her martini glass up, polished it off, and refilled it from her pitcher.

"Oh dear, I'm going to need another one, maybe two, if I'm going to talk about this," she said, taking a long pull of her vodka.

I waited. She sipped.

"Well, isn't this exciting," she began. "Almost as exciting as those key parties I told you happened in town back in the day."

The key parties. Oh God. Those were the parties where people put their keys in a bowl, pulled out a set of keys, and went home with the person who owned the keys, usually not their spouse. I didn't like where this was going.

"Well, I won't name names, other than to say that a lot of children born in that era might not be who they think they are."

"And who might they be?" I asked.

"Well, honestly, Piper dear, the way I heard those parties went, it could be anyone," she paused. "Not that I ever attended one, but I heard things, and I'm pretty sure that both of Grayson's parents, along with Horace Beddington, attended more than one of them."

Horace Beddington? The man who owned an old dump and sold used cars out front? Boy, that would be a fall from grace.

My phone buzzed. It was Jimmy.

"Excuse me, Gladys, I've got to take this," I said, standing up.

"Go ahead, Piper dear, I'll just pour myself one more little snifter."

I hit *accept call.* "Jimmy, what's going on?" I asked.

He was out of breath and sounded like he had just run a marathon.

"Piper, I was just coming back from covering the police commission meeting." He gulped loudly before he went on. "And when I came around the back and walked past the sally port, I saw them unloading Andy and leading him inside."

"Like he was in custody?"

"Well, it didn't look like a friendly visit, if that's what you mean."

This did not make any sense. If Grayson was the one who had the most to gain by silencing Charlotte, and the police knew the truth about his ancestry, then why would they bring Andy in through the secure entrance used to process criminals?

CHAPTER 36

In hindsight, my new plan to walk down to the police department and linger around outside in the dark might not have been the best idea. But after what I'd just heard about Andy, I couldn't stay away.

I knew Andy was innocent, and based on what I had just learned, there was a decent chance that Grayson was guilty of more than being a self-important elected official. For as long as I'd known him, Grayson had been so fundamentally attached to his connection to the town's founding father, I truly believed that the prospect of being exposed could have made him do almost anything. But murder? I still had a hard time imagining he'd go so far as to kill another person, even if she was blackmailing him.

I walked through the downtown area, past Franklin Street, now home to upmarket condominiums, and wondered if the people who bought those pricey homes knew they were situated in what had been the town's red-light district. It was the site of a brothel during Revolutionary times, or so Winnie had told me.

As I neared the police station, my heart beat a little faster. I did a pass in front of the building, peering into the lobby area from the sidewalk out front. When I didn't see anyone waiting, I decided to mosey over toward the edge of their parking lot. The sign at the entrance said *private*, but I kept walking. It was a bit of a thrill to slink around.

Police cruisers lined both sides of the lot. Despite Jimmy's tip about Andy being escorted inside through the sally port, there wasn't a lot of activity. However, Chief Sinclair's unmarked Crown Victoria was in his marked parking space, which could be a sign something was going down. The chief usually brought the cruiser home at night, in the event he had to respond to a call off hours. The only time it was here in the evening was when he was away on vacation.

The other side of the parking lot was filled with tall four-wheel-drive trucks; the type many of the firefighters, who worked out of the other side of the complex, owned. The police mobile command van sat parked in the rear of the corner, probably still recovering from its inaugural mission after Charlotte's murder.

I tiptoed farther into the parking lot, keeping an eye on the rear door of the police station as I looked at the other cars. Well, well, well, what did we have here? A black Audi station wagon with a license plate "DEFENDM," which I knew belonged to Andy's attorney, Darby.

"Hey, what are you doing out here?" a stern voice yelled at me, and I was almost instantly blinded by the flashlight in my eyes.

I blinked a few times to reset my eyes from the glaring light. Thankfully, a friend, not a foe, came into focus. "Richie, is that you?"

"Darn you, Scoop, what do you think you're up to?"

"Can you turn that off?" I asked. "I'm seeing stars."

He snorted. "I get that all the time from the ladies."

"Oh please," I said, glad it was dark so he couldn't see me blushing.

"So, again, what are you doing out here? Seems a bit late for a stroll."

I was tired of sneaking around and speaking in code. That and there was nothing more satisfying than telling someone else a juicy bit of gossip, just to see the reaction.

"Listen," I began. "I heard Andy was down here, that he was in custody, and I just heard about this thing with Grayson not really being an Adams, and I just—"

"You just thought you needed to do our job for us?"

Coming from a different police officer, that would have been intimidating, but I detected the hint of a smirk in the darkness.

"No—I mean, yes—I mean—come on Richie, what's going on in there?"

He looked over his shoulder at the rear door, where his partner had poked his head out of the sally port. His partner yelled, "You okay out there, Rich?"

"Yep, under control," he responded.

We walked to the other side of the parking lot, next to the crime scene van, where the overhead light didn't shine. He was inches away from me, and I had to stop myself from leaning even closer. I could smell his aftershave. Clean with a hint of spice. That martini Gladys had made for me was making me feel brazen.

"Listen, slow down, take a breath," he said.

In all honestly, I did need to take a breath. Between the excitement of my little cloak-and-dagger routine and being in a dark place with Richie, I felt like I'd just run around the block.

Richie looked at the rear of the police station again, then at the tall bays housing the fire trucks, which were closed for the night. I followed his gaze and realized we were the only ones around.

"Okay," he began. "Because we're friends, I'm going to give

you a little tip. But you didn't hear this from me, right?"

Boy, two off-the-record clandestine meetings in the dark with sources on one night. Watch out Woodward and Bernstein.

"Right," I said.

"Relax: Your pal Andy isn't a suspect," he said. "He's the lynchpin in the case. He had some very helpful information that we needed to make an arrest."

I waited, afraid to breathe or move in case it stopped him from continuing.

"So, he overheard a fight the night of the reception, the night Charlotte was killed," he went on. "We didn't necessarily believe his statement before because it seemed too convenient to shift focus from him to someone else."

So, they'd really believed Andy concocted a story to look less guilty? As much as I liked Richie, that made me angry. I asked him, "So what changed?"

He looked a little sheepish as he went on. "Well, another independent witness came forward, someone who had been out of town but heard the same argument Andy did that night."

I wondered who that witness was, but I was more interested in why Andy was at the police station that night, especially why he was using the sally port entrance intended for those under arrest.

"But why bring him in through the back, in the sally port?" I asked. "That seems really suspect to me."

Richie raised his eyebrows in response. "Do you really need to ask that one? Sometimes, people don't want to be seen, and sometimes, just sometimes, the cops want to maintain the integrity of their investigation without *someone*," he looked at me and raised his eyebrows, "getting in the way."

I knew I was stepping on their toes with my sleuthing around and asking questions, but really, I was just too impatient, and too naturally curious, to wait for them to tell me the good stuff.

"So, what was the fight he heard?"

Richie shook his head. "Sorry, you won't get that out of me tonight," he said. "But I will tell you, you should probably get yourself to district court first thing in the morning and get a good seat."

"Are you saying what I think you're saying?"

He winked, which I took to mean that yes, Grayson was going to be in court in relation to Charlotte's murder. This was huge. I owed him big time. I figured it was okay to share a little of what I'd figured out.

"Listen," I told him, "I have news of my own. But you didn't hear this from me, right?"

He looked confused and I forged ahead, eager to watch his reaction. "So, I have it on good authority that the parental origins for our boy Grayson can be tied back to one of those infamous key parties of the early seventies in our little Puritan village."

"You're kidding," he said, laughing.

"Nope! I have a highly placed source who confirmed this for me earlier tonight."

"Who?" he said.

This time I winked at him. "I never kiss and tell. See you in court in the morning."

He turned and headed back toward the rear entrance to the station, and I tried to contain my nerves. The case was coming together. I had a scoop, and by the next morning I'd be the one in the courtroom as the charges were made public. What a day. Two clandestine meetings, a martini, no dinner, and now a tip that the selectmen chairman was going to be arrested for murder. Who said this was a quiet, little Puritan village?

CHAPTER 37

In the end, it looked like the resolution in Charlotte's murder would happen in the same building where she died, the historic Exeter Town Hall. While her death came to light at the top of the town hall, when her lifeless corpse was stuffed in the redcoat jacket, her killer was brought out in the basement of the same building, home of the district court.

I had managed a few hours of sleep the night before, but it was not what I'd call restful. I was up before dawn, pacing around the carriage house, going over what I knew before the court hearing. I also alerted Hap about what was going down that morning, and he offered to send Jimmy as back up.

"Can you believe this?" Jimmy asked, as he sidled up next to me on the sidewalk in front of the court.

I shook my head. "Honestly, no, but it sounds like they've got the goods on him."

He looked around. We were the only people outside the court, so if we were lucky, no one had tipped off the TV news people yet. *Thank you, Richie*, I thought. With the case wrapping up, I wondered if he'd finally agree to that rain-checked dinner so I could repay the favor.

The door to the building was still locked, and I decided to take advantage of the time to use the ladies' room. My nerves were getting to me. Given the early hour, I was surprised to hear a toilet flush when I went in, but even more surprised to see the transient woman, Katherine. She jumped when she saw me.

"Good morning," I said, smiling at her.

"If you say so," she said.

I could tell she was not in the mood to chat further, and honestly, the reason I had gone in there was pressing on my bladder. "Well, have a good day," I said, hustling into a bathroom stall.

By the time I returned to the gallery of the courtroom, someone was unlocking the door, and I slipped in right behind her, eager to get a good seat. Jimmy, my shadow, followed me. Carol, the very efficient court clerk, met us at the window. She peered over the glasses on the end of her nose at us.

"So, we get both of you today, huh?" she said.

Jimmy nodded, clearly used to dealing with her more than I was. One of his regular jobs was to make a weekly trip to the court to search new filings for cases that might be interesting stories.

The clerk continued, "Well, listen, the judge is going to allow cameras today, but let's not make this into a circus, you hear?"

As if he had heard his name, District Court Judge Wally Smyth wandered into the clerk's territory, saw us, and remarked, "Well, well, if it isn't the fourth estate."

"Good morning, your honor," Jimmy responded.

The judge turned his gaze my way. "Miss Greene."

"Your honor."

I'd known the judge since I was a child, but here at the courthouse, the aura of procedure and civility remained, and there was no off-the-record type of chit-chat. Especially on a day like this. The court bailiff, a tall, well-muscled man with a healthy tan, unlocked the door to the court, letting us inside.

Jimmy and I found prime real estate at the front of the court on the antique wooden benches, which were guaranteed to make your rear end go numb, and staked our claim. And then we waited. A lot of life in the court was hurry up and wait. I knew this from going to court with my father as a child, but there were times—like this—that the waiting was excruciating.

Eventually, the side door to the courtroom opened, and a sheriff deputy, clad in a brown uniform, led Grayson in. Grayson turned toward the galley of the court, where only Jimmy and I sat so far, and shook his head, clearly dismayed that we were there to watch his fall from grace. He looked even worse than the last time I had seen him at the Historical Society. The orange jail jumpsuit did nothing to help his complexion.

The door to the court behind us burst open, and a slick defense lawyer I recognized because of his trademark snakeskin cowboy boots burst into the room like an actor in a play. His boots clickety-clacked all the way over to the defense table. The attorney was best known as the DWI doctor, the attorney with a giant billboard on the side of the highway that said, "The King of Defense," but I guess Grayson didn't know any better. Still, it was better than no representation.

Behind him, the prosecutor for the police department walked in with an unfamiliar attorney I assumed must be from the attorney general's office.

"All rise," the bronzed bailiff called out. "The Honorable Wally Smyth presiding."

Judge Smyth, now in his black robe and spectacles, climbed into his perch at the front of the court room and sat down. He looked around, probably surprised like me by the lack of a crowd in the gallery. He picked up a stack of paper.

"I have in front of me an arrest warrant charging Mr. Grayson Adams with one count of second-degree murder. How would the state like to proceed?"

The male attorney stood up. "Your honor, because this is a felony-level murder, the attorney general's office will be assuming jurisdiction. The state has attached an affidavit detailing the charges against Mr. Adams in the death of Carlotta Cabanovich, known locally as Charlotte Campbell. The state intends to prove that Mr. Adams deliberately caused the death of Ms. Campbell through strangulation, and based on eyewitness testimony, we can place him at the scene of her death, in this very town hall, moments before she died."

Mr. Snakeskin Cowboy Boots leapt up. "Your honor, this is all circumstantial and my client vehemently denies these charges!" he said, stopping to slick back a chunk of his hair. "We would ask for bail to be set. He is not a flight risk, he is an upstanding member of this community, and he looks forward to being fully vindicated in this case."

The two sides argued back and forth about bail, with the judge ruling that because it was a murder case, no bail would be granted, despite Grayson's former standing in the community. They didn't reveal any new details, anything more than I'd already heard from Richie the night before, but I got a copy of the affidavit on the way out, and back in the newsroom we pored over the details.

The paperwork spelled out how police knew that Grayson had blackmailed Charlotte to get positive press until she learned about his ancestry and started using that in a counter-blackmail scheme. She'd promised to hold off on a story about his background as long as he left her alone. But on the night of the reception at the town hall, Andy heard a fight in the stairwell outside the art gallery where the revolutionary revelers were partying. He went out to investigate and saw Grayson and Charlotte ("two people who were known to him," according to the dry police language). The document explained, "The witness heard Mr. Adams tell Ms. Campbell that she didn't know who she was messing with and that she was going to regret this decision, that she would never threaten anyone like this again if he had his way, and that she was going to her grave for this."

The charges went on to explain that another witness, whose name was blacked out, saw Grayson and Charlotte going up to the third floor of the building, and later saw Grayson leaving out the side door of the building, looking flustered. "He almost backed into the fire hydrant," the witness told police.

Forensics had confirmed that the suit Charlotte's body was found in did in fact belong to Grayson and that the lace from one of the colonial-era boots in his collection matched fabric fibers on her neck, thus confirming that she was strangled with his boot lace. The wire in Andy's truck had been just as he claimed, to put up the webcam for the chamber of commerce.

"Wow, that sounds pretty cut and dry," Jimmy remarked.

"I know," I said, but I felt so uneasy, I shifted in my chair. "Yet on some level, it's just hard to believe he could do something like that."

Sheila, who had arrived midway through this conversation, shrugged. "I guess it shows you never really know people, do you."

Jimmy got to work on a local color sidebar to my main story while I wrote about the court hearing. Then I picked up the phone to seek out reactions from town officials.

"I'd rather not get involved," Pansy Bolton sniffed when I reached her. "Let the court process happen first."

"Grayson's done a lot for the town," the town manager offered. "It's a real shame."

"He was always a little odd, now wasn't he," his neighbor said. I couldn't help but think of those crime shows where the people are always described by neighbors this way. "Something just didn't seem right."

I leaned back in my chair and took it all in. Jimmy was still frantically typing away. Hap was in his office, phone to his ear, where it had been all morning, and Clara was up front looking at pictures of her grandchildren on social media. The only person in the office who was not doing anything was Sheila, who sat quietly at her desk, looking off into space.

"Everything okay, Sheila?" I asked as I walked by.

She looked up. "Well, I feel kind of weird telling you this now when you're in the middle of a big story, but I just found out I got the fellowship."

After my meeting with Hap, I'd kind of expected this, but I feigned surprise as I congratulated her. "Well, that's great," I said. "When do you leave?"

"Two weeks."

"Wow, that's quite a turnaround," I said. "What will happen to your parrot? Can you take him with you?"

She looked legitimately distressed. "No, Clyde won't handle that kind of a move, and I will be in a dorm at the school, so it's not really the type of place for him. I guess my sister will look after him."

"I didn't know you had a sister," I answered.

"Yeah. We don't see each other that often anymore, but we always depend on each other at times like this."

"Well, good luck with that," I said. "We'll have to plan a little going away shindig for you."

"Oh, that's not necessary," she said, getting up to leave. "Really, don't go to any trouble for me."

Sheila had no sooner walked out the door when Clara, who had clearly been listening to the whole conversation, chimed in, "What do you think? Will she beam herself out there on a spaceship, you know with her little friends from that group?"

I gave Clara the look—the one that told her to be quiet—and she sighed in understanding before she returned to her grandchildren's photos.

As soon as I finished my story, I sent a quick email to Jack Harper. I knew it was a long shot, but the outcome in this case, with a town official, fake ancestry, and the fall from grace, was a compelling hook. Maybe I'd get lucky and the hot-to-trot editor would still consider it.

CHAPTER 38

I stopped at the Morning Musket on my way to the paper the next morning, more to hear reactions to the news about Grayson than for a scone. (Not that I would ever say no to a raspberry white chocolate scone!)

"What are you hearing, Jenny?" I asked, as I slipped in through the side door to the kitchen.

"Nothing definite, but it's been great for business," she replied. She pointed to the sizable crowd out front. "We sold out of cinnamon buns within the first hour."

"Can you believe it?" I continued, still grappling with the reality of Grayson, someone who had lived in this town his whole life, being a murderer.

"Honestly," she said, as she transferred some rolls onto the cooling racks, "I really can't. He sure has a lot of hot air, but he doesn't strike me as the type of guy who has the ability to actually do something like that."

"Well, I guess it shows that people will do anything when they're desperate," I said.

She shrugged and turned toward the ovens again, slipping on a worn potholder mitt as she slid a batch of cookies to the counter.

I helped myself to a coffee out front and found a seat next to

Winnie, who was alternating taking bites of muffin with digesting the hard copy of *The Exeter Independent,* which was spread out in front of her. It always made me happy to see someone reading an actual paper. She looked up when she saw me.

"Well, I guess this is it for the murder file," she said, then winked. "Can't say I'm not relieved that he won't be around to have me looking up those old files in the way-back room every day."

"Yes, there is *that,*" I said. "But, really, what did he think he was going to find out back there?"

"Oh, you know, maybe some old link between the other family and the Adams, something so he could still claim ancestry."

That was probably it. As Winnie and I chewed in silence, I listened in on the other members of the breakfast crowd, only hearing more of the same. People generally did not like Grayson, but they were mostly universally flabbergasted by the news of his arrest. I finished up my breakfast and headed for the newsroom, eager to find out how we were going to follow up on the story now that the news was out.

"Morning, Clara," I said, catching her again on social media looking at her grandchildren's latest antics.

"Would you look at her," she said. "Already sitting up on her own!"

I murmured something I hoped sounded positive in agreement, before asking, "Where is everyone else?"

"Oh, big goings on already today, Piper. Jimmy's off at an emergency meeting of the remaining select board, who are trying to figure out whether they need to have a special election to replace Grayson," she said. "And Sheila? Your guess is as good as mine. Haven't seen her yet today."

Until Hap arrived, I was in a holding pattern for the day. I suspected he'd assign me to help out with follow-up coverage, but I wanted to touch base with him first. I puttered around at my desk for a few minutes, checking work emails and then refreshing my personal email with hopes I'd have a response from Jack Harper. Still no word on the book proposal or whether he thought I should proceed.

"Well, would you get a load of that!" Clara called out. "It looks like we may be in for a treat."

I wandered to the front, where she was peering out the front window at the street.

A mustard-yellow vintage Dodge pickup truck with a slide-in camper in the back was sputtering and spitting out black exhaust fumes in our parking lot. Although it had New Hampshire plates, at first glance it was the kind of vehicle that could be from anywhere or going anywhere. The same could be said for the guy who got out. A man of undeterminable age, with a blonde ponytail and a cowboy hat, dropped the hat over the steering wheel of the truck and then turned and ambled toward our front door.

"Probably one of those alien people," Clara muttered. "Or one of Sheila's little friends, if you know what I mean."

I wasn't so sure. The guy looked more like Indiana Jones back from a treasure hunt. He opened the front door and sauntered over to Clara's desk.

"My name's Todd Tisden," he said, as he walked up her. "I heard someone was looking for me."

Todd Tisden, why did that ring a bell? It hit me after a second: the former reporter from *The Portsmouth Clipper*, the one who was supposedly on a banana plantation somewhere down south but who knew about Charlotte's background in Rockport. He certainly looked like someone who had been down south, with his well-tanned skin and tousled hair. Well, better late than never.

I stepped forward.

"That was me. Piper Greene," I said, opening the door into the newsroom. I motioned to my desk area, where I had a spare chair for guests like this, and he sat down, leaned back, and looked around.

"I've heard about this place," he began. "Independently owned, isn't that right?"

"Yes," I said. "The Henderson family runs it."

"Hmmph," he said. "Unusual these days, isn't it?"

I wasn't in the mood for a conversation about the state of the newspaper industry. Way back when I'd first heard of Todd, it was because he knew about Charlotte's past in Rockport, but since then, thanks to Winnie, I'd already learned about her time there, including her irresponsible reporting on Hank Tarr and his eventual death.

"Yeah, but this is Exeter. We do value our history and our independence here; it's kind of what makes the town special," I told him. Then, because I couldn't help myself, I asked, "So, what's the story with the truck?"

"Oh, the Jolly Dodger?"

You've got to be kidding me, I thought. He'd named this contraption after a pirate ship, although I guess that driving a wagon named Walter, I couldn't really cast judgment.

"Yes," I said. "It's a bit unusual, isn't it?"

He stretched back in the chair and crossed his legs in front. He had on Birkenstocks. With socks.

"Yeah, well, I needed a break. You know, the city around Portsmouth, it was getting pretty busy, lots of people." He stopped briefly and readjusted his ponytail. "So, I packed up and drove around the country for a while. Montana, South Dakota, California."

Here he shrugged. "And now I'm back."

I noticed he did not mention the elusive banana plantation.

"So, Piper, was it?" he said. "You wanted to know about Charlotte Cabanovich, or Campbell as she's been going by, according to the message you left for me a while back. Man, I can't believe she was murdered, that's what you said, right?"

"Yes," I responded. "Though it may be moot at this point, with the arrest and all." Then I thought, *though his input might help me with a good follow-up article in the paper.*

I filled him in on the murder, Charlotte, and the information that Winnie and I had pieced together about her time in Rockport, followed by her transition to a pen name when she arrived at the New Hampshire Seacoast area.

"I understand you worked with her in Portsmouth," I said. "And, based on my own dealings with her here, I can only imagine what that was like."

He grimaced. "She was awful, but I'm sure you know that, always undercutting me with my sources. I got a tip from one of my sources that she'd spent some time in Rockport. One weekend when I was down visiting a buddy there, I asked around, just out of curiosity. You know what it's like, being a reporter and all."

He said that despite his personal dislike for her, he had not been expecting to get such an earful about Charlotte and the destruction she had left in her path.

"And you probably heard about what happened to the poor selectman there," Todd said, and I nodded. "Well, the village was really upset about his wife and kids."

I prompted him to continue. "Yes? What happened to them? Did anyone know where they ended up?"

"Down the line to Gloucester I think, with some relatives who were fishermen," he said. "The selectmen's assistant, Katherine— I can't remember her last name but she was a really nice lady— kept an eye on them for a while. She even went down to see them from time to time."

Katherine. I got a little twinge, that feeling in my gut when a puzzle piece was falling into place.

"Katherine," I repeated to him. "Todd, what did she look like?"

"Your basic middle-age kind of secretary lady. Glasses, long hair that she wore in a single braid, kind of plain."

And eating Zagnut bars incessantly, I thought to myself.

"Todd," I blurted out, "I think she's here. In Exeter."

"What?" he squinted at me. "But why would she be here?"

"Well, honestly, I thought she was homeless at first," I told him. "She was walking around town with a backpack, kind of looking lost."

I told him about my last meeting with her, including her explanation that she was staying at the campground on the way out of town.

"Oh yeah," Todd responded. "I saw that place and marked it as a possible option to park my Jolly Dodger for a few days."

That feeling in my gut was getting stronger. Why would Katherine be here in Exeter, the town where Charlotte, whom many felt was to blame for the demise of Katherine's boss and close friend, Hank Tarr, was working at the paper? It was almost too perfect.

"Todd," I began. "I've got a funny feeling about this."

He raised his eyebrows in response. "What, like this isn't a coincidence?"

"Exactly."

CHAPTER 39

Although I'd never met Todd before, he seemed like the type of person who would make a good wingman.

"I've got to find her," I told him, jumping to my feet. "I just have a feeling about this."

He looked up at me slowly and blinked like he was trying to orientate himself. I imagined if we heard a fire alarm, he might sit there for a minute to make sure it was not a false alarm before finally evacuating, even if there was smoke in the building. I was going to have to light another kind of fire under him to get him moving.

"I mean, don't you think there's something to her being here, in this town? Like, she might be involved in the murder?"

He appeared to consider my words.

"Well, that's assuming it's really her," he said. He scratched his head and added, "Seems like a bit of a stretch if you ask me."

I had another idea. It was also a bit of a long shot but might be worth a try. There was one other person in town, besides Todd, who knew what Katherine looked like from his time working in the Rockport Town Hall as an intern. A person who could make the positive ID. The only problem was he was sitting over in the county jail charged with Charlotte's murder. But what if he was not guilty? The case did seem clear cut, in that he had motive, means, and opportunity. He was also loudly protesting his innocence, though to be fair, people always did that when they were charged with a crime.

It just seemed like too much of a coincidence that this Katherine woman, who had a real connection to Charlotte's past in Rockport, was in Exeter.

"Listen, I've got an idea," I told Todd, who was now wandering around the newsroom, looking at old issues of the paper and poking around. "We're going to the jail."

He did a doubletake. "Turning yourself in, are you?"

"No," I said. "We're going to see Grayson Adams. I believe he can help us sort this out."

I was talking a big story here but was really flying blind. I had never been inside the county jail. I did not even really know what the procedure was for getting inside. Still, I thought if we showed up over there, it might lead to something. As for why I was roping this man I had only just met into my scheme, something told me once he got some food into him, he could talk his way in anywhere. Even though he hadn't really agreed to go with me, I sensed he was game.

He didn't reply right away. Then he stretched, yawned, and said, "Breakfast? I'm starving. Do you think we could find something to eat around this town?"

"Focus!" I told him. I reached out and shook his shoulder. "We can stop over at the Morning Musket on our way to the jail. Get you a muffin or something."

"Well, what the heck," he said. "It's not like I have anything else going on today."

I thought, *That's an understatement.*

We did a quick stop at the Morning Musket, where Jenny was more than a little curious when she saw Todd. She gave him the once over and looked at me expectantly, but I didn't have time to dish, other than to mouth to her, "Colleague from another paper," on my way out.

"Shall we take my car"? I asked. Todd was still stuffing muffin crumbs in his mouth.

"Nah, let's take the Dodger," he said. "She might look a little rough, but she's solid."

If Gladys could see me now, I thought a few minutes later as I peered into the old truck, spying Duct tape holding the bench seat together. I could hear her calling out about what a grand adventure this was going to be. I climbed up, noticing a hint of marijuana, and hoped none of the police K-9s at the jail walked by the truck. He fiddled with the key and had to crank it twice before the beast sputtered to life. The truck was old enough that it had a long-handled shifter in the middle, which he pushed forward as we rattled off down the road. At this rate, I was not sure we would make it to the county jail, even though it was less than a fifteen-minute drive.

"You seem to know the way," I observed.

He chuckled, clearly coming to life a bit now that his stomach was full and our adventure was underway. "Oh, I've been there a time or two," he said.

As a journalist or a resident or both? I wondered, looking at him. All of these options seemed possible.

"So, what?" he said. "You think this guy, Grayson is it, is just going to talk to you? I hate to break it to you, but I think that's unlikely."

"It's worth a shot," I replied.

A few miles later, we rumbled into the parking lot of the county jail, which was part of the whole county compound, including nursing home, farm, and agriculture office. The only difference between the brick jail building and the other structures was the line of barbed wire around the perimeter. The Dodger ground to a stop next to a police cruiser outside.

"Should we both go in?" I asked.

Todd shrugged and then responded, "Sure."

Now that we were here, I was a little unnerved, no longer sure this had been the best idea. But somehow, having this completely nonplussed partner helped. Todd looked like he was going for a stroll in the park as he walked toward the front of the jail.

"So, what next?" I asked him, trying to act like I had done this before.

"Get out your license and anything in your pockets that might set off the metal detector," he advised.

I pulled open the front door, no small feat as it was heavier than me, and looked around. We walked through a metal detector and up to a thick glass window, where a uniformed deputy in a standard brown prison uniform peered at us from the other side. Todd slid his license through the little opening at the bottom and I followed suit.

"We're here to see Grayson Adams," Todd said.

"Are you from his lawyer's office?" the deputy asked.

"No, we're media," Todd said.

The deputy shook his head. "I don't think he's going to want to see you, but sign here and we'll call down to the unit and ask."

We both signed and walked past the deputy to a waiting area, which had a few shiny plastic chairs. "This might have been a mistake," I whispered.

But Todd, now fully fueled by his muffin, was indeed coming to life, and he appeared to be hitting his stride. "You might be surprised," he said.

About ten minutes passed before we heard a buzzer, which I

knew from binge-watching *Orange Is the New Black* was the type that indicated the locked door in the jail was opening. A guard in a two-toned brown uniform walked out.

"Well, it's your lucky day," he said. "He will see one of you. Pepper, is it?"

"Piper," I corrected.

He shrugged, and I thought, *Oh boy, I am going to be on my own here.* I nodded and tried to steady myself as I stood. He led me through another door and then to a little room, which had a narrow ledge, thick glass, and a phone.

"Sit there." He motioned to another plastic chair. "You can talk on the phone when he arrives."

I knew I was not coming face to face with a slasher serial killer. This was Grayson—the same Grayson who drank gin and tonics at the Tuck Tavern most nights of the week and still wore his high school varsity letter jacket. But being inside a jail like this still felt thrilling, in a dangerous kind of way. I heard another buzzer and looked up as Grayson walked into his side of the booth. He looked even worse than the last two times I'd seen him, though jail would do that to a person. He sat down and picked up the phone on his side, so I did the same.

"I shouldn't be talking to you," he said. "My lawyer told me not to talk to anyone."

"I know and I understand," I began, trying to hold my jiggling foot steady under the ledge. "But something has come up, something that I think relates to this case."

He did not respond, and I went on. "Do you remember a lady at the Rockport town hall, the administrative assistant, Katherine something?" I asked.

He nodded. "Yeah, nice lady," he said. "What's that got to do with anything?"

"I think she's in Exeter," I said. "And it seems like too much of a coincidence not to mean something. Have you seen a lady who looks kind of down on her luck the past few weeks? Backpack? Glasses, long braid?"

He sat up a bit, and I could see a new realization washing over him. "Was that her?" he asked. "You know, now that you say that, I do remember seeing that woman in town, but I didn't think much of it."

"So, do you think it was her?" I asked.

"There was something about her, but at the time I didn't put it together." He paused. "But what does that have to do with this, with my case?"

I could not believe I was going to have to spell it out for him. "Well, so, she was friendly with Hank Tarr. She worked for him; apparently she was like a doting aunt or something," I said. "And from what I've heard, she kept in touch with his wife and kids when they moved after he died."

His eyes registered this information. "And now she shows up in Exeter, right at the time the woman responsible for all that is killed," he said.

"Bingo."

So, Katherine had motive, I thought, *but did she have opportunity? How on earth would she have managed to get into the reception at the town hall, a ticketed event? And*, I suddenly realized, *there was another thing that did not make sense.*

"How could she have gotten her hands on your redcoat uniform?" I asked.

Grayson groaned. "You are not going to believe this," he said. "So, after I reported it missing, my buddy Brian fessed up. He took the uniform and stashed it over in the town hall, boots and all. He was planning to dress up and play a little joke on me. But something came up, and he wasn't at the reception that night."

Okay, so the uniform was at the town hall. And someone snooping around could have found it. But Katherine, she was an old woman, gruff but presumably gentle. Could she really be capable of murder?

"Do you remember anything about her, anything else that might be relevant?" I asked.

He sat for a minute, looking off into the distance, as if summoning that time of his life. "Well, she grew up lobstering. Her dad had a boat down in Gloucester," he said. "She helped out when he was short-staffed."

I had a sudden thought. "Grayson, I've got to go," I blurted, barely stopping to say goodbye.

My mind was racing about Katherine. Someone who knew how to use a pulley to haul lobster traps onto a fishing boat would certainly be able to piece together a makeshift pulley to hang a dead body on the side of the town hall.

CHAPTER 40

Katherine had been right in front of me the whole time. She had turned up in Exeter just after Charlotte's death, a mysterious apparition, only showing herself occasionally and on her own terms. She was like a wild animal, a sly cat, coming out after dark when people were not looking for her. But could a regular-looking, older woman like that really be a murderer? Or had she helped someone else carry out the murder?

There was only one way to find out.

I joined Todd in the waiting area and, for the second time that day, said, "Todd, we've got to find her."

He looked skeptical. "Really? I was thinking we might grab a beer or something."

"Later," I told him. It was barely mid-afternoon. "We have work to do."

We drove all around Exeter in his bumpy old Jolly Dodger, including Swasey Parkway, where I'd seen Katherine last, around the back of the downtown businesses, and out behind the camera shop where Andy worked now. Nothing.

"Let's try the campground," I suggested.

He grunted in agreement, before responding, "Well, why not? I need to reserve a space there anyway."

The campground sat off the road on the way out of town, just

274

before a sloping hayfield where our famous UFO sighting happened in 1965. I did not mention this to Todd. He didn't need anything else to distract him from the case at hand.

We rumbled into the campground parking lot, passing an array of campers with little flags hanging from their front doors, mismatched chairs, and firepits. I wondered where Katherine was staying. I could not imagine she had a camper trailer, but I had heard through the grapevine that the place had a few sites with trailers they rented out on a weekly basis. A neon sign flashed the word *OFFICE* near a small cabin on the side.

"You ready?" I asked him, but he was already lumbering toward the office, and I had to jig a few steps to catch up. An older woman with feathered hair reminiscent of the 1980s sat behind the counter. It looked like she hadn't changed the office décor since that decade either.

"I'm looking for a site for a few nights," Todd began.

She handed him a piece of paper, "Fill this out, and I need payment up front. Also, we don't tolerate any funny business here," she said, looking at me like I might bring that kind of vibe with me.

"That's fine," he said, opening an old leather wallet and sliding a handful of bills toward her. The money seemed to improve her attitude.

"Say," he said, "I'm looking for someone else who was staying here. Katherine, older woman, glasses and long hair. Is she around?"

"Nope," she said. "Checked out this morning."

You've got to me kidding me, I thought.

Todd finished up his paperwork, and we stepped out of the lobby.

"Want to get that beer?" he asked. "Seems like we can take a little break."

Talk about throwing in the towel at the first bump in the road. I said, "You know, I think I'm just going to head home. Can you drop me downtown? I could use a walk to process everything about Katherine."

A few minutes later, I was climbing out of the Jolly Dodger, waving farewell to Todd, though I suspected I'd see him again. I had a text from Hap who told me to follow up tomorrow with a story about Andy being cleared. His attorney, Darby, who it turned out knew him from childhood and represented him pro bono, was eager to shift the narrative. I pondered that as I began the walk from the newspaper office back to my carriage house. Andy might not even talk to me after all the snooping I'd done into his life. As I walked through the parking area of the apartments next to the town hall and headed toward the other side of the parking lot, something caught my eye. Someone was walking into the side door of the town tall—someone with a long braid of grey hair down her back.

I did not think; I just waited a minute and then followed her inside. I eased the door shut behind me so it did not make a sound, and then I watched from a distance. Katherine was moving at a good clip, her backpack bouncing on her back, as she walked to the other side of the well-worn wooden floor, banked a right, and started walking up the stairs.

I crept across the room, trying to walk as softly as I could. I waited until I heard her up ahead of me, then started up the old wooden stairs. I stopped every few feet to listen. What was she doing in here? We were headed back to the scene of the crime, the spot where Charlotte had met her demise. Perhaps Katherine had forgotten something up top? Something the police hadn't found that she needed to retrieve before she left Exeter?

Her feet were making a lot of noise tramping up the stairs. But then she stopped, and I heard a second set of steps. Someone else was in the building with us—someone Katherine was following.

I reached the second floor, the area where volunteers had an art gallery for the town, but the footsteps ahead of me kept climbing up toward the third floor, the storage area, and beyond toward the cupola. My unease started to grow even stronger as I realized I was following the same path that Charlotte had traveled on the night she died. Had she followed someone up these very stairs? Or was she already dead by this point and carried to the top by her killer?

I paused at the edge of the stairwell and peered ahead. Katherine put down her backpack, then began a slow climb up the narrow stairs into the cupola. I slunk across the room, to the bottom of the stairs, and tilted my head to listen. There was a reason my father had called me Miracle Ear. I could hear anything from a mile away.

"Come on, I know you didn't mean it," Katherine said. "You don't have to do this, you know. People will understand, really."

"No, they won't," a second voice answered.

A second woman's voice. A voice I knew. Sheila.

"Sheila, honey, I know you're not thinking straight right now, but come on, come down, let's talk somewhere a little safer."

What the heck was going on up there? Was Sheila in on it with Katherine?

"Listen, old woman," Sheila responded, her voice harsher than I'd ever heard it sound before. "You don't know what it was like. Do you have any idea what it's like to haul lobster traps every weekend? And every day over summer vacation? What it's like getting the smell of bait out of your hair? What it's like when the other kids make fun of you all the time?"

"Sheila, I do know. Remember? I've been out on a boat or two in my day. I tried to check on you, make sure you were okay."

"Yeah, when it was convenient, but my sister and I, we were basically on our own. Our mother might as well have died with him. She was like a Zombie after that, going through the motions without really being there."

Wait, was I hearing this correctly? Sheila was Hank Tarr's daughter?

She wasn't finished. "You know," she said, "once we moved, we had to do our part, earn our keep. Up before dawn to pull lobster traps, all summer long. And during the school year, too. We never could join any clubs; we never went on any class trips. We wore clothes from the church thrift shop, and sometimes there wasn't enough to eat. My hands are still calloused from those wretched years."

Oh God, poor Sheila. It sounded like she'd been used as free labor for her lobstering relatives. I didn't envy her.

"Let's get down from here, honey. Please!" Katherine begged.

"What are you doing in Exeter, anyway?" Sheila asked.

"Your sister was worried about you. She thought you might refuse to see her, so she told me where you were and asked me to check up on you. She gave me your new last name, though I knew it already. I'm so sorry your marriage didn't work out. I did keep tabs on you, sweetheart."

Sheila muttered something unintelligible, and Katherine continued, "I kept an eye on that other reporter at the paper, too, the one in the carriage house. I thought you might be friends, but I never really saw you together. I wanted you to have friends, to have a good life."

So that's why she'd hung around long enough to drop her Zagnut wrappers out back. I leaned forward ever so slightly, trying to hear a bit better, and inching forward so that I could see inside.

"Come on, Sheila, this isn't a safe spot!" Katherine said. As I watched, she eyed the open side of the cupola, which had no safety railings to prevent someone from falling out. "What are you doing up here, anyway?"

"Nothing, really," Sheila said. "Taking one last look of where I killed that awful woman who ruined my family before I leave this town."

What? I tilted my Miracle Ear up again.

"Oh, Sheila, I was hoping that wasn't what happened." Katherine sighed heavily. "You know, you need to make this right. Don't let an innocent man take the blame for this."

"Listen, Katherine, I know you checked in on us when we were kids. I know, and I will never forget that," Sheila said. "But you need to drop this now, or else."

Oh crap. I was going to have to do something here. I briefly considered my options, and then I heard Katherine scream. I ran the last two steps and moved into the small alcove.

"Sheila," I called out. "Stop! Come on, please."

Sheila had a feral gleam in her eye, no longer the gentle features writer I was used to seeing in the newsroom. She had her arm around Katherine's neck, and I could tell she was really strong. Those years of hauling lobster traps must have given her a lot of upper-body strength.

"Great," she sputtered. "I should have known you'd be here. Always turning up at these things, aren't you?"

"Sheila, listen, this isn't you. I know this isn't you. Can you let Katherine go so we can talk?"

"That's what *she* said too—Charlotte—when I lured her up here that night. 'Let's talk, let's go downstairs,'" Sheila said, looking off into the distance. "You know, I didn't plan it, any of it. I didn't even make the connection that she was the person responsible for my father's death until I'd been at the paper for a while. I overheard her talking to Grayson out back late one night. He was going on and on about the Rockport scandal, and it hit me."

Katherine gasped for air as Sheila tightened her grip on her neck again.

"But then that night at the reception, I decided to finally ask her if she remembered me, remembered Hank," Sheila said, her voice breaking. "And you know what she said to me? She said, 'What are you so upset about? I did you a favor.'"

Wow. Even for Charlotte that was harsh. There was no way that writing an unsubstantiated story that resulted in a man losing his business and eventually dying by suicide was doing anyone a favor. Especially two little girls whose lives were forever changed.

"Sheila, please," Katherine tried once more, her voice coming out in a gasp. "Please!"

"And that did it," Sheila continued, unmoved by Katherine's pleas. "I heard what she said about doing us a favor. And by the time I got back to the paper later that night and saw her, I snapped. I told her I'd gotten a tip that an informant wanted to meet her in the cupola. And once she hurried back, I followed her up. I wanted her to feel the pain I felt the rest of my childhood."

I had to calm Sheila down. "I understand; she was horrible," I said, keeping my voice gentle. "Is that why you put the redcoat jacket on her? To let everyone know she was a traitor?"

Sheila paused for a minute, then pulled up her sleeves,

revealing long red scars down her forearms. "Not even close. She scratched me so hard I was bleeding. I couldn't let anyone see that, so I took her shirt to wear out, and then I covered her in the jacket."

So much for that theory. But I knew I had to keep her talking. "Sheila, I'm so sorry. Let's go downstairs, cool down," I urged.

She shook her head. "It's too late," she said. "There's nothing left for me here."

Sheila suddenly relaxed, let go of Katherine, and turned to look out toward the downtown area. Then she put one hand on either side of the cupola, pulled herself to the ledge, and started to edge her body over the side.

CHAPTER 41

"Sheila, no! Stop!" I yelled as she leaned forward.

And that was the last thing I remembered before something heavy pushed me forward and I slammed my head onto the old wooden floor. I came to in the back of an ambulance, with one of the Exeter paramedics, an older man with wiry salt-and-pepper hair and a big mustache, looking at me. I blinked at the bright white lights inside the ambulance.

"Well, that was quite a bump you got," he said. "Are you nauseous?"

Oh boy, he did not have to say that twice. My head was pounding, my stomach felt queasy, and the light hurt my eyes. I closed them again to get some relief.

"What happened?" I asked.

"Well, I'm not supposed to talk out of school," he began. "But it was quite something. Apparently, this guy, Todd something, saw you all going up into the cupola, and he decided to follow you. He got there just in time to see Sheila trying to jump out, so he pushed past you and grabbed her. It was really just dumb luck that he saw you go up when he did."

And clearly knocked me over in the process. "Did he get her before she jumped?"

The paramedic nodded. "Just in time! He literally grabbed

her right as she was sliding over the edge. He pulled her back in and held her in a giant bear hug while the other woman went to call for help."

Wow, I thought. That was going to expend Todd's energy for a while based on what I had seen of him so far.

"So," the paramedic said, "we're going to get you up to the hospital so they can take a look at your head, get some imaging, though unofficially I'd say you probably have a concussion."

There was a knock on the back of the ambulance, and he opened the door. An anxious-looking Hap and Jimmy both peered in at me.

"You really scared us," Hap said. "How are you feeling?"

"My head feels like it's been hit by a bus," I admitted.

"Well, when you're up for it, Jimmy's going to come see you at the hospital, get your account of what happened, for a story."

The news never stopped. My misfortune was giving Jimmy an internship opportunity to write a huge story that he'd never forget. I nodded, regretted the movement, then closed my eyes again. My head had not hurt this much since that spring break in Cancun when I'd made the mistake of doing tequila shots with the locals.

I felt a firm hand on my shoulder. The paramedic said, "It's okay to close your eyes, but we don't want you to go to sleep right now, okay?"

I murmured that I understood, felt the ambulance begin to move, and tried not to drift off as I digested everything that had happened.

At the hospital, they determined I did in fact have a significant concussion and would need to spend the night. I was told to avoid using computer screens and phone screens for a week at a minimum, which was going to put a damper on my ability to read about the whole situation that was unfolding. Chester called me, delivering a lecture about the dangers of trying to take investigations into my own hands, but I tuned most of it out. Beneath all the bluster, he did sound genuinely concerned.

Richie dropped in for a brief visit. He also seemed worried, but before I could grill him with questions, he was called back to work. The next morning, Gladys and Stanley came with the car and drove me home. After the hustle and bustle of the hospital ward, it felt wonderful to be back in the quiet carriage house again.

The next week passed in a blur. Richie didn't call or come by, but initially I felt far too lousy to even really think about it. I did manage to take a phone call from Jack Harper, who told me we would talk about a book proposal when I was recovered, but that he felt my personal role in the case's ending strengthened the chance it would find a publisher.

Gradually my energy improved, and even though I was supposed to limit reading, when the next edition of *The Exeter Independent* was published, I devoured the coverage. I felt a sense of pride at Jimmy's coverage and at my work as his mentor leading up to that point.

Calamity in Cupola Leads to Arrest in Editor's Murder
By Jimmy Malloy

EXETER__A *former features writer for* The Exeter Independent *is under observation at a psychiatric hospital while authorities mull whether to charge her with murder.*

According to eyewitness reports, Sheila Bradbury confessed to killing Charlotte Campbell during a tense confrontation in the town hall cupola. Bradbury reportedly blamed Campbell, whose real name was Carlotta Cabanovich, for falsely accusing her father of embezzlement in the months before he died by suicide.

Lara Bricker

Piper Greene, senior reporter for The Exeter Independent, *was a witness to Bradbury's confession, and sustained a concussion when she was knocked to the ground during the cupola catastrophe. Freelance journalist Todd Tisden is being credited with both stopping Bradbury from jumping and rushing to Greene's aid. Greene is recuperating at home and expected to make a full recovery.*

"It was just such a shock," Greene said. "Sheila was always so kind as a reporter, but it was clear that night that she is a deeply troubled person. I'm so thankful that we all made it out of that cupola alive."

Police Chief Frank Sinclair said authorities are waiting to proceed with charging Bradbury until after they receive the results of her mental health evaluation. He praised all those involved for their work in bringing the case to resolution.

"Ms. Greene certainly did some things that we would not suggest civilians take on themselves during the course of this investigation, and put herself in harm's way, which we definitely do not advise. But her dogged pursuit of the truth did play a role in finding out what really happened to poor Ms. Campbell," Sinclair said. "We wish her a speedy recovery."

Select Board Chairman Grayson Adams, who was initially charged in the case, has been released from police custody. All charges were dropped. Adams would not comment on reports that he is contemplating a civil suit against the police as a result of the false arrest.

The squeak of the hinges on my side door drew my attention away from the newspaper as Gladys tiptoed in. She had been doting on me like a little bird, flitting around me every few hours in the carriage house.

"Oh, Piper sweetheart, are you sure you don't want the afghan

285

on your legs," she asked, as she fluttered around my living room. "How about some tea with lemon?"

She sat on the loveseat, settling in to rehash "the excitement" as she called it, for what felt like the hundredth time. She said, "I just can't believe you went all the way up to the top of the town hall like that. I know you are curious and all, but really dear, even for you that was a bit much."

"I know, I know," I told her. "I wasn't thinking ahead at the time, only wondering what that Katherine woman was doing."

"Oh her," Gladys said. "I heard from that fellow, Todd—you know, the adventurer—that she's been holding vigil at the psych hospital since that poor girl Sheila was taken over."

I said, "That doesn't surprise me. Katherine seemed to view herself as a mother figure to Sheila in a nostalgic kind of way. But wait, why did you speak to Todd?"

"I wanted to thank him, of course!" she said. "He saved your life!"

Before she could continue, there was a knock at the door, and Gladys hopped up. "Another of your fans, no doubt," she said, opening the door. Then she brightened and announced, "Speaking of the adventurer!"

Todd Tisden strolled in, looking a little more put together than the last time I had seen him. He'd had a haircut and was wearing a button-down shirt, albeit a wrinkly one. There was no cowboy hat to be seen.

"Sorry I didn't come by sooner," he said, as he looked around at my home, not trying to hide his nosiness. "I had to get some things sorted out."

That sounded awfully organized for him.

"That's okay. I've not been much in the mood for company," I said.

Gladys beamed over at him. "Oh Todd, do tell Piper that story you told me about seeing the grizzly bear in Montana." She looked at me. "He's quite the renaissance man, Piper, and a bit of a naturalist, like Jacques Cousteau."

Oh boy, I thought. *Gladys does love her fascinating people.*

"So, are you moving on then?" I asked Todd. "Back off in your Jolly Dodger?"

He grinned, almost sheepishly, as he looked from Gladys to me.

"Well, funny story," he said. "So, I went down to give an interview to your intern, Jimmy, there at the paper about the way everything went down. And while I was there, I talked to Hap. With Sheila gone, he's in need of a features writer, and, well, we came to an agreement, a trial period of sorts."

My mouth dropped. Then I said, "*You're* my new coworker?"

Gladys clapped her hands with glee. She gushed, "Oh, this is exciting, Todd dear. This means we can hear some more of those adventuring stories, doesn't it?"

He shrugged, but I could see he was warming to Gladys the way most of us did after spending a bit of time with her.

"I'll have to tell you about what I saw when I got to Wyoming," he said, pausing for effect the way people do when they like to tell a good story. "I climbed the Devils Tower, in the winter, ice as far as you could see."

"Ooh my," Gladys said. "That does sound dangerous, doesn't it, Piper?"

But I was feeling drowsy again, ready for a break. "Yes," I said. "I'm sorry to be the wet blanket here, but I'm fading again."

"Oh, you go right ahead there, Piper. I'll walk Todd here out," she said.

"Well, thanks for stopping by," I said. "Will you be staying at the campground for a bit then?"

"Well, actually, I'm looking for somewhere to park the Dodger for a bit. That place isn't really my scene," he said. "Do you know of anywhere else around?"

Gladys clapped her hands again. "You know, we have plenty of space on the other side of the carriage house. Why don't you stay here for a bit? Piper here checks in on me to make sure I'm still ticking, but it would be nice to have someone else around while she's recuperating, now wouldn't it, dear?"

A picture of Stanley and Todd singing showtunes together flitted through my mind, and I tried not to laugh. "Sure," I said. "The more the merrier."

Gladys and Todd wandered out and I closed my eyes. The door hinge creaked loudly a moment later. "Really, Gladys, I'm okay," I called out.

"Well, that's not the welcome I was expecting," a deep voice responded.

I opened my eyes. The elusive Richie Collins had reappeared. He was not in uniform and had a take-out box from the Morning Musket.

"Jenny asked me to drop this off for you," he explained, as he handed me the box.

Oh, Jenny, that was clever, I thought, silently grateful for her not-so-subtle attempt to move things along in the romance department.

"Thanks," I said. He settled into the loveseat. "I'm not going to fit into my grown-up pants if she keeps up this daily pastry delivery."

He laughed at that and paused to look at me. "So, now that you're more coherent than the last time I saw you at the hospital, how about you tell me the whole story about what happened up in the cupola?"

God, was he always on duty?

He seemed to pick up on my expression and shook his head quickly. "No, not as a detective, just as your friend, as someone who was worried about you."

I opened the box of pastries and held it over to him. "Well, if we're just two friends, have a treat, and maybe we'll talk."

He selected an éclair the size of my forearm, and I picked up my current favorite, the raspberry white chocolate scone. Jenny, always thinking ahead, had added some napkins and plates in the box, and I handed Richie a plate, then took one for myself. I savored the first bite: the butter, vanilla, and creamy chocolate were the perfect combination with the local raspberries, now in season. We sat chewing in silence for a few minutes. Jenny's baking had that effect on people, but Richie's éclair was making a mess. Gladys had trained me well, and I offered him a napkin.

"You've got a little chocolate right there," I said, pointing toward the side of his mouth.

He smiled and leaned toward me. "Is that so?" He was so close I could feel his breath on my face. "I know another way to deal with that," he said. His expression changed and my heart did a little flipflop.

And just like that, he bent over and gave me a feather-light kiss. I hesitated only briefly before I returned it. Oh my, Jenny's pastries really did have magical powers. He pulled back ever so slightly. Neither one of us moved or said a word for a moment, until he whispered. "Now, can we agree that you'll stay out of trouble for a little while?"

I laughed out loud at that. "Now, Richie, after all this time, don't you know me better than that?"

He leaned back onto the loveseat and shook his head in defeat. "Okay then, Scoop, how about you tell me the story now." He stopped and winked at me, "Now that we're just two close friends eating breakfast."

I finished the last bite of my scone, and that's exactly what I did.

About the Author

Lara Bricker is an award-winning journalist, podcaster, former private investigator, certified cat detective, and true crime author. She is one of four crime writers on the hit podcast, Crime Writers On and the author of the true crime book *Lie after Lie: The True Story of a Master of Deception, Betrayal, and Murder.*

Her work has appeared in the *Portsmouth Herald,* the *Exeter News-Letter,* the *Hampton Union,* the *New Hampshire Union Leader, Woman's World* magazine, *USA Today,* and the *Boston Globe.* In 2008, she covered the first death penalty case to go to trial in New Hampshire in almost fifty years for the Associated Press. As a news reporter, she has received numerous awards from both the New Hampshire Press Association and the New England Newspaper & Press Association for her crime and investigative reporting.

Lara lives in Exeter, New Hampshire with her husband Ken; teenage son Will; dog, Buddy; and most importantly, her three cats, Rocky, Zelda, and Pippin. She can often be found walking around Exeter pondering where her next local murder mystery will take place.

www.larabricker.com

Dead on Deadline